# JUBILEE

# ELIZA GRAHAM

**ISIS**
**LARGE PRINT**
Oxford

Copyright © Eliza Graham, 2010

First published in Great Britain 2010
by
Pan Books
an imprint of Pan Macmillan

Published in Large Print 2011 by ISIS Publishing Ltd.,
7 Centremead, Osney Mead, Oxford OX2 0ES
by arrangement with
Pan Macmillan
A division of Macmillan Publishers Limited

**British Library Cataloguing in Publication Data**
Graham, Eliza.
Jubilee.
1. Aunts - - Fiction.
2. Missing children - - Fiction.
3. Families - - Fiction.
4. Genealogy - - Methodology - - Fiction.
5. Elizabeth II, Queen of Great Britain, 1926- - -
Anniversaries, etc. - - Fiction.
6. Domestic fiction.
7. Large type books.
I. Title
823.9'2–dc22

ISBN 978–0–7531–8674–9 (hb)
ISBN 978–0–7531–8675–6 (pb)

Printed and bound in Great Britain by
T. J. International Ltd., Padstow, Cornwall

# jUBILEE

For Lauri and Jeanette Day

# Part One

# CHAPTER
# ONE

**Rachel**
**Silver Jubilee day, 1977, and June 2002**

By the time the kitchen clock struck seven I knew that my cousin wouldn't be coming back. I abandoned my rehearsal of the cool response I'd planned for her return: I *always knew you were just mucking about, Jess* . . .

While we waited for the men to finish searching the hedgerows and the white snaky curve of the Ridgeway path above us, I watched my aunt. Evie sat at the kitchen table twisting the fabric belt of her new dress as though she was trying to wring the anxiety out of herself. She caught me staring at her and managed to twist her features into something halfway to a smile. This attempt to reassure me made me feel even more frightened. "Come back!" I shouted silently at my cousin. "It's not a game any more."

I was still clutching my Silver Jubilee mug with its Queen's head and coat of arms. I wished I could go upstairs and put the mug away but I felt bound to stay here at the table with my aunt, as though any movement could jinx the search for Jessamy. We sat in silence, listening to the kitchen clock tick-tocking until the noise seemed to drill itself into my chest.

"I'm going out," I blurted out after five more minutes had passed. "I'm going to check the stables again." I put down the mug and rose.

Evie gave a start. "No." She reached across and grabbed my wrist. "Stay there."

I wriggled my wrist free. "Let me. Please."

She ran her hands over her face. "Rachel, we've looked a dozen times. We've been all over the farm."

"There are places we hide . . ."

"I know them all. The elm the lightning hollowed out." She sounded almost fierce. "The little hollows in the sheep field. Your father and I used to hide in them, too."

She gave another of the strained smiles. "We've combed this place, every inch. And you and I need to stay here, in case she comes back. Imagine if she returned, cold, tired, scared . . ." Her voice cracked a little on the last word. "And there was nobody here."

I stared hard at the kitchen table. Jessamy and I had been making Union Jacks out of red, white and blue Plasticine and they still sat at the end of the table. I reached across for one of them and squashed it in my hand. Some of the blue Plasticine squelched into the white strips. I clenched my fist again. The red ran into the white and now it didn't look like a flag at all. I kept on squeezing it until I held a dirty grey ball in my palm. "We need to check on the ponies," I said.

She put a hand to her mouth. In the field outside the house stood a new chestnut, a surprise for Jessamy.

4

Evie had arranged for him to arrive while we were at the Jubilee party.

Eventually I must have fallen asleep, the spoiled Plasticine still in my hand, because I came to with my head resting on the oak table. ". . . again in daylight," a man was saying.

"Thank you." Evie's voice sounded like a stranger's: polite, detached.

But in the morning they found only half a dozen deflated Jubilee balloons and some crumpled Union Jack paper napkins, blown into ditches and hedges.

I returned to Winter's Copse six weeks after the Silver Jubilee party, when my summer holidays began. My father, Evie's twin brother, Charlie, had done what he could to protect me from the newspaper and television coverage of the disappearance but I'd caught a few glimpses of myself, huddled behind Evie as she stood in the kitchen doorway, before Dad could switch off the television. "Craven villagers are still perplexed by the disappearance of Jessamy Winter," the reporter started.

Whenever I could escape the insistent tones of a school teacher I let my cousin's image drift back into my mind.

This evening Evie was making me tea: scrambled eggs on toast, and I was laying the table. I set three places. Evie turned from the range with the saucepan of eggs, and her eyes widened at the sight of the three table mats and sets of cutlery.

She let out a quiet moan. The saucepan in her hand dipped so that the yellow contents slopped on to the table. "Sorry," she said, raising her other hand to her mouth. "Oh God, I'm sorry, Rachel. It's just . . ." The words seemed to jam in her throat. She rocked herself backwards and forwards; more of the scrambled egg spilled out of the pan, pattering to the scrubbed kitchen floor.

It was then that the fact of Jessamy's disappearance hit me with an almost physical violence. I stared at the stupid, wretched, third place I'd set and knew that she would never lift the knife and fork, never drink from the water glass again. She'd never ride that new pony still waiting for her. It was my birthday next week and I was going to be ten. Jess wouldn't be there when I cut my cake. If there was a cake. Perhaps there would never be cakes again.

These days, in my job as a freelance marketing consultant, I write copy and do a bit of simple design work. I work with sophisticated photo enhancement programs on the computer. It's possible to excise an image and replace it with something else: an unwanted wedding guest can become a tree or bush. But before you carry out the replacement you're left with a cut-out of the missing person's body, filled only with an amorphous grey vacuum.

As Evie's scrambled eggs splattered out of the saucepan I saw my cousin's outline at the third table setting, with a vacuum where her body — that vital, energetic mass — had been. And that outline followed me round my life as I progressed to all the places where

Jessamy should also have been: university matricula-
tions and graduations, weddings and funerals.

But eventually life filled in the vacuum so that I
started to look through it. But nothing could fill in the
vacuum for Jessamy's mother.

The Golden Jubilee was approaching; only weeks away
now. Evie had already sent me the invitation to the
village party, with its official Jubilee logo on the top.
Twenty-five years since my cousin had disappeared.
Everyone watched old film coverage of the Coronation
and the Silver Jubilee on television. Parties were
planned; bunting was ordered.

But for Evie the anniversary could only ever be that
of the last time she'd seen her daughter.

# CHAPTER
# TWO

**Evie**
**Coronation Day, 2 June 1953**

The red jelly in the half-eaten trifle looked like drops of blood against the yellow custard and real cream on the top. Splashes of orange squash had stained the white tablecloths and the balloons tied to the fence had already started to deflate.

Evie clutched the table and closed her eyes for a second. A metal coil tightened round her head. When she opened her eyes again the jelly still looked like blood. She swallowed hard and looked away. The children were eating more slowly now, their eyes glazed as though they were inebriated, tin-foil crowns sliding down their heads. One or two would almost certainly be sick. Several of the adults also looked a little green, though that might have been the cask of best ordered especially for the party, rather than the food.

Sandwiches, cold sausages, cold beef, lemonade, tea, fairy cakes, buns, trifle, chocolate cake: a cornucopia to celebrate the new queen, the new hope, the modern age. All consumed within an hour. Perhaps these new Elizabethans would never again feel that desperation to taste something sweet and rich in the mouth that Evie remembered from the years of rationing.

New Elizabethans. To distract herself from the spoiled food and her throbbing head Evie rolled the phrase silently round her lips. She liked the idea of being a New Elizabethan. The old Elizabethans had been a vivacious lot: explorers, pirates and poets. Perhaps their twentieth-century kin would be equally entertaining. Her headache seemed to subside. Feeling better, she looked along the table for her next chore. Some of the older folk were sitting back in their chairs, eyes slightly glazed. Hard to imagine them exploring and writing sonnets. But the children . . . Perhaps they'd live great lives. Perhaps she herself might be a writer. But if she'd been going to do something clever in her life she'd have made a start by now. It was too late now: twenty-three, married, with this —

"Evie!"

Day-dreaming again. The earthenware teapot in Evie's hand was needed at the far end of the trestle table. Fiona Fernham gave her a fierce wave. "That tea will be good and stewed now. Give me the pot if you're just going to stand there staring at nothing." She gave Evie the kind of glare that one of her illustrious land-owning forebears might have given a retainer.

"Sorry." Evie walked over and handed the pot to Fiona. If you were female and aged between sixteen and sixty and resident in the village of Craven you weren't granted a day of leisure to celebrate your new monarch's anointing at Westminster Abbey. It fell to you to decorate tables, drape bunting, shell hard-boiled eggs, cut sandwiches, refresh tea-pots, and walk backwards and forwards all afternoon bearing heavy trays. Relaxation was only for the young, the old and the male. Still, at least these exertions meant there was no time to brood.

Matthew caught her eye and he gave her a long, slow wink. "Pay attention, Eve." His face was tender. He must have overheard the exchange. For all his softness she knew he wouldn't have liked hearing her spoken to like that. She was a Winter, by marriage at least. The Winters were landowners, successful farmers, even through the gloomy interwar years.

Evie flipped her apron at him and made a face to lighten the moment. Matthew's mother sat beside him, a small dribble of tea falling down her chin. But her eyes were bright. Perhaps she was remembering the Coronations of the past: the Georges and Edwards. VE Day. And VJ Day, too, though that had been more muted because the boys weren't home yet. All this remembering. There were things Evie preferred to forget. Her hand shook as she picked up an empty plate.

She didn't feel sick, exactly. Just exhausted, with the occasional throbbing head and hot stabbing pains beneath her navel. Oh God, if only she could go home and curl up somewhere warm. But she couldn't because people — she meant Fiona — would guess what was wrong with her. Pregnancy was the desirable condition for someone eighteen months' married. To be incapable of keeping a baby until term was

10

reprehensible, especially if your husband needed someone to hand his farm —

"At least try and clear up that mess!" Fiona was almost shouting now, pointing at the jelly splodges on the table as though Evie herself had spilled them on the cloth. Matthew used his knife to scrape up the worst of it onto his plate. "Oh not you, Mr Winter! I meant Evie." The coldness in Fiona's voice when she said Evie's name showed that the dislike was more than purely social.

"No trouble for me to help," Matthew said in his slow, deep voice. "You ladies have been working all afternoon."

But Matthew was Male and not intended by Providence for drudgery. Evie eyed him. He looked calm enough but you could never tell. Sometimes too much noise distressed him. And large numbers of people eating at the same time were difficult for him, too. She noticed the crumpled-up paper napkin beside his plate and wondered whether he'd hidden half a bun in it. Sometimes she still found food hidden in drawers or placed behind the cushions on the parlour sofa. At first she'd thrown it away but now she simply left it where it was and never mind the mice.

Evie took a cloth from her pinafore pocket and dabbed at the red stains on the cloth. You could never get them out, not completely. Even after a boil wash pinkish tints would remain. She felt her husband's gaze on her and looked up to see Matthew regarding her with that expression that was peculiarly his own: half quizzical, half sad. She never knew sad for what, exactly. He'd lit a cigarette now that the meal was over and blew gentle puffs of smoke and his face was still soft as he watched her.

Matthew didn't know about the pregnancy yet. She hadn't been sure enough to raise his hopes. Or dash hers, she thought. But they were probably already dashed.

The children were on their feet now, clamouring for three-legged-races and egg-and-spoon. The fake sable-edged robes they'd worn for the pageant lay crumpled and trampled on the grass. Evie looked at their pink cheeks and shining eyes. New hope. A fresh start. She had to look away.

I still have so much, she told herself briskly. Think of all those war widows. Or those women whose children were crushed to death by bombs in London, Bristol or Portsmouth. Or those even more wretched women all over Europe whose entire families were deliberately murdered.

She finished clearing the table and went to put the scraps in the swill bucket, hidden behind the hedge, the smell of the wasted food making her want to retch. The pigs would like it, though. When he'd first come home, Matthew had stared at the pig swill and she'd known he was thinking how men in the camp would have fought over it.

Philippa, who lived in the cottage next to the shop, was rinsing plates in a bowl of soapy water on an old table, her hands wrinkled by long immersion.

"Weren't we clever to miss the worst of the rain?" It had rained most of the morning.

Evie smiled and nodded, inhaling the smell of new grass to ease the nausea.

"How's Matthew?"

"This is a good day." At least she'd asked outright. Some of the others gossiped about him behind their hands. "He still hides food but the dreams don't seem as bad. This cool weather makes his bad foot ache, though."

"Nearly eight years and still they're not right." The woman's face suddenly took on a guarded expression, as though she'd said too much. Evie wished she hadn't stopped. But she couldn't ask her for details. Before the war Philippa had walked out with Jonathan Fernham, Fiona's brother, for a while, but when he'd come back he'd done no more than occasionally partner her in mixed doubles or lead her round the village hall in a stiff foxtrot.

"Did you watch the ceremony on television, Evie? We went to my mother's to see it." Philippa handed Evie another bowl to empty. Evie watched the jelly and cake crumbs slide off the bowl into the swill bucket, where they joined more cake crumbs and a pint of cream that had turned too much to be used at the party. In the war they'd have done something with all that food. Again her stomach protested.

"I saw it."

The girl polished a plate with her drying-up cloth. "Those gorgeous dresses. Imagine having all that silk and taffeta."

Evie nodded, although she hadn't paid much attention to the Queen's costume.

**13**

"Like something from a film." Philippa wrung out the cloth. "A life of glamour. That's what the Queen has. Not like us." She put her hands to her lower back. "Though you don't need the posh frocks and jewellery."

Evie put a hand to her face.

"You've just rubbed jelly into your cheek. Here." Philippa flicked it off with the cloth. She gazed at Evie. "How do you do it, Evie?"

"What?"

"I remember you when you first came here, a scrawny little kid from south London. Nothing special. But now . . ." She didn't sound envious, only slightly reproachful. Evie had got her man, after all.

Evie shrugged. "I don't think I'm all that special. My mother was pretty, as far as I remember. But by the time I'm twenty-five I'll be a weathered old hag from all those winter nights in the lambing shed."

Philippa turned back to the washing-up bowl, shaking her head. "And Matthew adores you and you live in the prettiest house in the village."

And only one thing was asked of her.

"Fetch me some more plates if the kids have finished with them. I'll freshen up this bowl first." Philippa tipped out the soapy water onto the grass, where the suds gleamed like small crystal balls before popping.

"I'll fetch you some hot water from the urn." Both women jumped at the voice. Martha Stourton stood at the hedge, unsmiling, watchful, her pale eyes huge in her face.

"Thanks!" Philippa answered.

14

Evie retreated behind the hedge. First Fiona Fernham and now Martha: this was going to be a day of avoiding women who didn't approve of her. The grass was nearly dry here now and she could risk her new frock for a minute's peace and quiet. She'd promised herself that she wouldn't brood today, she'd let the past go, fold back the memories and pretend they'd never been taken out again. She removed her pinafore and laid it on the grass to protect the full poplin skirt. "There's enough material in that frock to clothe all the women in the village," Matthew had joked when she'd put it on. Then his eyes had softened and he'd put his arms around her. "It shows off your neat little waist. You're fit for a queen yourself."

It might have been her imagination but the dress already felt slightly tight around the bust and stomach. Could she still be pregnant after yesterday? She felt the muscles around the tops of her legs and in her pelvis tighten, as though they were trying to hold on to the foetus.

The grass was soft and springy from all the rain. It made a comfortable resting place. Nobody would see her here. From her pocket she retrieved her Woodbines and lighter. Mrs W didn't like smoking in the house. She could barely talk but her hands would flutter in her lap at the sight of a cigarette packet.

From here Evie was looking up towards the White Horse. Its front legs were hidden by the curve of the hill and it looked more like a kangaroo. Small black figures walked around beside it; not everyone was marking the Coronation, some had travelled out here to look at the horse, now restored again after its ignominious wartime camouflaging. Above the horse, hidden by the slope, the Ridgeway cut its way like an east-west scar across the Downs. Sometimes, when she walked up there, Evie could almost imagine a call blown on the breeze, or the treading of hooves behind her. She never turned round in case she saw the ghosts of the men and beasts who'd tramped the footway all those centuries ago. And she only ever walked on the eastern section of the path, never to the west of the White Horse.

Evie let her eyes close for a moment. Sleep had been elusive for the last few nights but wanted to snare her now. Her chin slumped onto her chest. The packet tumbled from her hand before she could even remove a cigarette.

"Taking a break?"

Her eyes flew open. Martha, back from fetching water. She sat up. Martha always made her feel guilty for taking a minute's break. If Evie sat on a hay bale or leaned against the fence posts for a sip of tea from the Thermos, that would be the moment Martha conjured herself up from nowhere to suggest with just a flash of those green eyes of hers that Evie lacked commitment. "Just wanted a rest."

"I see." Martha's eyes seemed to glide along Evie's body. Perhaps she'd guessed.

"I'll just finish this. Would you like . . ." She gestured at the cigarettes.

"Thanks." Martha took one and lit it with her own lighter, standing beside Evie as she smoked.

"Funny how peaceful it gets as soon as you step just a few yards away from the crowds." Might as well try for some conversation, Evie thought, difficult as it was with Martha.

"Especially now the silver band's stopped." Martha took a draw of the cigarette. "Bit different from London."

She liked to refer to Evie's early childhood in the city, as though underlining her incomer status.

"I don't really remember London." She forced a note of neutrality into her words. "I was so young when I came here."

"Ten." Martha made it sound like a contradiction.

"I should be getting back. Philippa needs the plates cleaning." She was gabbling.

"I saw you up on the hill earlier on, Evie. Didn't you want to watch the ceremony on television? Matthew bought you a set, didn't he?"

The last sentence made it plain what Martha thought of such uxoriousness. "He thought his mother would like to see it." She felt her cheeks burn and turned her head so that Martha wouldn't see and forced herself to stare at the trees and the distant lettuce-green Cotswold hills to the north. But the older woman simply stared at her for another second before drifting away towards the tables.

Evie stayed where she stood, giving herself another minute, just until the worst of the pain subsided. Should she tell Matthew now? He looked so happy, sitting with his mother at the trestle table, enjoying the

**17**

celebration. If she told him, he'd worry. Wait another day.

She should have told him this morning, when it had started.

She'd come inside to join Matthew and Mrs W. She wasn't really that bothered about watching the Coronation but it had started to rain again. Just like D-Day had been, cold and wet, not like early summer at all. Matthew moved up on the sofa so there was room for her, grimacing slightly as he moved his left foot. "Tea's just brewed, Evie. Here, let me pour you a cup."

"No, you stay there, I'll do it in a moment." She looked at the square wooden cabinet, received with such pride and anticipation just days ago. The picture wasn't bad, smaller than the cinema but you could make out the shining brass on the horses' harnesses and the details on the carriages. Shame you couldn't see the colours, though. So many people on the streets: thin faces, and tired-looking, still, some of them. The war had only finished eight years ago, after all. Perhaps the cheers and shouts were a release of emotion. People looked at that young woman in the carriage with her smooth skin and they thought she was drawing a line under it all.

Evie considered whether this would ever be possible. She gave her husband another little smile and looked back at the television screen

"Just look at those arches they've put up over the Mall," Matthew marvelled. "It's like something from ancient Rome." The Queen's coach was coming closer.

The camera angle changed and Evie saw the backs of the spectators' heads, then the sides of their faces as the camera moved round to get a clearer shot of the monarch. What did she feel, this young woman, as she saw all those people? Perhaps she was flattered, gratified. Or perhaps she was secretly terrified, longing to run away and spring on one of the horses they said she adored.

How many tens or hundreds of thousands of them were in London to see this procession? Little children, old people, middle-aged women in their best hats, soldiers in uniform. Happy, smiling faces.

Mrs W's shawl had fallen off her lap. Evie rose to retrieve it for her, moving closer to the television screen just as the camera changed its angle, focusing on the crowd instead of the coach, so their faces were close to Evie's eyes. How extraordinary that she could look at these excited strangers while sitting in their own parlour, eighty miles away from the Mall.

A cramp squeezed her abdomen. And she felt the back of her neck prickle with cold sweat even though the coal fire was lit in the grate.

A cool tingle ran down her spine. It was going to happen again and there was nothing she could do to stop it, to hold on to what might have been a child. Somehow she managed to pick up the shawl and tuck it round her mother-in-law's lap.

"Robert." Evie had to strain her ears to pick up the word. The old lady raised a finger and pointed towards the screen. Evie glanced at the television and saw only the blurred black and white faces of thousands of strangers. A quick glance at Matthew's relaxed expression told her he couldn't have heard his mother murmur his brother's name. Evie sat back again and forced herself to breathe slowly. Mrs Winter was confused again; she couldn't possibly have made out an individual in that throng.

Robert was dead. That's what they'd told Matthew when he'd come home from the hospital. Your brother died in a barn fire. He fell asleep and left a cigarette alight and the dry hay caught fire. He is buried underneath one of the yews in the churchyard.

"There," said Robert's mother slowly again. Evie'd never even been certain whether Mrs Winter had understood that Robert had died those eight years ago. Impossible to tell whether the information had pierced the old lady's expressionless eyes.

Evie touched her arm. "The picture's not very clear, is it? You can't make out the details?" She gave the arm a gentle shake. "Where did you think you saw him?"

Mrs W's eyes focused on the square box. The carriage had reached the Abbey now.

"First the Duke of Edinburgh and then the Queen alight from the royal carriage," Richard Dimbleby said on the television.

The old woman's lips opened. "There," she said again, her eyes focusing somewhere in the direction of the television. Something about the flags and crowds must have made Mrs Winter remember a previous Coronation. Perhaps Robert had enjoyed watching the news film at the cinema and that was why she was thinking about him now.

20

"You're right, mother, she's there now," Matthew said. "Going in a young wife and mother and she'll come out a queen. Doesn't she look young? Barely older than our Evie."

"There," the old woman said again.

"I'm just going to check on that heifer." Evie stood, her eyes on the window behind the television. The room felt stifling, despite the unseasonable chill outside. Remembering Robert was making her feel dizzy.

"She'll be fine, love. Leave her till later. You'll want to watch the ceremony."

"I don't mind." She left the room, praying he wouldn't make a fuss, but he didn't, Matthew never did unless something triggered one of his bad turns; then he'd grow uneasy if she left his sight. She forced herself to walk unhurriedly through the house to the kitchen, where she swapped her court shoes for a pair of boots in which to negotiate the muddy farmyard. The heifer looked up as she approached the shed, eyes no longer dull, nose damp and twitching. Good. She could go back inside now, into the companionable fug of the parlour. But she didn't. She found herself walking out of the yard. She needed space — her feet found their own way across the field and through the gate. The faint outline of a sheep track led up to the Ridgeway. Years ago she and Charlie had stood up here looking down as smoke curled from the roof of the barn.

Evie's feet pulled her into a run uphill, towards the ribbon of clear sky forming over the grey skies. She passed Martha Stourton's cottage and was careful to take quiet steps, in the shadows, until she was outside the view of anyone looking out of a window. Her lungs protested as she dashed forward but she kept going. It started to rain and almost immediately her frock became a cold flapping sheet around her legs. Evie headed slowly back down the hill towards the farm, her head bowed down, her mind dipping backwards into the past. She found herself standing by the back door again and rubbed the raindrops off her face.

From the drawing room came the sound of Richard Dimbleby's voice, still narrating the Coronation from Westminster Abbey. A blast of trumpets snarled out. She could slip off this bloodied dress and leave it to soak. Lucky she'd planned to wear the New Look-style frock she'd made to the party on the green.

It could be as though it had never happened.

# CHAPTER
# THREE

**Robert**
**Camp at Ban Pong, Thailand, November 1942**

Dear Evie,

I lost the earlier letters I wrote: they must have dropped out of my pack as we marched out of Changi camp in Singapore for the last time. I could rewrite them from memory but haven't the heart to list it all. How Matthew and I were redeployed from the Berkshires when we reached India and sent out with men from other regiments to Singapore. The last days trying to hold out against the Japs, hiding out in a small village when the fight was over, capture, humiliation (they made us line the roads and drove their dignitaries past us to laugh).

This will be another letter I write but can never send to you. But just pretending you read what I write helps me enormously. You're just a kid of twelve so perhaps it's as well you don't. Perhaps it's a bit odd, me writing to you rather than to Mum. Or Martha. But when I think of you I feel calm, like I used to.

We'd seen bad things in Changi, but when we heard the rumours that the Japanese wanted to build a railway between Burma and Thailand, I assumed that was all it was: a rumour.

But it wasn't.

November now, not sure of the exact date. I think about you back on the farm. Have you slaughtered a pig? Is the farm manager ploughing? Have you had frosts? I love the first frost, the way it makes your cheeks glow and makes the horses toss their heads when we take them out in the harness. I would give anything for just an hour's frost to refresh us. "Never thought I'd miss the cold," Matthew said just this week. "I used to hate getting up when the windows had frozen up inside. But imagine sleeping in a room where you know no insects will bother you." Good old Matthew. We've done our best to stick together, joining the same regiment and then managing to get me sent to Singapore with him when he was redeployed. Otherwise I'd be with the Berkshires in India. Most of the officers are very sympathetic but warn us that it's up to the Japs as to whether we stay in the same camp.

A thousand miles in a goods wagon to Ban Pong in Thailand, the nearest point on the Thai railway system to the coastal plain of southern Burma, two hundred miles away across the mountains. The Japs want to cut a railway across these peaks. Even we British couldn't do it. They're insane, Evie. Just writing that sentence could get me shot so I must hide these letters very carefully. Even just having this blank exercise book is dangerous. I pulled it off a desk at the school in Singapore we were holed up in and somehow I managed to keep it with me. How long ago that seems now. But I can't face writing about what happened back there again, so I'll just start from here, from the start of our work on the Burma railway.

When we reached Ban Pong they marched us through the town. The Thais stared at us without much curiosity. From the gardens of the bigger houses came the scent of tropical blossom and flowers. I smelled something I recognized: jasmine. I tried to hold on to that smell, Evie, so that I could draw on it when we reached the camp and they stood us outside the stinking hut that was to be our quarters. Someone started laughing. "Look," he said, pointing up to the tall teak trees. We looked up and saw the black vultures in the branches. "They know they'll be fed." Then we were all laughing, but it wasn't laughter like there is at home when the cricket club piles into the Packhorse on a Saturday evening after a match. I looked at us in our filthy clothes, already thin, some shaking from the effects of disease, and I wondered if we were actually already dead and hadn't realized. Perhaps this was hell. Matthew managed to grab a bed-space next to me. Thank God, thank God for letting him be here with me. "No snoring, Bobby," he said. And we might have been on Scout Camp on Boars Hill.

Our nearest neighbour, i.e. the person just inches away on the next mat, is a man called Macgregor, a Savile Row tailor in peacetime. "Could you measure me for a new dinner jacket?" Matthew asked. "This one seems to have lost its shape." He pointed to the ragged shirt he wore and even Macgregor, a solemn Scot, laughed. "Aye, you'll be needing to take in the seams a little, too."

A few days later. Haven't written because I have had my first attack of malaria — that stagnant pool beside the hut, I suspect. Not too severe. Poor Matthew, he's still not right after his bout at Changi. When I had the fevers I dreamed I was at home, at Winter's Copse. I ran out onto the lawn at the front of the house in bare feet, and it was cool and lush. I fell down and rolled over and over in the dew until I was soaked through.

Then I woke and saw I was lying in sweat-drenched clothes and instead of the coo of wood pigeons the harsh shrieks of the guards filled my ears.

# CHAPTER
# FOUR

**Rachel**
**March 2003**

One click of the DVD remote and Jessamy stood before me.

The television screen showed me a giggling, prancing nine-year-old with a mop of dark hair. I could almost feel electricity crackling round her. This film must have been shot in '76, the year before the Silver Jubilee party. I guessed it must be early June because the lawn was still a soft, almost fluorescent, green and lush; it would have felt like a silk carpet under Jessamy's bare feet. In fact, 1976 was later to turn into the year of the drought. I, too, was only nine that summer, but I remember how later on the heat enveloped the village, trapping us all inside the oven it created.

Looking at this DVD, such oppressive sunlight seemed impossible; everything on the screen was soft, the light radiant rather than glaring.

Winter's Copse itself looked much as it does these days, sheltered by the oak, chestnut and beech trees which had given it its name, its chalk walls and muted orange brickwork unchanged. The smaller size of the plants and shrubs in the garden was the only clue that we were looking back over a quarter of a century. Evie had been a busy gardener back then, always hoeing, digging and mulching. But it was Jessamy who grabbed all the viewer's attention. She grinned at the camera and lifted her arms above her head like a ballerina, bending a slim leg. Then she sprang forward into a cartwheel, legs perfectly straight as they moved through the air, and another and another before cantering towards the apple tree. She made a graceful jump up to the lowest bough, catching it with her hands and swinging her legs through the O she'd made with her arms and flipping her body through so she was standing again. She always was quick to take a risk if she thought it would be exciting. Her legs and arms had attracted many bruises and cuts from failed attempts to scale walls or jump water troughs and her knees were seldom without scabs. These never seemed to detract from the grace of her limbs, though.

I wondered who was taking the film. Perhaps Matthew, Jessamy's father. He'd once owned a cine camera, I recalled. It hadn't been used since his death from lung cancer in 1972. Perhaps Evie hadn't known how to use the camera. More likely she'd never had the time to learn: after the shock of her husband's death there'd been the farm to deal with.

Jessamy released the bough, with another smile at the camera, and darted towards something outside the frame. I knew it must be the hutches beside the fence which housed her beloved guinea pigs. As she ran she turned and called out over her shoulder. There was no sound to this film so her words were lost, but I imagined she was pleading for them not to stop filming her. Jessamy always loved being the centre of attention, the star, the focus. And that's what she was for her mother. Not surprising, really, after such a long wait for her birth. Her mother had married Matthew Winter in 1952 and Jessamy hadn't arrived until 1967. But I didn't want to think about Evie's problems conceiving.

I've noticed that there's always one child in each clan who's the golden one, the one your eye is drawn to. Jessamy held that position in our family. I've noticed, too, how these children seem more likely to end up prematurely dead or involved in some tragedy. Maybe the gods really do love them too much. Or else they envy those shining faces and supple limbs.

I couldn't watch this footage without my eyes pricking. Perhaps we were all once children playing outside on a sunny lawn in some endless, blissful summer, adult worries hidden beyond the dark shrubs at the bottom of the garden.

Yet there was a shadow falling on Jessamy in this film, a real shadow, not a metaphorical one. It wasn't that of the person holding the camera, as far as I could calculate; it fell from someone observing the scene at some distance to the right of the camera. Not Matthew: he'd died four years earlier. The shadow might have been Evie herself but I could make out the edge of her peony-printed dress at the other side of the garden. She must have been tying back an early rose or pulling bindweed from a shrub. Evie was never one for pushing herself forward into the frame, even though her beauty

usually drew all eyes to her. Her modesty was one of
the things I loved most about my aunt. Perhaps she'd
never shaken off her sense of being an incomer in this
village, even though she'd lived at the farm for over
sixty years. "I wasn't born here," she'd said once. "Not
like you, Jessamy." And Jessamy had wriggled with
pride. "I'm a native, aren't I, Mum?" And Evie's smile
had been full of love.

I'd felt a prick of jealousy. Like my aunt, I hadn't
been born on the farm. I was only a visitor. But Evie
had spotted my discomfort. "You've been coming to
stay since you were a baby, Rachel. You belong here
too." And Jess had flung her arms round me.

"I wish you could live here all the time." And her
breath had been warm against me, scented with the
Heinz tomato soup we'd had for supper. Her hug was
so tight I could barely tell where I stopped and she
started. Sometimes this lack of boundaries pushed me
into situations I found frightening: she'd put me up on
her pony and insist I rode at a jump I knew I wouldn't
manage. Or she invented one of her terrifying games
and made me join in: climbing out of the bedroom
window, or running across the field the bull lived in.
But I could never resist the lure of that wide grin, those
sparkling eyes. "C'mon, Rachel, dare you!"

But now the shadow in the film was preoccupying
me. Whose was it? I tried to assess its height and
breadth. But my efforts came to nothing. It might just
be that of a passing neighbour, come to drop off a cake
or collect eggs. Anyway, it was hard to concentrate on
its grey outline because Jessamy was moving again,

turning cartwheel after cartwheel, her limbs long and tanned, her movements smooth and accomplished for such a young child. The shadow swayed slightly as she passed over it. I found myself clenching my hands, willing its darkness away from the girl.

But I was also feeling another reaction to the film, an emotion I tried to push aside as it was unworthy and immature. Where was I when this film was shot? I told myself I was being ridiculous. It was too early in the summer for me to have come to stay at Winter's Copse for the school holidays. And this obviously wasn't one of the weekends Dad drove me over for a brief visit. None of this logic soothed me. I was jealous, envious of Jessamy's life at the farm without me. "There's always a home for you here," Evie had told me more than once. "We miss you so much when you go back to school." But nobody in this film seemed to be missing the absent niece and cousin. Perhaps they never thought of me at all when I was away. Uncle Matthew had died and Evie and Jessamy had drawn even closer together in their loss.

I wasn't going to let myself revert to being a prickly little girl. "I'm going to pull myself together," I'd told Luke as I left the flat to come down here. "Sorting out the house will be cathartic. And when I come home again you'll find me a changed woman. No more weeping. No more hormones. I shall redecorate our bedroom and book an exotic holiday for us. And I'll reinvigorate my business. Clients will come flooding in."

He'd looked down at the suitcase he was carrying to the car for me. "I'm worried it'll all be too much for you."

"No." I took the suitcase. "I can manage."

"I don't doubt that." He sounded sad.

"You know what I'm like: I need to keep busy." I patted my jeans pocket to make sure I'd got paracetamol with me. At least I didn't have to worry about taking painkillers now.

"Are you sure you're OK to drive?"

"It's been twelve hours since my last drink." My head gave a rebuking throb.

"I didn't mean the alcohol."

I knew he didn't.

"Do you really have to do this now, Rachel? Couldn't it wait?"

"I need to start clearing the house." I picked up my suitcase. "And plan the funeral now we can go ahead."

"You could plan it from here. You don't need to be in Oxfordshire to make phone calls."

My hand tightened on the handle and I laid the case in the car boot. "There's the dog. I need to find a home for him. I need to talk to letting agents. I need . . ."

I need to be at Winter's Copse, I wanted to say. I need to feel my aunt and cousin are close by. Even if they're both dead. I need to come to terms with the shock of Evie's death, so sudden, so unexpected. Perhaps something of Evie will still linger in the house. Perhaps there will be answers.

"Don't stay too long," he said, gently. "We need to make plans, contact the clinic —"

"No." The word took me by surprise. "No more clinics. We need to move on, plan our lives round something different." The cross-London rush to the clinic for daily blood tests. The nasal sprays that made me retch. The injections I had to administer at home. The sense of failure, growing stronger every day so that it had started to affect every part of my life. I could barely write some simple copy for an advertisement which I could once have dashed off. "All the embryos are gone, anyway."

"We could try to —"

I held up a hand. "I can't bear the thought of producing more. It makes me feel like a brood mare." I sounded brattish but Luke just nodded and closed the boot.

"Perhaps it's wise to leave things."

And as soon as he said this I felt my emotions rush in an opposite direction. I'd wanted him to try and persuade me it was worth trying again.

I pushed the stop button and ejected the disk. Evie had gone to all the trouble of having this home movie transferred to a DVD just before Christmas. I knew this because I'd found the receipt from the computer company in Wantage that had carried out the transfer for her.

She'd placed the DVD in her desk with her will and details of her solicitor and of various insurance policies and other papers I hadn't yet had time to examine. Evie had meant this footage of her daughter to be seen in the case of her death, probably by me as I, along with her solicitor, was an executor and had the task of clearing out Winter's Copse and selling everything that couldn't be rented out along with the property itself.

She could never have expected death to come so suddenly, though. Cardiomyopathy, the post-mortem had revealed, a condition I'd had to look up on the internet. Inflamed heart muscles. Evie had never mentioned heart trouble to me. Perhaps she hadn't realized. It seemed unfair that a woman who still tramped up and down the hill and maintained a huge garden with barely a moment's breathlessness had suffered such catastrophic heart trouble. Luke had raised his eyebrows over the post-mortem results, too. "Your aunt seemed one of the healthiest people we know. Perhaps the strain of not knowing what had happened to Jessamy had worn her down. But you should ring her GP, Rachel, see what she thinks."

The GP had been kind but mystified. "Evie came into the surgery about four months ago to have her blood pressure checked," she said. "I listened to her heart then and it sounded fine." There was a pause. "I'm just looking through her notes again but there's no sign of anything like a virus that might have damaged her heart."

"When I rang her two days before she died she told me she was planning to dig up one of her flowerbeds and try a whole new planting scheme for the summer."

"Nothing giving her problems on the farm?"

"Not that I'm aware of. She sold the livestock a few years ago. Thank God."

I'd shuddered at the images of the burning pyres of sheep and cattle in the foot and mouth disease outbreak in 2001.

Evie's doctor could add nothing more except her regrets.

In the last two days I'd emptied drawers and cupboards, written to the telephone company to have the landline disconnected, informed Evie's bank and building society of her death and phoned friends and family on my mobile, ticking actions off a list and feeling as though I was moving underneath an ocean, limbs weighed down by the pressure of the water. We hadn't even had the funeral yet: that would have to wait until the crematorium was less busy. Flu season.

As the house emptied it seemed to reflect my own state: a vacant womb that couldn't contain what it was supposed to contain. Only Evie would have understood this. "Not being able to have a baby made me feel I was worthless," she'd told me after one of my failed IVF treatments. "We were surrounded by animals who could reproduce whenever they were required to, year after year, and I couldn't even carry a baby past a few months."

I felt like that every time I walked to our local shops at home, tripping over buggies and prams and toddlers, all of them mocking my barren state.

"Until Jessamy," I'd said.

"Until Jessamy," Evie echoed. "When I got to four months with her and realized I wasn't going to lose this baby I couldn't believe it." And there was a fierceness on her normally gentle face.

My mobile trilled, breaking in on my remembering and alerting me to a text. "Cd come down 2 help . . ." Luke. "No point, all going well, thanx, xxx," I texted back, feeling even worse. But I'd manage. I always did.

And I didn't want Luke here just now. Admitting this made me feel shame, but it was true. Sometimes mad thoughts bubbled up and wanted to burst from my lips. I wanted to tell him to ditch me and find himself someone else, someone who could produce a child or who wouldn't care about not having children.

Evie's dog Pilot whined gently at me as I passed him in the hallway. "What am I going to do with you?" I stroked his smooth dark head and went upstairs to my cousin's bedroom and sat on her bed, staring at her chest of drawers and wardrobe, the bookcase that Evie had long ago emptied of books and toys. Little of Jessamy remained in this house except the DVD film and some photographs. And yet I often sensed my cousin's presence in Winter's Copse. Sometimes I found myself turning suddenly, half expecting to see that broad grin, that way she had of standing, thumbs tucked into the belt loops of her skirt or trousers, ready for action, for a walk down to the village shop to buy sherbet fountains or Curly Wurlies.

My pulse was still racing. The film had shaken me. I hadn't been expecting to see Jessamy leaping across the garden. I hadn't braced myself for it. "Did you think I'd forget Jessamy, Evie?" Like a loon I almost listened for an answer. Nothing. "I'll never forget her, I promise," I went on. When I'd watched that DVD I'd felt myself falling through time, back to when I myself was nine or ten again, spending much of the summer with my widowed aunt and my cousin at Winter's Copse while my parents were abroad. I was once again that child who swung on ropes and collected eggs, who fed calves and rode the pony round the paddock, who shared Jessamy's bedroom and giggled with her after lights-out.

Evie always greeted me with outstretched arms. My aunt, so reserved and dignified with adults, was a different woman in the presence of children. She'd show us how to do magic tricks with cards and coins and how to make explosive mixtures of bicarbonate of soda and vinegar. She said that the house was too big for such a small family. I knew from conversations with her in the last months of her life that my aunt had wished for more children. Sometimes, looking at her fine, straight nose and perfectly shaped forehead, I could picture her as the matriarch of some Italian dynasty, sitting at the head of a long table and indulging her grandchildren.

I went back downstairs to the television set and laid the DVD in a cardboard box with the photographs and the diaries I'd put aside to read. Had Evie ever intended me to see these? Perhaps she'd have burned them if she'd known death was on the way. She'd left Jessamy's little medal in the box, too, the last prize she'd won. I remembered my aunt twisting the medal's ribbon round her wrist that afternoon as we waited and waited for its owner to come back to the party.

I took the box into the kitchen and looked at the gap on the dresser where Jessamy's Silver Jubilee mug should have stood as part of an unbroken chain linking Queen Victoria's Coronation to the Golden Jubilee of Elizabeth II last year. Victoria, the two Edwards, the two Georges and Elizabeth II herself: all commemorated in this collection of china. Evie had valued continuity even though she wasn't much of a one for chitchat about the Royals. I can't ever remember her expressing an opinion about the divorce of Charles and Diana, for instance.

What should I do with these mugs? Sell them along with everything else of value that I didn't want, I supposed. Our London flat was small and minimalist. The mugs wouldn't work alongside the stripped wood floors and modern art.

Perhaps I'd just leave them here when the house was rented out. Twenty-five years was the period Evie had decided upon. If the case of Jessamy's disappearance hadn't been resolved by then, I was to inherit Winter's Copse. The house owned by the Winters for hundreds of years would pass out of the family. I picked up the newest of the mugs, the Golden Jubilee one given to my aunt just months ago. Something rattled inside it. I pulled out a small lead knight on a horse. He'd been painted once but the colours had peeled off. Enough of the pigment remained on his face for me to see he'd once been carefully coloured in. Lancelot. Or perhaps

Galahad, who, I thought I remembered, had been the knight pure in heart who'd found the Holy Grail.

Evie'd never recovered her grail, her lost child. It had slipped from her grasp and remained in shadows. I replaced the mug and its contents on the shelf.

A little cowardly part of me wondered whether Luke had been right and I should have delayed the task of tidying up her affairs, not that there was too much to do. But who else was there? Evie's face, still in its final repose, flashed back into my mind. I pushed the image away and swapped it with a happier one: Evie waving Luke and me off after a weekend's visit to Winter's Copse.

"See you next weekend," I'd called, throwing her a last kiss.

"Drive carefully," she told me. I turned at the door and looked back at her. She was wearing a dark blue wool dress, a scarf pinned round the neck in the elegant manner only she could effect and flat ballet pumps. She'd looked like Audrey Hepburn. That had only been about ten days before her death.

When I went to the hospital after her death she was lying in a small, quiet side room, wearing that same blue dress and scarf. Evie's heart had given up in the morning at home. I'd pictured her wearing old trousers and a jumper to walk the dog, but perhaps she'd been planning to go out to lunch with a friend. The scarf was pinned very carefully round her neck. Evie always joked that nobody except her understood scarftying and only she could arrange her scarf correctly. Surely the scarf would have been taken off while they did all those horrible violent things they did to people's hearts when they were trying to save them. Someone must have retied it after she'd been pronounced dead.

"It was lovely that you took the trouble to tie her scarf the way she liked it," I told the nurse, when she knocked on the door and brought me a cup of tea. She blinked.

"Oh, that wasn't me." She frowned. "Can't remember who was on duty then." She'd opened the door. "Stay with her as long as you need."

I'd stooped down to rest my lips on my aunt's smooth cheek, scared she'd smell of death but determined I should carry out this last gesture of affection. Her skin felt smooth and soft. She smelled slightly of the scent she always wore and of the herbal shampoo she'd used for the last thirty years, buying it by mail order when local shops stopped stocking it. It was the realization that Evie would never again need to wash the long hair she'd worn tied back in a bun that made the tears flood my eyes. She'd never again hand me a cake or a pie to take back to London.

I fell forward onto my knees and wept for my aunt in a way I hadn't for my own father following his death in a car crash, or for my long-vanished cousin. I couldn't have cried more for Evie had she been my own mother and I stopped only when exhaustion bowed me over her bed, my head resting on the scratchy white hospital sheet with its chemical scent.

"You've gone," I said now, addressing her empty kitchen. "Where are you now, Evie?" Surely if her spirit lingered anywhere it would be somewhere here at

Winter's Copse. But all I heard in answer was the squeak of the birdfeeder swinging as a woodpecker, harlequin coloured in black and red, fed from it. Someone had kept it topped up with bird food. Probably Evie's cleaning lady.

I listened for a few more seconds until the woodpecker flew off, then tried to get back to the letters I was writing at the pine table.

I kept having problems with the word "executor" and misreading and mis-writing it as "executioner". That's what my executor's jobs felt like, too, as though I was rummaging through boxes and drawers and killing off my hopes and dreams. I finished the letter and decided to tidy up. As I picked up the cardboard box the contents shifted and I noticed the scrapbook lying underneath the farming diaries I'd scooped up from the filing cabinets. This was a scrapbook as I remembered them from the seventies when scrapbooks were made of dull-coloured sheets of thick paper with plain covers, rather than flowers and seashells and God-knows-what-other whimsy.

I pulled it out and opened it. Every sheet was stuck over with cuttings. They came from a mixture of local and national newspapers and started around the time of the Coronation. With a sick feeling I flicked through until I reached the events occurring at the Silver Jubilee party. I felt my insides knot together as I read them. There was my own nearly-ten-year-old face peering out from one of the cuttings as I stood beside my aunt, my eyes wide and blank. The photograph must have been taken the morning after the party. I remembered the journalists coming to the door. We hadn't been expecting them and, unsuspectingly, Evie had opened up. *Grieving widow begs for news of missing Jessie . . .* Nobody had ever called her that. *Farmer's wife loses only child . . . Little Jessamy vanishes as country toasts Queen . . . Gypsies questioned about missing child . . .*

I replaced the scrapbook in the cardboard box and decided to put the box in Evie's office.

But in the office my energy seemed to ebb away, as though the act of reading the cuttings had sapped me. I sat at my aunt's desk and looked at the photographs I'd gathered up and placed here so I could decide which ones I wanted to take back to London with me. The one of Jessamy as a ten-year-old, of course, sitting on her pony with a beaming smile, her back straight.

I also wanted the picture of Uncle Matthew aged, I estimated, in his fifties. The colour in the old photo had faded but I could make out the smile on his face. He was kneeling in front of a tractor in the farmyard, his hands in front of him, back straight and parallel to the ground like a cat's. His eyes were sharp and he was observing the tractor as though it was another cat. Probably checking a repair had been carried out correctly. I imagined my aunt spotting her husband at work and running inside to grab a camera, unable to resist the shot of a man in love with his work. Evie and Matthew had had a happy marriage. "It shook me terribly when he became sick," she'd told me once. "He always seemed so strong. It was lung cancer, nothing to do with the diseases he caught in that camp, but I always wondered whether it weakened him in some way, like his . . ." And she'd broken off, shaking her head.

I smiled at Matthew's picture and put it aside, turning to a black and white photograph of Evie and my father Charlie, at roughly the age Jessamy had been when she vanished. It had probably been taken by their mother, my grandmother, because they were standing in the doorway of a mock-Tudor semi. If I hadn't known of Evie's origins, I'd have imagined my aunt to have been born in some neo-classical pile in the shire counties, but she'd been a south London girl and proud of it. She and my father looked bright, expectant, in Fair Isle cardigans, gas masks slung over their shoulders, with no idea that they would never return to that house. There was something of Jessamy in Evie's features: they might have been sisters at that age.

The fourth photograph, a black and white print, was of two young men with bare chests and stick-thin legs, behind them palm trees and a barbed wire fence. Matthew, with his brother, Robert. I'd never met Robert, who'd died in a fire on the farm just after the war.

The men were smiling but the smiles were almost like grimaces. They were standing in a Japanese prisoner-of-war camp somewhere in the Thai jungle and someone (fellow prisoner? guard?) had taken this photograph of them because today was Christmas Day 1942, as evidenced by the small branch they'd decorated with paper chains and stuck in a tin pot in front of them.

They didn't look like survivors. It was beyond me why my aunt had kept this photograph in the frame. Matthew certainly didn't look his best after months of privation, not at all like the smiling man in the tractor picture. If I'd been given this photograph to use in my work I'd definitely have needed my software to smooth out the lines in his face. The silver frame was attractive, though. Perhaps I'd take out the picture and replace it with a photograph of Evie herself. There'd be plenty to choose from: Evie had the kind of face that the camera loves; it was — had been — almost impossible to take a bad photograph of her. I undid the clasps at the back and removed the velvet-covered board, giving it a gentle shake to dislodge the photograph onto the desk.

As it came out I saw that there was another picture there, hidden behind the group shot. I turned it round so it was the right way up and found myself looking at a photograph of a young man of about eighteen in uniform, with roses behind him. "Matinee idol," I muttered to myself. Examining his features I felt a glow of admiration. This man was beautiful, in a completely masculine, nineteen-forties style. He also looked familiar and the roses were obviously those still growing round the front door. I glanced again at the picture of the two men in the camp and recognized him, or his ghost, in the figure standing next to Matthew.

"You're Robert," I said. God, I was going mad, talking to myself like some old biddy. "Jessamy's Uncle Robert." I glanced back at the portrait photo. "What on earth did they do to you out there to make you lose your looks like that?"

The young and handsome Robert Winter smiled back at me. I noticed that the smile reached his dark eyes, slightly wrinkling the skin around them. But their expression remained melancholic. "Did you know what you were getting into when you signed up?" I asked him. "Was there any warning —" I stopped, thinking now of my cousin, of how her disappearance had come as a sudden hammer blow.

The clock on the fireplace struck eleven. I coughed, trying to dislodge the stone that had suddenly threatened to choke me. I was supposed to be going into town to talk to the mason about headstones. No time to search for a photograph of Evie to place in the silver frame. I replaced Robert's photograph under the glass and fastened the clasps behind the backing. "You can stay there for now," I told him.

As I left the room I glanced back to make sure I'd turned off the electric heater. I caught sight of Robert Winter's dark eyes. They looked different again from this angle, seeming warning or reproachful. Perhaps that was why Evie had swapped his photo for the group picture.

I should probably stick every one of those photographs in the cardboard box so that I didn't have to look at them again.

Pilot, Evie's black Labrador, stood as I entered the hall, anticipating his walk by furiously wagging his tail. Evie had given him at least one long outing a day. "Later," I told him.

He gave me what sounded like a sign and flopped down again. "Sorry," I added. "I promise I'll take you out soon." In London my day had been organized round the demands of my clients. Down here it had always been the animals who dictated the timetable: cows to be milked twice a day, chickens to be fed, horses to bring in and out of the field. Even as small children Jessamy and I had been bound to certain tasks such as collecting eggs or feeding calves. I hadn't minded. It had been magic.

"You could be a country girl, young Rachel," Martha had told me, nodding approval as she came upon me collecting eggs. "You're making a better fist of it than your dad ever did. Charlie could never find all the eggs. But he and Evie came here too late in life."

"They were only ten," I had protested. "That's not much older than I am now."

"They were incomers. Them and that Eyetie."

"Eyetie?"

"Italian. Carlo, his name was. A POW. He helped on the farm. Spent most of his time taking naps if he thought he could get away with it. Luckily Mr Edwards, he was the manager while the Winter lads were away, and I were here to keep things going round the place."

And she nodded her head in apparent satisfaction and shuffled off. Martha never stayed long in the farmyard, preferring the open fields above the farm, where we'd see her striding around, her silhouette on the ridge like an exclamation mark against the pale sky. I hadn't seen Martha yet, probably been putting it off because they said she was now so eccentric and I didn't feel strong enough for eccentrics. She'd been kind to me, as a child, though, and I'd have to pay her a visit.

I'd related Martha's comments to Jessamy as we'd curled up together in her bed that night. She scowled. "Martha's got this thing about Mum being an incomer. Don't tell her what Martha said, it'll make her cross." She wriggled closer to me. "Martha's right about you, though, you belong here. When we're grown up you and I'll live here together all the time," she whispered. "We'll share the work between us. You can have your own cows and horses. And sheep. Do you promise, Rache?"

"Yes," I whispered back.

"It's a solemn oath." She sounded as though we were in church and lightning would strike me if I broke my word. "Like they used to make in olden times."

But she'd been the one to break the oath, involuntarily.

# CHAPTER
# FIVE

**Robert**
**Camp at Nong Pladuk, Thailand, January 1943**

Dear Evie,

We managed some kind of celebration for Christmas, with a pretend pudding made of rice and a few currants someone had bartered for. We even had alcohol, brewed from vegetables or rice. It would make good rust-remover. So you see, we do keep our spirits up, Evie. Note the pun! I try to look at the animals, to admire the hornbills with their strange casques on their beaks, and the macaques. You'd smile to see how they carry their babies on their backs. Not so sure you'd smile at the scorpions and snakes, though.

These letters are becoming more like diary entries but they serve a purpose. There are rumours they're going to move us on again. I'll write again soon, Evie. And I pray I'll come home soon, too.

# Part Two

# CHAPTER
# SIX

**Rachel**
**A few days before the Silver Jubilee, 1977**

"Just one more go," Jessamy begged.

We were in the farmyard, admiring our latest game: an obstacle course constructed from milk churns, hay bales, a rusting Ferguson tractor and whatever else we could find. We'd been up since six because the early morning light had flooded the bedroom and woken Jess and then she'd shaken me out of my sleep. Any time spent awake in bed was time wasted, she said. As soon as we'd heard Evie pull the bolts of the back door open to let out the dog we dressed and came down to play before breakfast.

"It's too easy for you." The low beams of sun shone on the fragments of old man's beard floating round the farmyard so they looked like fairies.

"You nearly managed it, too, Rache. You'd have done it if you hadn't fallen off the bale."

I nursed my sore wrist. "You'll just win again anyway."

"Make it harder for me."

"How?" I considered increasing the drop from the bales. If I put one on top of the other Jess wouldn't be able to spring down as neatly onto the upturned oil drum. But I'd never be able to hoist another one up on top.

"I know." From her pocket she extracted a handkerchief. It was large so it must have been one of her father's. "Tie this round my eyes. Then I can't see."

"You want to do it blind?"

"Why not?"

"You'll fall off the bales. It's too risky."

"No I won't." She was already tying it round her eyes. "Can't see a thing. C'mon, Rache. Take me to the starting line."

I moved her by the shoulders to the broom we'd laid on the ground. She set off, hand in front of her, finding her way to the row of bricks and walking across them sideways with easy, neat movements. "This is peasy," she called. Then she found the bales and climbed up, crawling over them like a monkey on all fours. I thought she'd climb down the other side but she sprang down in a neat gymnast's jump.

"Come on, girls!" Evie called from the kitchen. "Breakfast is ready." I smelled the bacon.

"Let's finish it off later," I said.

"I'm nearly there." She was running towards the wall now. Once she'd scaled and jumped down the other side and crossed the water trough, she'd have finished the course.

She'd almost finished when Evie's black Labrador jumped up from his vantage point by the milk churns and ran towards the kitchen door. He always was a greedy dog and he must have smelled the bacon frying. He didn't knock into Jessamy but his shadow must have passed over her face, disorientating her so that she changed direction by a couple of inches. Now she was running towards the steel tow bar of the trailer. "Stop!" I screamed. "Wrong way."

Too late.

The tow bar caught her on the shins. She let out a cry, arms flaying as she struggled to stay upright. My held breath seemed to choke me. She fell very slowly onto a wooden crate. I ran to her. "Jess!" Her fingers pulled at the handkerchief's knot. Her shocked scream had brought Evie tearing out of the kitchen. "What have you done?" She ran across the farmyard and pulled the blindfold off Jessamy's face. "Oh sweetheart." Her eye was already swelling up. "You must just have caught it on the corner of that crate. And look at your legs. I'll wrap some ice cubes in a cloth and put it on your eye. You'll have some more pretty bruises to show everyone." She put an arm round Jess's shoulders. "Why do you have to take these risks? That's the second bad bang to your head in a fortnight. One of these days you're really going to hurt yourself."

"I just can't stop myself." Jessamy spoke through sniffs. "If I see something I have to try it. I can't let myself be a coward."

"Stay there," Evie ordered. "I'll bring the compresses out."

Jess sat on one of the bales. Already I could see the shock passing from her face.

"What's going on?" Martha stood in the yard, a jar in her hands. "Brought honey down for the girls." She handed the jar to me and scowled at Jess's eye. "What's happened to you, missy?"

I saw the mischief flicker over my cousin's bruised face.

"Mum hit me again." Jessamy said, giving me a wink. "She's so strict."

As I caught sight of Martha's face I saw horror mix with contempt. "Jess was just —" I started to tell her.

But Martha's lips were already set tight.

Evie came out with the compress: a drying-up cloth she'd soaked in cold water.

"Vet's coming at ten, isn't he?" Martha said.

Evie let out a sigh. "Yes." I saw Jessamy glance towards the cowshed.

"Don't mention the cows," she'd whispered to me when I'd first arrived. "Mum's worried about them."

"Why?"

"TB. Perhaps."

I didn't know what those letters meant but I knew that they struck fear into farmers. "What will happen?"

"They prick the cows' skins and if the cows react to the pricks it means they could have TB." Jessamy swallowed and looked away.

"And then?"

A shrug. "I don't want to talk about it."

When I woke a few days later on the morning of the Jubilee Jessamy's bed was empty. I went to the window and peered out but there was no sign of her in the yard.

54

I put on my dressing gown and went downstairs. The dog wagged his tail in his basket by the door. Jessamy was walking towards the house, very slowly, her hands in her jeans pockets, her head bowed. Perhaps she was still mourning the death of the three cows the vet had put down. When she saw me she gave a start.

"Where've you been?" I asked.

"Wanted to check Starlight's water." I knew it was a lie; we'd gone to the field last night and topped up the pony's trough with the hose. I stared at my cousin. Her eye was healing well; the black bruise turning to yellow. Jess's bruises always went down quickly. She gave a shrug and walked past me. Perhaps she'd been checking on the remaining cows. Didn't want me to see she was worried about them. Jessamy'd been quiet since the three had been slaughtered.

"You're up very early, girls," Evie said behind me. "I've got something for you. Look in the bread bin." It was a loaf of bread coloured red, white and blue. "Just a bit of fun," she said. "There may be another surprise later on, after the party." Her eyes sparkled. "I thought we all needed cheering up."

"What is it?" Jessamy cried. "Tell us."

"No." And she refused, even though we bombarded her with questions, and set us to work with various tasks. "No surprise unless these are done first." There were plates and cutlery to count out into wicker baskets for transporting over to the village green. The morning passed in a haze of errands and panics over tablecloths and serving spoons. Meanwhile Evie took a hammer

55

and nails and a length of chicken-wire out to the hen house to mend a hole.

I went out into the yard and found her talking to Martha. Evie and Martha rarely spoke to one another more than was necessary for running the farm. "They've never got on," Jessamy had told me once. "Martha wanted to marry into the family, you see. But Robert died. And Mum married Dad. So there was nobody left for her."

I moved behind the slurry bin, feeling shame and curiosity all mixed together.

Evie clenched the hammer. "I can't deal with any more bad news."

"Don't you want to look at these ewes?"

"I'll come up later." She shook her head. "I'm just praying that's the end of this run of bad luck."

"Farming's a tough life. I always told you that," Martha hissed. "I'm glad you've sorted that henhouse. I see the fox took two more chickens last night."

I hadn't seen the bodies. Evie must have cleared them away.

"Or was it the gypsies?" Martha went on. "I saw them hanging around in the lane yesterday. You need to make sure everything's properly locked."

"We shouldn't blame them for every single mishap." Evie sounded weary.

"They took that saddle last week, I'm sure of it."

"We don't know that."

Martha snorted as she walked away. I peered round the bin and saw Evie stand motionless for a few seconds. She put down the hammer and nails on top of a milk churn — unlike her not to replace them in the work shed immediately — and walked very slowly back towards the kitchen, her face puckered up into an expression I couldn't read. I ducked back into the shadows behind the corn bin until she'd passed me, waiting there for a few minutes so there was no risk she'd know I'd been listening.

I meant to tell Jess what I'd seen but as I re-entered the kitchen Evie thrust a Pyrex bowl of strawberries into my hands. "These need hulling. Then there's cream to be whipped." And I was swept up into the maelstrom of Jubilee preparations.

The telephone rang about ten minutes before we left and Evie took the call in the farm office, so we couldn't hear. She came back to the kitchen with a flushed look on her face and a smile. "All according to plan," she said.

"What is?"

"You'll find out."

"I almost don't like surprises." Jessamy stuck out her lower lip. "It drives you mad not knowing."

"It's only fun for the one who's keeping the secret," I said.

"I hate keeping secrets." For a moment Jessamy looked quite solemn.

For the party itself Jessamy and I both wore long white socks with our cotton summer dresses. Because our legs were skinny they often fell down around our ankles, revealing the bruises on Jessamy's leg that matched the one on her eye. "You look like you've been in a fight," I told her.

She laughed but then once again that strange expression passed over her face and was gone before I could comment on it.

Apart from the bruises my limbs seemed very similar to Jessamy's but were actually inferior in all respects. Jessamy had never been beaten in a race by any girl her age in the parish and few of the boys of her own age could run faster than she could. She never appeared big-headed, though, taking her athletic successes for granted but not referring to them. Lucky Jessamy, golden girl, born with all the good fairy godmother gifts: pretty, fast, clever and popular.

"I wish I was you, Jessamy." The words popped out now as I gazed at my cousin, fresh from her latest triumph in the egg-and-spoon race on the village green, where the party was in full swing. Evie turned to me, her brown eyes anxious. "You always win everything." I went on, knowing I'd made a mistake, saying all this, but unable to stop myself. "I'd like to win just one thing, just once."

Jessamy's eyes narrowed but she said nothing.

"I don't understand why there have to be so many races at a Jubilee party." Evie sounded tired. "It's supposed to be a day of fun, not an athletics contest. But you're a good runner, Rachel, too, just like your father. I remember how he could whizz up the hill behind the house. I could never keep up." She squeezed my shoulder and the soft sleeve of her floaty dress brushed me. It felt like a butterfly wing against my arm.

58

I'd already noticed people looking at my aunt today. People always did. This afternoon she'd put on a silk smock dress, tied loosely round her waist, and swept her hair off her face using a thick hair band.

"I might not enter the sack race after all." Jessamy spoke casually. "Horrible scratchy old bags. And I'm tired now." In fact she seemed so full of energy that it was almost crackling round her.

I peered at my cousin but her face was closed. She dug at a daisy on the field with the toe of her white plimsoll. I wanted to ask her what was up but there wasn't time.

"Off you go then, darling." Evie smiled at me. I crossed to the starting line, where the ladies from the parish council were laying out sacks.

"Jessamy not competing this time?" I turned to see Martha standing beside me.

"No."

She turned to look at her for a moment. I was conscious of the concentration in her expression. "Shame. She always does well. The Winters were always good at sport and running."

"So was Aunt Evie. And my Dad." Martha blinked and looked away. There were five of us in the race, two big boys from the senior school in Wantage, a girl my age, and a smaller boy. I looked at the older boys' sturdy legs and didn't rate my chances. But when the pistol fired and I started jumping I struck an easy rhythm, unlike my larger competitors whose legs were too long to fit comfortably into the sacks. The finishing line raced towards me.

Evie beamed at me. Jessamy gave me one of her silent looks from underneath her dark lashes. I could tell she was really pleased for me. But there'd still be some part of her which wished she'd competed and won.

"Let's go and look at the Jubilee cake before you run the relay," Evie said. We were both on the same team. Jessamy would be running first to build up a good lead and I was to follow. There'd been long practices on the lawn back at Winter's Copse, using some old bed legs as batons.

"Hope I don't drop the baton." Nervousness sent ripples through my stomach. Jessamy had been good about standing down from the sack race for me. If only I could repay her by doing well.

"It's just for fun," Evie said again, sounding suddenly flat. "But you won't drop the baton. Come on." She put a hand behind each of our backs and steered us towards the tea tent.

A huge rectangular fruitcake sat on a silver-foil-wrapped platter, iced in white with the Queen's coat of arms in different-coloured sugars. A photograph of the Queen in a silver frame stood next to it on the table.

"When will they cut it?" Jessamy asked, examining the ribbons round the cake.

"Not for a while yet. There'll be a loyal toast first."

"What's that?" I asked.

"Like a kind of congratulations to the Queen."

"And then they'll give us our mugs?"

Jessamy was obsessed with the silver-rimmed mugs showing the Queen's head. "Let's go and look at them again, Rachel." The mugs were stored in a cardboard box under the table displaying the Jubilee cake. We knelt on the grassy floor to study them. Each mug nestled in its own cardboard square inside the box. Jessamy stroked their rims. I knew she was imagining hers on the dresser at home. Not long to wait now. I watched the tip of her tongue as she placed it between her teeth, a sign that she really, really wanted something so much that she was almost scared of admitting it.

"Come on, girls, it's your race soon," Evie called. "No, it's not Zandra Rhodes, just something I ran up myself," she told a woman from the village, who was touching the sleeves of her silk dress and cooing. "Hurry, you two!" We walked to the starting-line, Jessamy brushing crumbs from her mouth. Nobody who didn't know her as well as I did would have noticed that her chin was now more firmly set. I crossed my fingers that the baton change would go well.

Jessamy left me to go down to the starting point and I stood in position facing her thirty yards down the track. She pulled up her socks so that they covered the bruises on her legs.

The starter fired the pistol and Jessamy seemed to blast from the starting line, ahead of the other four runners within four paces, increasing the lead all the time. She was nearly at the other end of the course and I was standing, palm stretched out for the baton, my face muscles aching from the strain of concentrating. My fingers were almost clasped around the black plastic when the baton fell to the grass. I scooped it up and managed to propel myself forward at the same time but the precious lead had been lost. The boy from the pub was breathing down my neck. I clenched my teeth and pushed myself harder and harder, still just holding the lead, perspiration beading on my brow. I handed the baton over to the third runner and glanced back up the track. Jessamy's eyes were on the runner. The fourth girl had her hand outstretched. The change was smooth but the team beside us were already level now. Our fourth runner, a sturdy girl from a farm in the next hamlet, threw herself up the track, arms pumping away. Her opponent was already an inch ahead. I closed my eyes. A cheer from the crowd told me that the race was lost. I joined in the clapping, unable to meet Jessamy's gaze until the other competitors started drifting away. I stole a look at her. She was smiling at the winners but I spotted the blankness in her eyes that changed to something almost like confusion.

Evie was coming towards us. "Well done, you two!" she told us. "Let's go and get you both some orange squash."

"I'm not thirsty."

"Jessamy . . ."

"I'm going to look at the mugs again," she called as she ran off.

"I'm sorry," I shouted after her, not caring that people could hear, would know exactly what I was sorry for. Jessamy Winter's cousin had let her down in a race.

She glanced over her shoulder. ". . . don't know what to think any more," I thought she said.

Evie and I looked at one another. "It's because I dropped the baton," I whispered. "She doesn't know what to think about me any more."

"It's just a village race," she said. "You ran well, Rachel. I haven't seen you sprint like that before."

"I've been practising."

"It paid off." She smiled at me and I felt better. "I remember your father running up the hill one night." Her expression was dreamy. "I thought my heart would burst trying to keep up with him." It was the second time she'd brought up this memory.

"Why were you running up the hill at night?"

Evie didn't seem to have heard me and steered me towards the drinks stand. "I don't know what's got into Jessamy." Out of the corner of my eye I caught sight of my cousin heading across the bright field towards the darkness of the tea tent. Perhaps Jessamy had decided she really did want another look at the mugs. Over the chatter of the crowd I heard her laugh, just once. I wanted to run after her but perhaps it was better to wait until she came to me, when she'd worked out *what to think*.

Then she was gone, taken up into the black interior with its trestle tables of Victoria sandwich, scones and buns and the big earthenware teapots borrowed from the village hall.

Evie found me orange squash at the stand, keeping up a stream of conversation all the time. Trying to distract me from my humiliation, probably.

"Now I wonder where that cousin of yours is." She sounded more relaxed.

"She went into the marquee." We walked across to it.

Evie peered at the crowds queuing for tea and buns. "She's not here. Perhaps she's gone outside again to play with her schoolfriends." She frowned. "Very naughty of her to leave you out."

I wasn't surprised. I deserved exclusion.

"I hope she's not going to miss out on the loyal toast and cake cutting." Evie looked suddenly weary; unusual for my aunt, who generally never sat down except for meals. She'd have been forty-seven that summer and now I noticed the lines around her eyes. For the first time it struck me how hard it must be for her: farming without Uncle Matthew. A neighbour tapped her arm and she turned. "Yes, just the three reactors . . . Thank you. We're hoping that's the end of it," I heard her say. Those three slaughtered cows again.

As we left the tent to look for Jessamy I spotted three of the gypsy children peering out from behind the tea tent. They'd been invited to the party along with everyone else but preferred to linger on the periphery, only occasionally venturing inside for currant buns and squash. Jessamy liked the gypsies, or tinkers, as some people called them, admiring their skills on horseback. The older girl, Rosie, went to school with her. They didn't look like what I imagined gypsies should be, being fair-haired and blue-eyed. "Irish originally," Martha said. "Riffraff."

"I like Rosie." Jessamy's lower lip had stuck out. "She's kind. Her dog's got puppies and they let me play with them."

I stayed by my aunt's side for the rest of the afternoon, shadowing her as she moved from one group of friends and neighbours to another. Everyone seemed to have a word for Evie. She might not have been born in the village but she'd come to live here at an early age and then married one of its oldest families. Evie Winter had a certain status.

We were summoned to the tea tent for the loyal toast in front of the Jubilee cake. ". . . God save the Queen!" Mr Fernham, the chairman of the parish council, ended, the smile on his face spreading across the park. The ladies from the choir launched into the National Anthem and we all joined in. I was thinking how Jessamy would have enjoyed watching plump Mrs Chivers's bosom quiver as she trilled. Mr Fernham's sister wore a look of almost religious fervour on her thin face. He sang in more measured tones, as though contemplating the meaning of each word.

Then Miss Fernham took the cake off to slice it into pieces for handing round. With her brother she hoisted the cardboard box of mugs on to the trestle table. One of the cardboard squares at the top of the carton was now empty, I noted. The children's names were called out: youngest first and upwards in age so that Jessamy and I came roughly halfway through the list. Each child trotted back to its place clutching a mug.

"Jessamy Winter." Mr Fernham looked towards Evie and me. Evie shrugged. "Rachel Parr." I took my mug from him and muttered a thanks. His gaze lingered on me for a second. Perhaps I had an orange-squash moustache. I walked back to my aunt, wiping my mouth.

"I really thought she'd be back in time to get her mug." Evie sounded tense now.

Jessamy had already cleared a space on the dresser shelf so that there'd be room for the new Silver Jubilee mug beside the Queen's Coronation mug.

"Have you any idea where she might have gone?" Evie asked.

I shook my head.

A muscle twitched in the side of Evie's face. "I'm going to ask Mr Fernham to put out an announcement over the loudspeaker."

"Not yet!" Something about the idea of an announcement made Jessamy's disappearance suddenly seem frightening.

"Why ever not?"

"It's too soon."

"We need his help, darling." She sounded curt. Probably thought I was behaving like an idiot.

Evie and I went to the stewards' tent and Evie explained about Jessamy. Mr Fernham was very calm and picked up his loudspeaker to issue a short message asking Jessamy Winter to report to the stewards' table by the tea tent. So strong was the confidence which he injected into this broadcast that I turned my head to look for Jessamy running across the park towards us. But she didn't.

Now my slight impatience at her absence was growing into concern because of all the trouble she'd be in if she didn't return, rather than because I thought something bad had happened to her. My aunt was tolerant of Jessamy's whims but I could tell by the small vein pulsing on one temple and her tight grip on my arm that Jessamy wouldn't just get away with a few cross words. It would be bed with just a piece of toast for her: lights out and no talking. How could she have been such a fool? But then that baton sliding out of my hand onto the grass shot back into my mind. This was all my fault.

I could feel my aunt's tension in the fingers she kept wrapped around my arm. I thought of Uncle Matthew, barely remembered now except as a kind and silent presence around the farm. He'd scooped me up many times when I'd fallen off the bicycle I'd been learning to ride in the yard and had let me hold the new lambs. I wished he'd been around this afternoon to soothe my aunt. I was aware of how feeble any attempts on my behalf to do this would be. Dad should be here to support his sister but he was in Majorca building a marina and holiday apartments.

We waited. It was time to sit down at the trestles for sandwiches and cake and people began to amble over. One or two cast sympathetic glances at us as they passed. "Not found her yet? Little minx." "You'll have something to say to her when you get her back."

I refused to join the other children, superstitious that if I sat down with them I was accepting that my cousin wouldn't be back this afternoon. I stood with my aunt beside the stewards' tent. The balloons tied to the awnings and table legs had started to deflate. Paper cups and plates littered the grass and some of the smaller children were rubbing their eyes and whining. I kept expecting Jess to run across the grass in that easy loping gait of hers to join us. "Where's my mug?" she'd ask. "Hope you saved me a piece of Jubilee cake." I stared at the gate until my eyes ached with the effort of making out an outline of her figure that wasn't there. I closed them, counted to ten and then opened them, hoping she'd be there.

But she wasn't.

Mr Fernham appeared with two plates of the sliced cake for us. "Fiona made it. It's very good."

Evie crumbled off a piece and put it into her mouth but I murmured an apology.

People were starting to push back their chairs, their meal complete. In a moment they'd start moving slowly towards home, happy to put their feet up and watch the TV coverage of the celebrations in London, weary after an afternoon of rich food and games. Evie and I would walk through the fields to the house and Jessamy would be sitting in the kitchen. Evie'd tell her off, but not harshly; she'd gone beyond anger now. I felt her anxiety pulsing from her in little waves. But Jess would be back at home. She'd look stricken for exactly one second and then she'd give that shrug of hers, say she was sorry, and mean it, and accept whatever punishment her mother gave her without a word of complaint. I'd say sorry too for dropping that baton. Jess didn't bear grudges.

"I could run back to the farm," I offered. "See if she's there and then run back here."

"No." Evie clutched my shoulder. "Stay with me." She had something wound around her hand and wrist; I couldn't work out what it was at first. Then I recognized it as Jessamy's egg-and-spoon medal. The red ribbon was cutting into Evie's slender fingers. The red matched the polish she'd put on her nails that morning.

It seemed Evie needed me as much as I needed her. The realization made me feel strange, as though the grass beneath my plimsolls was tilting and threatening to tip me over. Again I wished that there was someone else here with me, an adult.

Volunteers were stacking chairs and clearing plates. Mr Fernham reappeared. "I think we should organize a search for Jessamy." He shook his head at Evie. "Nothing too serious, but we could knock on doors, check whether she's playing somewhere inside."

"I don't think she'd leave the party willingly," my aunt said.

"And who would she go with?" I put in, my eyes sweeping the green. "Everyone's here."

Mr Fernham scratched the back of his head and went off to organize the search party. Evie turned to a neighbour to ask her to check her garden for Jessamy.

While Evie's back was turned. Martha approached me. "Nobody would harm that precious child."

I pressed my lips into an expression resembling a smile, wishing I found her words more reassuring, and walked on, remembering the half-conversation between Evie and Martha I'd overheard that morning in the farmyard.

"Martha's completely mad," Jessamy had told me once. "She's the great-great granddaughter of one of the last Welsh drovers, the men who herded the animals along the drove-ways before the railway was built. He was crazy. That's what they say at school, anyway. And so's she. But she's nice to me."

Everyone always was.

Evie had finished the exchange with the neighbour. "Let's go home and wait, Rachel. Oh."

"What?"

"I forgot about the pony."

"Pony?"

"I bought another pony. So you can have one each when you ride. And he'll be company for Starlight. I arranged for him to be delivered while we were out." Evie bit her lip.

I felt a little ashamed at how my excitement about the new pony intruded on my worry about Jessamy and prayed it didn't show.

Evie gasped. We'd turned a bend and in front of us stood a girl in a dress the same yellow colour as Jess's, back to us. I felt my aunt stiffen and my own heart pump.

Then the girl turned and we saw her round, spectacled, face and blonde curls. Not Jess. Evie's breath came out in the form of a long sigh and her grip crushed my hand so that I cried out.

# CHAPTER
# SEVEN

**Evie**
**October 1977**

On an afternoon as golden and still as this Evie could still hope for the best. Children did turn up months after they'd vanished, it wasn't impossible, the police had said. Evie should keep her hopes alive.

"Alive," she repeated silently to herself. She pushed her hands into the pockets of the old duffel coat she wore. The word seemed almost incomprehensible now; she'd said it to herself so many times. *Jessamy is still alive, somewhere she is alive.*

"I'm pleased to plant this tree in honour of the twenty-fifth anniversary of the Coronation of Her Majesty the Queen." Jonathan Fernham drove his spade into the earth and brought up a clod. It smelled sweet, almost tangy, like something you might want to eat. No frosts so far this autumn and still plenty of golden leaves on the oaks and beeches. Warm enough not to need a coat. Jessamy had left the Jubilee party four months ago without as much as a jacket, wearing just that flimsy cardigan over her primrose-yellow summer dress. On a day like this it wouldn't be nearly warm enough. Evie tried to push the image of her daughter shivering out of her mind. Impossible. She shouldn't have come today but some foolish hope inside her believed that Jessamy might somehow find out that the Jubilee tree was to be planted, might manage to make her way back to the village green.

No signs of a struggle back at the party in June, the police had concluded. No reports of a child being dragged off the field. And heaven knows, there'd be witnesses enough, with the celebration still in full swing. "Your daughter has seemingly vanished off the face of the earth," the sergeant had told her the afternoon following Jessamy's disappearance. "Is there nothing more you can tell us? Nowhere she might have gone? What about other family?"

And she'd run through the family tree with them again: Matthew, her husband, dead. Her brother Charles and his wife. "So it was just you and the other little girl at the party?" the sergeant had asked.

"That's right, Rachel, my niece."

"And she doesn't know where Jessica is?"

"Jessamy. No."

He'd looked displeased at the correction. "No quarrel between Rachel and Jessamy?"

"Jessamy was a little annoyed that a baton had been dropped in a relay race at the party, but that was as much her fault as Rachel's." Evie knew Jessamy had felt anger only for herself. "They've always got on well."

The sergeant didn't even bother to write this in his notepad.

"Nothing going on at home?"

72

"Nothing." She thought of the TB. "We had some cattle slaughtered earlier in the week. Jessamy was upset about that but she's grown up on the farm, she's used to things going through hard patches."

The sergeant's pencil remained motionless in his fingers.

"Did she have her own passport or was she still on yours?"

"On mine."

"Good." He wrote something. "Any other family?"

"Only my brother now. He's divides his time between the south of France and Surrey. He came to collect Rachel at lunchtime."

"We'll need to speak to him."

She gave him Charlie's number in Weybridge.

"No trouble with the gypsies?"

She shook her head.

"Nothing stolen?" He gave her a knowing look. "That's not what your neighbours say."

"Sometimes eggs go, the odd hen, too. A saddle disappeared from the stables a week or so back. But that could be anyone." There were occasional whispers in the village of stolen dogs, too, sometimes. Evie had no doubt that some of the rumours were justified, the Jacksons were no saints, but stealing a child? The small surviving part of her still governed by logic knew it would be insane for them to do that. And why would they? They had no particular reason to dislike the Winters and Jessamy and Rosie played together at school.

"Maybe." He closed his notepad and stood, muttering something about detectives coming to talk to her later. She watched him tramp up the lane. He'd be going to speak to Martha.

When his footsteps had faded Evie had let herself slide off the chair on to the quarry stoned floor, where she'd pulled her knees up under her and huddled like an infant, trying to hide away from it all. She'd stayed there, motionless, until darkness had fallen and the range had gone out and the dog came to sniff her, begging to be fed. Thank God Rachel hadn't still been here to see her like this. Charlie had begged Evie to let him stay at Winter's Copse with her but she'd almost pushed him out of the door, superstitiously believing that Jessamy would return to her in the dark and quiet, when her mother sat alone with the dog at the kitchen table.

But she hadn't.

"You all right?" Freya Barnes's dark eyes were focused in a look of deep concern. "You don't have to do this, Evie, if it's all too much. I'll go back to the farm with you if this is all too much."

"I'm fine." Thank God for Freya. People had muttered about the West Indian woman when she'd first arrived a year ago. Freya was ignoring all the whisperings and had even managed to get a part-time job in the school. She would have been teaching Jessamy this term.

Evie watched Jonathan Fernham insert the sapling into its hole and remembered a time, years back, when she had planted trees — pear and damson — in the

74

garden. Jessamy had still been in a pushchair then, her cheeks creamy and smooth as the flesh of a hazelnut against her brown hair. A hazelnut, safe in its shell. Never so safe again. Matthew had still been alive then, too, a quiet, comfortable presence around the farm.

Freya gave her a complicit grin and winked. Freya had never shown any embarrassment on the subject of Jessamy and perhaps that was why she and Evie had become close friends over the last months.

Even Freya could never be told Evie's nightmares; how she sometimes dreamt of a ghostly blacksmith descending the down the afternoon of the Silver Jubilee party and stealing Jessamy in reprisal for a night Evie and Charlie had once spent in his magical smithy. Or of a band of shadowy drovers sweeping her daughter off as they herded monstrously formed animals along the Ridgeway to some hell that no human could penetrate.

Mr Fernham trod in the earth round the planted sapling. The little tree looked like a thin young girl, liable to be blown away in the first autumn gale. Evie felt a pang for its tender roots and slight waving boughs.

Jessamy lived, she surely lived. Evie closed her eyes briefly and spoke silently to her daughter, begging her to come back.

# CHAPTER
# EIGHT

**Robert**
**Camp at Nong Pladuk, Thailand, February 1943**

Dear Evie,

I look at the city boys with their thin arms and hollow chests and know each sleeper we lay will cost a life. I thank God for those years of good food and physical work at home. The times Matthew and I carried food pails to animals or drove in wooden posts. We have muscle and stamina.

When we worked at home there'd be a cool breeze blowing off the Downs. We'd bring a flask of tea or a stone bottle of ginger beer. Sometimes at harvest Mum would walk up with a jug of cool lemonade for us. I wonder how my mother is now. She wrote to me before Singapore fell. You must have helped her write that letter, Evie, because I recognized your writing in places. I lost what she sent me. But I still have that wonderful letter of yours, Evie. It's about the only thing I didn't lose on the journey from Singapore. Sometimes we see Thai kids playing and I wonder what you're doing at home. It's strange to think of you sleeping in our old bedroom, playing with our old toys. But it's a good thought.

A week later. We've been moved from the railway itself to a camp further up-river.

And there are new guards. They seem to speak a different language: perhaps they're Koreans. On a brighter note (perhaps the only bright note) we have a pet! It's a baby macaque, a boy. Macgregor found him in the jungle and even his stern Scottish heart melted at the sight. He's something we can look after and we seem to need this, even though it means we give him rations (we're allowed to trade what we are paid for our labour for food). Perhaps it reminds Matthew and me of the animals we've cared for at home. We've called him Stanley.

## Two nights later

Little Stanley has already earned his rations, Evie. When we came into the hut to sleep he started to shriek and would not stop shrieking. The men around us were cursing and shouting at us to stop the bl..dy racket. He seemed to be staring at my mat so I pulled it up. Curled underneath it was a scorpion, couldn't make out what kind as it was dark. Extra rations for Stanley tomorrow!

## Following night

I try, I try so hard, Evie, to keep the dark away, to concentrate on what's good: the comradeship, the jokes, the conversations, but days like this make me wonder if it's worth the effort. Clinging on to the light seems too much.

# Part Three

# CHAPTER
# NINE

**Evie**
**Golden Jubilee, June 2002**

If Evie closed her eyes it could be twenty-five years ago. Or fifty. The Union Jacks. The marquee. The breeze picking up, making the bunting whirr above them and the children shouting. Time passed. Years went by but they'd all come back to this part of the green to mark the Queen's reign.

What did the Queen make of all the Union Jacks and balloons, the commemorative china and the cakes? Was she flattered, overcome? God knows Elizabeth II had had her share of family woes: break-ups, flighty in-laws and cousins, fires. But she'd never lost a child; never that, so she could still be considered fortunate.

Lost. Once again Evie paused to consider the implications of that word. Lost suggested that you'd put something down and forgotten where it was. It suggested that the fault somehow lay with you. Had she been at fault at the party twenty-five years ago? These days parents seemed to keep their children under closer scrutiny. It hadn't been like that a quarter of a century ago; not in this village, at least. Children had come and gone pretty well at will, subject only to school hours and household chores. And Jessamy had been at a village party, surrounded by friends. She'd been ten, not three: old enough to remember repeated warnings about not going off with strangers.

As she had so many times before Evie ran through everything that Jess had done in the days and weeks leading up to the Jubilee. And there was nothing. Her daughter had been playing outside quite a bit; but it was early summer, with long, light evenings. And Martha had been out on the farm, keeping an eye on things. Officially Martha was the shepherd, but the role had always encompassed more than watching sheep. Martha helped with the cattle, the crops. She was everywhere. Too much so, perhaps. If it hadn't been for the centuries binding the Winter and Stourton families together Evie would have found a way to pay her off years back. But she had never been able to do this.

No, if there'd been strangers hanging around Jessamy, Martha would have noticed them. Nor could the gypsies have had anything to do with this. The afternoon after the disappearance police had been seen leaving the caravans the gypsies lived in during the summer months. That night every pane of glass in the caravans' windows had been shattered. Evie had walked past to see them picking the shards off the grass. Her cheeks had burned and she'd wanted to tell them she was sorry. Rosie was helping her mother to pick up the glass. Her feet were bare. Suddenly she'd squealed and held up her foot, a red drop of blood already forming where she'd stood on a shard. Evie had walked on.

Sometimes she woke from her sleep convinced she knew what had happened to Jessamy, had seen it all in her dreams, clear and distinct. But even as she grasped for the images they curled up round the edges.

The wind scooped up paper plates and spun them over the lawn. It blew scraps of conversation, loudspeaker announcements and children's shrieks out of earshot. Tablecloths fluttered as it caught them. Evie felt on edge. But of course she did. They'd all been so kind to her, giving her tea and finding her somewhere more sheltered to sit, but it was impossible for her to settle here this afternoon. She scoured the green, walking from group to group, looking, always looking, sometimes turning on her heel as though someone might just be slipping out of view behind her. Perhaps a child eating a bun or the laughter of a group of young lads would trigger a memory. It could be anything, anything at all.

And if Jessamy were going to reappear this was surely where she'd come, to the same place from where she'd vanished twenty-five years earlier. A portal, that's what this party might be, a gateway to the past. Evie was proud of herself for having picked that word up from a children's science fiction programme.

She pictured a parallel universe in which Jessamy had not disappeared, in which she was still at this party with her mother, organizing the sack races or pouring cups of tea, chatting to people she'd known all her life. For the first years of Jess's disappearance it had been easy to imagine that her daughter still moved beside her. Evie had seen her outline clearly. A quarter of a century on, the details seemed to have blurred. Would Jess have worn her hair short? Would she have put on a dress this afternoon or would the cold wind have made her favour trousers?

Jessamy must be here, somewhere: by the face-painting stand, or looking at the display of Coronation photographs beside the marquee. It was just a question of willing her to appear, wanting it hard enough so that the atoms would rearrange themselves into her form. Time was supposed to be relative so perhaps Jessamy's ten-year-old self was still actually here. If only she could call out to her daughter, warn her not to leave the park . . .

Enough.

Pilot wagged his tail as her gaze fell on the park gate. Dogs weren't allowed on this fenced-off section of the green. That had changed since the Silver Jubilee party, when spaniels and Labradors had accompanied their families to celebrate the monarch's twenty-five years. The dog caught Evie's eye and his tail thumped against the grass. She longed for his silent company, his warm head against her sandaled foot, his breath comforting on her bare skin. As a group of latecomers pushed the gate open he raised his head and pricked his ears. Did he, like her, check to see whether Jessamy was with them? But of course he wouldn't have a clue who Jessamy was. Once, foolishly, Evie had given Pilot the still-unwashed nightdress her daughter had worn the night before the 1977 Jubilee party. He'd sniffed it with his usual gentlemanly politeness. "Find, Pilot!" she'd urged him. "Find her for me!" But traces of Jessamy would long since have vanished. He'd given his tail a single wag and dropped his handsome black head to the flagstones, confusion obvious in his eyes. "Sorry," she'd said. "Oh God, I'm sorry."

As though looking at herself from the outside she saw what others must see: a batty, ageing woman with foolish hopes, who held her grief behind a mask of control so that some probably considered her reserved. She just couldn't cry in front of anyone else, not even Freya.

The wind seemed to sharpen its edge and Evie could feel her cheeks burning in its rasp. She lifted her head to see if clouds were massing on top of the down but the sky was still clear. In this light the hill was etched sharply and it looked like a wave about to crash down upon them, wiping away the flags and balloons, the cake with the Queen's head on it and the children running races, sweeping them all away in a morass of red, blue and white. She should warn them of the calamity close at hand. They wouldn't believe her. She wouldn't have believed it either, twenty-five years ago. Despite the cool air, she felt perspiration glow on her brow.

*Come back now, darling. Walk out of that tea tent with a plate of chocolate brownies or a scone and jam. It's not too late.* She closed her eyes and opened them again. Nothing.

"Evie?" Freya stood beside her. "How are you coping, my dear?"

She managed a nod.

"They were needing help in the tea tent. I said I'd find volunteers."

She rose; she'd be no worse off in the tent. Why wouldn't Jessamy come and find her in there? It had, after all, been the last place she'd been sighted before her disappearance at the previous Jubilee.

Evie followed Freya across the field. Around them children whooped as they balanced eggs on spoons. Adults chatted. It all looked so innocent. Things in this village always did.

The hedge beside the tea tent rustled. Evie caught a glimpse of eyes, blue, mocking: the gypsy children, travellers, they were called now, standing out in the lane. The two smallest were Rosie's. Just like their parents all those years ago they wouldn't come into the park. Perhaps they'd always regard themselves as outsiders, not part of the pack. Who could blame them? Some in Craven would always blame them for Jessamy's disappearance although they'd been questioned again and again and their cars and caravans checked for her fingerprints. With nothing found.

Evie shivered again. Perhaps it would have been better to have stayed at home today. But it would have been cowardly. And part of her had been so sure something would happen here today; she'd imbued the date with such significance, as though the celebration bunting and the gilded carriages in the Mall could magic Jessamy back to her.

She was aware of people looking at her as she took up her place in the tea tent. They must realize the significance of this date, too. Some of them hadn't even been living in this village when Jessamy had vanished, but knowledge of the disappearance had been passed on to them along with information about post office opening hours, where to find a cleaner, and the best place to buy eggs and honey. *There's that old woman up at Winter's Copse, Evie Winter. Her daughter went missing. Never found.* She could tell when the newcomers had found out about Jessamy, tell by the sudden interest mixed with awkwardness in their expressions when they met her in the post office.

Evie's mind went back to her own arrival with Charlie, to how the villagers had come to examine the evacuee children in the village hall. The older children, especially the boys, had been taken first. Useful on the farm. She and Charlie had almost been the last to be selected because they were twins and the teacher wouldn't let them be separated. Not everyone had room for two children. They'd stood in the hall and people had walked past them saying kind things but leaving them there. Evie had felt like an unfavoured animal in a zoo.

She sliced cakes and poured tea in the marquee for an hour until one of the young mothers from the new estate came to relieve her. She suddenly knew she had to go home. And immediately. As she walked out of the tent towards the gate, Freya, now manning the pin-the-tail-on-the-donkey stand, raised an arm in farewell. Freya would explain her disappearance to anyone who needed to know. She'd already told Evie that she shouldn't go to the party, that she should drive out for the day or go for a long walk, perhaps even go to France for the long weekend.

Martha sat on one of the straw bales set up around the edge of the field, watching the children playing football, a look of complete concentration on her face. Perhaps she too was remembering Jessamy running races and playing with her friends in this very park. Evie continued towards the gate and untied Pilot's lead. They walked up the lane towards the farm passing the houses with their delicate brick- and stonework walls and thatched roofs. She passed the village hall, a modern structure on the site of the old hall where in another lifetime she and Charlie had arrived as evacuees from London. As she always did she peered up the alleys in case Jessamy was standing there in the shadows. But why would a grown woman hide in the gloom?

As Evie walked the breeze seemed to pick up her foolish hopes and disperse them.

# CHAPTER
# TEN

**Robert**
**Camp at Nong Pladuk, Thailand, March 1943**

Dear Evie,

I was a fool to hope things might be going better. I just don't know how to tell you about what happened today.

A Korean guard came past the workshop where we were sharpening tools, Stanley the monkey was playing quietly beside us with some strips of bamboo. The guard stopped. I thought he was enjoying the sight of the animal. Sometimes there are moments when you can see that we're all fellow human beings. I bent my head down towards the bench. A shadow flickered over me. I turned just quickly enough to see the sweep of the guard's gun. He skewered the monkey on his bayonet. Stanley took one last gasp of air and looked at us. I thought I'd be safe with you, he seemed to say. Then he gave a shudder, and some blood ran out of his mouth. I thought Matthew might strike the guard, I clutched at his arm.

On the farm animals are killed all the time: for meat or because they're old and sick and suffering. I was never one of those lads who'd torture flies or frogs. "The boy who torments an animal is the boy who'll grow up to torment his fellow humans," Dad used to tell Matthew and me.

I shouldn't write and tell a kid like you about these things, but just putting them on paper helps. I'm going to try and pull myself out of it. Tomorrow I'll write about our work.

## Next day

I've been moved out of the workshop so my main task at the moment is hammering drills into rocks so that charges can be blasted. We also cart the stone away and cut trees and drag away the logs. Splinters cut our fingers and palms and each splinter seems to cause an infection, so that our hands are always swollen and yellow. I almost prefer the rock work, though that, too, leaves the hands bleeding and cut. At home, felling trees was fun: I looked forward to hitching the horses to the logs and pulling them out of the copse. Here it is us who are the horses. Sometimes the Thais use elephants but these are better treated than we are. I wish you could see the elephants, though. Must try and draw them for you. And the barges on the river with their painted eyes. You see, I can still find the good things to concentrate on! I am trying, Evie, really I am. I know I could let myself slip. Some of them here already have and their minds are disordered. I'm so afraid I'll

90

Matthew still very feverish, I wish I could find him some quinine, but I will not let them put him with the other sick men. Who knows what might happen if I wasn't there to keep an eye on him? I've always been good at looking after people and animals. Dad said I'd have made a good doctor or vet but I only ever wanted to work on the farm and I wasn't good enough at maths.

My other main concern is to find another hiding place for these letters: somewhere dry. Almost impossible in this place.

# CHAPTER
# ELEVEN

**Rachel**
**March 2003**

"Sit, Pilot!" I shouted but it was too late. The dog had heard the faint clink of the lead and was already bounding towards me. "Stay." He wagged his tail and kept on coming. Where should I take him? I tried to remember where Evie had gone for walks. Sometimes, if she had the time, she'd walk him up to the Ridgeway, the ancient droveway carved along the top of the hills. It was a walk I loved, with its ancient earthworks and monuments, and its view of the Vale and the distant Cotswold escarpments. But as it was already growing dark I decided to take the dog down to the village and round the Green. Jubilee Park, it had been renamed, somewhat grandly, after the Silver Jubilee.

I opened the back door and the dog shot past me, spinning in delight. I smiled and realized that those muscles in my face felt almost stiff from lack of use.

Pilot propelled me down the lane into the village. He obviously knew the walk to the park well. There was a fenced-off section where dogs couldn't enter but the rest was just open space, with three oaks of descending size in the middle. Daddy tree, mummy tree, baby tree. The largest was the Coronation oak, planted in 1953. Beside it was the tree commemorating the Silver Jubilee and beside that in turn was the sapling planted just weeks ago to commemorate the fiftieth anniversary of the Queen's accession. I strolled towards the family of oaks as Pilot dashed across the green in a series of excited loops, feeling guilty that I hadn't brought him down here before now.

Evie had been present at the planting of the Silver Jubilee tree, but not of its predecessor, the Coronation oak, or its successor, the Golden Jubilee tree. Perhaps she'd been recovering from one of the many miscarriages she'd suffered. What was it with the women in our family and their problems bringing a child to term? Perhaps Jessamy would have been better at it than I was. She mightn't have needed to make appointments for embryos made with donor eggs to be inserted inside her. Stop it, I told myself. Trying for a baby is over, don't torment yourself, don't indulge yourself.

At the time of the 1977 oak planting only months had passed since Jessamy had vanished. Despair must surely have replaced hope by then, but maybe Evie had still half expected to see her daughter walking back towards her across the green. I hadn't seen my aunt for some months after the disappearance of Jessamy. My mother had been overcome by one of her rare and powerful maternal impulses and had bustled me off to the south of France with them, promising a tutor. At the time this had seemed a huge improvement on the stuffy girl's school in Reading I'd attended and I was happy enough to comply. In fact, nothing educational had been arranged and I'd spent the autumn wandering around St Tropez, wondering what was happening back at Winter's Copse and fretting about Jessamy. And Evie. Every time my father brought back a day-old *Times* with him, I'd scan the pages to see whether they'd found Jessamy.

"I should be back there helping to look," I told him. My father wasn't one for demonstrativeness but he picked up my hands and squeezed them.

"Your aunt will need you," he said. "Not for the search, but to cheer her up. Perhaps you could go and stay over Christmas. That'll be a tough time for her."

"Nonsense, Chas." My mother's disapproval creased her brow; something she hardly ever let happen because she worried about lines. "It's morbid for the child to act as support to her aunt. Dangerous, too. Supposing whoever it was who kidnapped Jessamy came back for Rachel?"

My father had scowled at her in a way that made her look away. "We should be supporting my sister. She's all alone on that farm waiting for news."

And I had pictured Evie sitting by the range in the kitchen, the dog at her feet, willing the telephone to ring or someone to rap on the door. My stomach churned and I wanted to be sick.

I should have gone to the damn Golden Jubilee party back in June. But friends had offered us their house on

94

Kos. Sunshine. Swimming. Sex. Perhaps the combination would help my body relax and do what it was supposed to. And, to be honest, I'd been half relieved to miss the party and the whispers as people reminded themselves of what had happened at the last Jubilee.

"Have a wonderful holiday," Evie had told me. "Make sure you have a good rest, both of you."

Perhaps Evie herself could have done with a relaxing holiday. Who knows, perhaps time away would have done something to help her heart.

I forced myself to concentrate on Pilot and his zigzag race across the green. I'd promised I wouldn't torture myself.

Pilot raced towards me. "This has all preoccupied me too much for too long," I told him. "We've given it our best shot." We certainly had: our consultant was world-renowned.

"There is no obvious reason why you shouldn't conceive," he'd told me. "But I'd like to run some tests." One test had led to another and then we'd found ourselves having attempt after attempt at IVF, each failure marked by nights of tears and Rioja.

Evie had died and that very morning I'd probably been fussing about an appointment at the IVF clinic. And the IVF hadn't worked anyway. It was as though I'd been mocked for my blinkered, obsessive desire to procreate.

"As if there weren't enough people in the world anyway," I told Pilot.

I walked briskly back to the Jubilee oaks, the dog striding out beside me. The wind blew the young

Golden Jubilee oak so that it looked like a small, lost wraith. Just like a missing child, in fact. I pushed the image back behind a mental door and slammed it shut but it hammered its fists on the wood and screamed for attention.

# CHAPTER
# TWELVE

**Rachel**
**March 2003**

As I'd promised myself, I started to fill cardboard boxes with small items from the house which any prospective tenants wouldn't need and which, I supposed, I'd have to take back to London with me. Evie's sewing basket. The old pack of cards she'd used to teach Jessamy and me rummy. An old Scrabble set, which I remembered Evie taking out on Sunday evenings during the summer holidays when I was staying. I stared at the objects, almost as though I expected them to hold some explanation of what had happened to Jessamy. But all I saw was a collection of faded objects.

What on earth was I going to do with them? Perhaps the tenants wouldn't mind if I stored them out of the way in the cellar. There wouldn't be much room at home. Our flat was so different from Winter's Copse, with its passageways and half-rooms, its bookshelves and cupboards full of interesting things, its floorboards that creaked and sighed according to the time of the day and the warmth of the sun. Yet Winter's Copse had its share of perfectly proportioned reception rooms. It was Queen Anne and had been built by Samuel Winter, the first Winter to come to the village in the late seventeenth century. He'd farmed the acres first as a tenant and had married a rich merchant's daughter from Oxford, enabling him to make the landowning family, the ancestors of the Fernhams who still lived in the village, a generous offer for the land. "The Fernhams didn't like giving up land," Evie had told me. "Samuel Winter must have paid a big price." And Jessamy's eyes had glinted with pride. Martha had been out in the field, too, helping us gather the last of the blackberries, hooking her shepherd's crook over the furthest branches so we could pull the ripest berries towards us. It was a fine early September afternoon.

"The Winters did well," she said. "They got the land and they wouldn't give it up. And you're the last of the line, young Jess. We need to show you how to care for the farm."

"I teach her," said Evie. "I pass it all on."

"My family have lived here as long as the Winters," Martha went on, seeming to ignore her. "We know how things are done here." The berry she had picked dripped red juice onto her fingers.

The Winters had survived the agricultural downturns of the nineteenth century, when cheap grain and meat had flooded in from America and the colonies, and the slump of the thirties. "They were never afraid to take risks, to try new things," Evie said. "One of the first threshing machines in the county was used on the farm. And the Winters were one of the first to switch

98

to a new breed of sheep in the nineteenth century because it produced better meat yields." I could hear her voice telling me this with pride, could see Jessamy smiling with pleasure at her clever ancestors.

I left the Coronation mugs on the dresser, not feeling strong enough to deal with them today and went into Evie's study. I'd already taken some of the paperbacks into the charity shop and placed the really good things, including a King James bible and some silver, in storage at the bank. Apart from the Jubilee mugs and the diaries and photos all that was left were some black bin liners of clothes I hadn't had time to take down to the charity shop.

I picked up a silver-framed photograph of Evie and my father from the desk. Five years since he'd died in a car crash on one of the winding roads above his latest south of France property development. My mother was in Dubai now, enjoying her new incarnation as rich expat wife of Barry, another property developer. Her latest email had described champagne receptions and shopping expeditions. "Found the dearest little frock for you, darling," she'd told me. "Just delightful. Barry sends love." I knew the dear little dress would be a skimpy black evening number and wondered where she thought I might wear it.

"Don't give up too much of your time to sorting out Winter's Copse," my mother had continued. "After all, you've still got twenty-five years until you get hold of the place. And you need to get on with making me a grandmother!"

How typical of her to cut right to any self-interest I might have felt about what I was doing here: she had always found it hard to accept my affection for my aunt. Perhaps she'd been jealous of Evie and the time I spent with her. "I want to do it," I told her in my email reply. "The house has many happy memories for me."

The notion that I needed to do this as part of saying goodbye to my aunt would never have occurred to the woman who'd given birth to me.

As for the line about making her a grandmother, I wondered if she'd ever listened to a word I'd told her in the past about the trouble we were having conceiving. I'd already explained about the donated eggs procedure we were considering if the next IVF round using our own embryos failed. There'd been a silence on the phone. "I *suppose* it would be like having your own baby," she'd said at last.

"It's just me now," I told Evie and Dad in the old black and white photograph. They smiled back at me and I almost imagined they could hear me, so I chatted on like a loon. "Isn't it funny how you just happened to come to this house in 1940 and not anywhere else in the village?" I hadn't meant funny as in comic, more that our lives would have been utterly different if Charles and Evie had been taken in elsewhere. Or stayed in London. In which case, I reminded myself, they'd have probably been killed alongside my grandmother when the bomb landed on the house in August 1944. And Jessamy and I would never have existed. So I wouldn't have been standing here in this house anyway. A logical disconnect, Luke would have called this chain of thoughts.

Luke. There'd been nothing very logical about the night we'd spent at home after the last IVF failure. The evidence, in the form of greasy take-away cartons, most of them still nearly full, and empty bottles, had spoken of yet another attempt to anaesthetize ourselves from the reality of our situation. "I know we shouldn't be drinking like this but I just can't help it." I'd filled my large wine glass again. I'd had to wash the glasses before we could drink from them, so dusty had they become in the last months. Luke had been keeping me company in my abstinence from alcohol.

"I'll probably regret this in the morning," Luke held out his own glass. He'd be worrying about how he was to keep control of 8E next morning in the classroom with a hangover.

I put a hand to my brow as though to push away the reflections, and focused instead on the evacuee aspect of Evie and my father's childhood. Most village families had taken in children from towns and cities, Evie had told me once. But usually they'd hoped for sturdy boys who could help on the farm or with digging allotments, or a single girl who could be squeezed into a small spare room and act as a companion to a woman whose son or husband had joined up. Twins of ten were another proposition altogether.

"Robert must have wanted a teenage lad, too," she'd said. "It would have been so useful for him on the farm. But he chose us. That shows he must have . . ." Her mouth closed on the unspoken words.

"Must have what?" I asked.

"Nothing," she'd said. "We were so excited when we left London on the train with all our classmates. I don't think we understood that we weren't just going on holiday." Her expression altered. "But our poor mother knew, despite her brave face. I think the reality only dawned on me when we were standing in the village hall. It was a terrible place with a tin roof, stifling in summer and freezing in winter, reeking of damp lino and mildew. Most of the people who came to take in evacuees just walked past us, though a few old ladies cooed over your father. He was such an attractive child."

"So were you."

She laughed. "Not then. I was too thin-faced for a child. But they couldn't have Charlie without me. Mum had made our teacher promise they wouldn't split us up because we were twins."

"It must have been awful, waiting to be chosen." I shuddered, remembering netball teams chosen by the most popular girl in the class, how she'd select her friends and leave me standing alone, unwanted. How much worse this selection of evacuees must have been.

"Being evacuated seemed like fun at first. I remember the train with its cream and brown livery, how smart it was, and the charabanc from the station to Craven. But then we reached the village hall and I thought Mum would think I hadn't tried hard enough to look appealing." For a moment my aunt's face was that of a child's. "She'd even found some wool to knit us both new cardigans so we looked our best: mine was red and Charlie's was blue. With smart horn buttons. But it didn't seem to be working." She paused. "Then Robert Winter came in and saved us."

# CHAPTER
# THIRTEEN

**Robert**
**Kanburi, Thailand, late March 1943**

Dear Evie,

I'm starting to realize that nothing can save us from this ordeal but I'm still trying to keep my chin up. We're in another camp, thirty miles or so north-west of Ban Pong. It's called Kanburi or something like that, hard to tell whether the Australians have cut out a few letters from the proper Thai place name. The town itself has shops and some good-sized wooden buildings, running down to the river.

When we were told we were marching to our new workplace some of the men looked at one another. I didn't know what they meant by those looks. I do now.

We were responsible for moving all the tools and equipment we needed for our work constructing the railway. No mules. We were the mules. At home I could carry tools on my shoulder without thinking about it. I could heave a sack of feed in one easy movement and carry it across the farmyard. "You're strong," you told me.

I'm not strong now. By the time we'd reached this camp I'd dropped most of my tools at the side of the track. The guards could have killed me for that but I scarcely cared any more. We slept each night in the open, with nothing to protect us from the mosquitoes. Or the snakes and centipedes and scorpions. I felt the darkness rolling over me and I wondered whether I should just let myself drop over the edge of the path so that I'd shatter on the rocks below. Only knowing Matthew was beside me stopped me from doing that. We didn't say much. We didn't need to.

The first few weeks we were here I managed to get a job cutting strips of wood into signs and painting them. Good work to conserve energy. But then I was thrown out of that post. I think they saw I was too strong to waste. So now I break stones on the ground they're clearing for the railway. Each work day is ten hours long. I watch the tracks lengthen and I think of all those Japanese soldiers heading north-west for India.

I long for someone to tell us that the war is over and that they are coming to save us. I don't even know who the "they" are. Last night two British officers were hauled out because they'd made and hidden a radio. They will be made to stand in the open for two days and nights. And that won't be the end of it, the Japanese build punishment on punishment. They stand you out. Then they beat you. Then they let the doctor patch you up and then it starts again: stand out, beating. Or perhaps a visit to the secret police treatment centres in the town. And the worst is what happens in your head.

A radio. All those evenings at home before the war when we sat in the parlour and listened to the wireless. Mum was better then, not confined to bed. Matthew'd listen to the news with us, though he didn't like the wireless as much as I did. Mum liked the dance bands — she'd been quite a dancer herself before the stroke.

I used to be called a steady lad. Reliable middle order batsman, they said, just like his brother, just like all the Winter men. Mum knew different. Sometimes, when I was small, and there was an animal to be slaughtered on the farm, she'd find a reason for me not to be there. "Go down to the shop, Robert," she'd tell me, handing me a sixpence. "I need tea." And I'd go, even if I knew she didn't need the tea, even if I was ashamed because I knew I should be there watching the slaughterman with his sharp blade and quick strokes. Mum knew my secret: that I'm not like my brother, that when I see bad things they won't leave my imagination. Stanley will always have that bayonet through him in my mind. I can't replace the picture with one of him chattering to himself as he played with our tools.

But it helps when I pretend I'm back at the farm. You and Charlie are playing tag in the farmyard. You're good runners, like hares darting from the barn to the henhouse and stables. Sometimes I join in and you scream with delight as I catch you. Then I realize that the screams are real and they're coming from the officers as the guards beat them. I try and pull myself back into

Winter's Copse but the screams keep me here, in this hut with its stinks and crawling insects.

Do you remember when I first saw you in the village hall? When I came to take you home with me.

# CHAPTER
# FOURTEEN

**Evie**
**1940**

He unlaced his boots at the entrance and approached the line of children in his stockinged feet, stopping in front of them to examine them. For a whole minute nobody spoke. Even Miss Moss ceased her chatting with the WRVS lady who'd driven them here from the station. The thin woman sitting in the corner with the clipboard watched the young man intently.

Evie felt the warmth of his eyes on her face. She stared at him and couldn't keep her eyes from his. He was probably the most beautiful boy she had ever seen. Evie's chest suddenly felt tight. She stared at the fire extinguisher on the wall until it blurred. He smiled and there was a note of apology on his face. Evie hardened her face. He walked away.

And turned. And came back to look at them again. The young man nodded slowly and padded over to the desk, where Miss Moss, the schoolteacher, handed him some papers.

Unsure what was to happen next, Evie and Charlie remained in the line.

The young man walked back to the door and replaced his boots, which, Evie saw, were caked in mud. He turned. "What are you waiting for, you two?"

The thin woman in the corner made an exclamation. "It's all right, Miss Fernham," the young man said. "I know what I'm doing."

"They're from south London. Are you sure it's appropriate?" She spoke in a clipped voice.

He gave a single nod.

Evie sought Miss Moss's eyes. "Off you go with, erm, Mr Winter, Eve and Charles." Miss Moss's fingers pulled at a loose thread on her angora jumper. "His mother is waiting for you at home. I'll see you both at school on Monday. You can tell me all about the farm."

"The farm?" Evie must surely have misheard.

"Apparently the Winters live at Winter's Copse, the biggest farm in the parish." She made a gesture with her hands like a woman shooing away pigeons. "Off you go, you've been chosen now."

Chosen. They had been chosen to live on a farm. But why? The children picked up their suitcases.

"You like chicks?" Mr Winter asked as they joined him at the door. She noticed the way his eyes crinkled up at the corners. His hair was thick and shiny like a film-star's. "Ducklings? We've got both. In spring we have lambs, too." He held out his hands. "What am I thinking of? Give me those cases, you both look all in."

And they handed them over and followed him out of the hall and up the village high street. Most of the gardens had flowers in them: roses and honeysuckle and other plants she didn't recognize. In London

**109**

people had started digging up gardens to grow potatoes and carrots. There were cats, too, sitting on walls, enjoying the last of the sun. Apart from their own footsteps the only sound was of cows mooing somewhere behind the cottages. Evie nudged her brother. "D'you hear that?"

They turned off the street and up a narrow lane leading uphill. Charlie slowed. Evie tugged at his hand to hurry him. Mr Winter stopped, and walked back to them. "I'm going too fast, aren't I?" He rolled his eyes. "Sorry. I'm not used to kids. How old are you two?"

"Ten," said Evie.

The young man whistled. "Tiddlers." With one smooth movement he hoisted a case up under each arm and held out a hand to each of them. "Come on, I'll give you a pull up the hill."

His hands felt warm and rough. Her suitcase had left a red welt on Evie's hand but he held it gently so it didn't hurt.

He turned through into a field with lots of trees in it. "The orchard," he said proudly. "Best apples in the parish. Pears too. You like pears, Master Charles?"

Charlie nodded, still too shy to speak. Mr Winter grinned and suddenly looked hardly older than them. "My big brother Matthew says I've got a knack with fruit trees. They do well for me."

So there was an older brother, too.

Then the house was before them. Evie stopped. It was enormous. Posh. It made their own house in London look teeny. The white walls with their soft orange brick detail seemed to be growing out of the

**110**

fields, as though the building was a living, breathing thing, part of the landscape. Trees waved their boughs all around it.

"I like your house," she told Mr Winter. Immediately she was aware that like wasn't a big enough word for what she felt. Winter's Copse, was its name, it said so on the sign.

He turned to smile at her and his eyes were like warm toffee. "It's the prettiest house in the village, if you want my opinion. But I'm prejudiced."

Uncertain what the word meant, Evie nodded.

They didn't enter by the front door; he walked them round to the back, through a side gate. The garden was long and given over to grass, with flowerbeds of lupins and delphiniums beneath the stone walls. A black and white collie rose and wagged its tail but the young man waved it away. "The kids are too tired for you tonight, Fly."

Inside the kitchen copper saucepans hung from the ceiling and the range was warm. A slim girl about the same age as Robert stood at the table, arranging plates and cutlery. "Thanks, Martha," Robert said. "You can go now."

The girl's eyes, a curious pale green in colour, narrowed. Evie felt her sweeping cold glance take in every detail of her appearance: the new cardigan, the not-new skirt, the slightly scuffed, if highly polished, sandals. She gave a brief nod, her glossy dark hair falling over her shoulders.

Evie's attention moved to the chairs round the kitchen table. The day had started early. "Supper in a minute," Robert said. "Martha's got it ready. I'll just take you upstairs first."

They followed him up the broad wooden staircase.

"Mother's in here," he said quietly. "You'd best see her tonight, before she gets too tired. She had a stroke a few years back, just after Dad died, and now she can't move or talk much." He nodded at them to enter the bedroom, which was dark because the curtains were drawn. It smelled of menthol and lavender. A woman sat up on her pillows to peer at the children. She wore an old-fashioned lace cap. Evie noticed the spectacles folded on top of the bible on the bedside table. Perhaps she couldn't even see without them. "Plenty of milk," she told her son. "To build them up. Pretty little things." And the lids covered her watery eyes. Mr Winter beckoned them out of the room.

"You're in this room." He opened a door on the other side of the landing. Two beds, a chest of drawers and a wardrobe. A striped rug on the wooden floor, some cross-stitched verses from the Old Testament on the walls. A big bookcase against one of the walls, its shelves packed with children's books and toys, which must once have belonged to Robert and his brother. On the floor sat a large model castle with knights defending its ramparts. Charlie gave a short exclamation. He'd left a toy fort at home in London but it was nothing in comparison with this one.

"Used to be ours," Mr Winter said. "Matthew's and mine. We collected all those knights and painted them." He laid a suitcase on each bed. Evie flopped down beside her case. "Have a wash-up," he said.

"Bathroom's at the end of the landing. Then come down. Martha's made us a stew for supper. I'm no cook."

"Can we play with it?" Charlie's eyes were still on the fort.

"That's why I put it in here for you."

"Robert," the girl Martha called up the stairs. "Supper's ready."

He gave a little start. "We'd better go down. She doesn't like it if we let the food get cold."

The stew had real beef in it, just small pieces but you could tell it was the proper thing. Martha served the children. The ladle paused as she came to Evie's plate. Evie looked up, enquiringly. "Your hands could do with a scrub, young lady." Evie felt heat spread across her cheeks. She'd washed her hands in the bathroom but she'd missed the smear of soot on the top of her left hand.

Robert laughed. "Not to worry."

"Didn't your mother make you wash before meals?" Martha served the stew. Evie nodded, humiliation flooding her. And more than humiliation, the image of her mother came to her, standing in the kitchen and serving the tea: not stew but dripping on toast . . . Something blocked her throat and for a moment she couldn't breathe.

A hand stroked her arm. "Been a long day, hasn't it?" Robert said. "Eat up now, you'll feel better for the food." Evie nodded and picked up the knife and fork. Her brother shoved forkfuls into his mouth. Evie tried to be neater but it was hard when her stomach was almost touching her back with hunger. "Thank you, Mr Winter," she muttered with her mouth full of carrot.

"Call me Robert." He looked amused. "I'm only eighteen."

"I'll be off then." Martha folded the dishcloth over the tap.

"Thanks, Martha. See you tomorrow." Evie felt herself relax as the girl and her sharp eyes left. Fly the collie padded into the kitchen and rested his head on Robert's lap. His master ran a palm down the dog's head and smiled at the children.

When they'd finished he took their plates. "I'll wash up now," he said. "We'll have to share the chores in the future as Martha only comes in once a day, rest of the time she's out on the farm."

"She doesn't live here then?" Evie felt relief.

He rolled up his sleeves. "She lives in a cottage up the lane. Tomorrow you'll have to help with the dishes, but you two need to rest tonight." His movements in the sink were quick and deft, she noticed.

"Why did you choose us?" Evie asked. "All those other people said they could only take older children. Or that they couldn't take in two."

He turned to consider her as though she were a grownup asking an important question. "I'll tell you why, Evie Parr." His eyes really were the colour of toffee as Evie remembered it from before the war, with long, thick lashes. "I'm always right about the creatures that'll do well here. Matthew says I'm better at choosing livestock than he is. He's away being trained for the army now but he knew he could leave things with me." His expression grew more serious. "When Matthew and I go off to war we'll have to get in a farm manager. Martha won't be able to manage by herself."

"You're going to war too?" Evie felt as though a cold boulder was dropping down through her body.

"All the Winter men have gone off to fight when they've needed us, even though farmers don't have to. We're both joining the local regiment, the Royal Berkshires." He must have noticed the panic on her face. "But don't worry, Evie. It won't be for a while yet. I said I'd wait till we can find a good manager. And mother's here as well to keep an eye on things."

She crossed her fingers that finding a manager would prove an impossible task.

Next morning he took them for a tour of the farm, starting with a climb up the side of the hill. "The White Horse is up there," he said, pointing at some curved lines above them.

"A horse?" Charlie squinted.

Robert laughed. "You can't see it; it's cut into the chalk. It's been covered over for the war. Else German airmen might use it to navigate. But it's old, thousands of years old, maybe more. People were living up here before Abraham was born."

"What did they do?" Charlie asked.

"Hunted. Made tools. Worshipped their gods. Come on, here are the sheep." They climbed a stile. "The lambs are putting on weight nicely." They barely looked like lambs now, with their chunky bodies. Evie was disappointed. He laughed at her face.

"Not so sweet as they were in February, I'll grant you. These are Hampshire Down sheep. They fatten up well. There used to be hundreds and thousands of sheep up here but times grew hard for sheep farmers and now we're the only farmers in the parish who keep our flocks."

"Why?" asked Charlie.

"Matthew and I worked out that if a war was coming people would want meat that didn't need shipping halfway round the world." He nodded at the black-and-white faced lambs. "Reckon he had a point. Martha and I think the farm wouldn't be the same without the sheep."

"Does Martha know a lot about sheep?" Evie asked, trying to make the question sound casual.

"Her family were shepherds up here for hundreds of years, before the land was all enclosed. Many families had flocks on the Downs." Evie felt a pang of envy for Martha for belonging so completely to the green hill and the sheep. "There's not much about a sheep that Martha doesn't know," Robert went on. "See that field there?" He pointed at a square below them. "That's where we put them in the winter so they can feed off turnips."

He plucked a flower from the grass and showed it to her. "Look, Evie, this is an ox-eye daisy." She took the white flower from him. "And this," he pulled up a plant with yellow heads, "is yellow rattle."

"Yellow rattle," she repeated.

"Can we go back to the house now?" Charlie asked. Evie knew he'd be wanting to play with the toy fort.

116

"We've got to see the cows first." Robert nodded down the hill to where the cows grazed in the meadow. When they reached the cattle the grass looked so juicy Evie almost imagined wanting to chew it herself.

As they walked through the farmyard he took her by the arm. "This is going to be your special job."

"What?"

He pointed at the chickens scratching at the ground. "Putting the hens and the ducks in at night. And feeding the cat." He nodded at the stone wall at the far side of the yard, where a tabby stretched out. "While I'm away it'll be good to know you're keeping an eye on the things here."

At night, while they sat round the kitchen table with the wireless on, he'd read to them from an old book he and his brother had enjoyed as children. The stories were about knights on quests and the beautiful women they fought for. While the women waited.

The days seemed to speed up. Sunday afternoons, letter-writing time, seemed to come one after the other without a second between them. Evie looked at the calendar in the kitchen with its scenes of south coast seaside resorts and realized that three months had passed.

"Charlie doesn't like the animals as much as I do but he likes playing out in the barns," she wrote to her mother. "Robert says I'm a reel help on the farm and have a way with animals. If you come down here one weekend I'll show you the chicks, only they're quite big now, not fluffy any more." She drew one for her mother, then put down the pencil for a second and closed her eyes. Before she'd left London she'd pressed the image of Mum on that last morning deep into her memory: wearing her best dress and a hat that was almost new, faint shadows beneath her eyes. Now Evie had to struggle to remember the exact shade of blue of the dress: periwinkle or navy? She had a photo of Mum and Dad with the two of them, taken on a south coast beach a year back. But of course it didn't show colours.

She wouldn't make the mistake again. She'd be sure to remember the colour of Robert's toffee-brown eyes. And the exact shade of his hair and the pinkness of his lips. She'd never ever forget those. Would he forget her? He'd been so kind to her and Charlie but perhaps when he was away with all the other soldiers the children's images would slip from his mind. Evie sat up in bed. This couldn't happen. From the drawer of her bedside table she pulled out her writing pad, kept for the weekly letters to her mother. What should she say? She felt embarrassment prickling at her skin and stuffed the pad back in the drawer and curled up.

But sleep wouldn't come. It could be months, years before Robert came back. More than a school year, perhaps. Evie sat up again and switched on the light. This time she didn't let awkwardness stop her. "I will look after everything on the farm for you," she wrote. "Don't worry about anything. When you come back and I have grown up I would be very happy to stay at the farm to help you or maybe even as your wife. I just wanted you to know this in case you forgot wile you were away. From Evie Parr."

Before she could change her mind again she tugged an envelope out of the drawer, folded the sheet and sealed it up. She'd put it in his jacket pocket at breakfast time and hoped he wouldn't notice it until he was well on his way by train.

Next morning, his last before he went off to basic training, Robert produced a Box Brownie and took some photographs of Evie and Charlie with the farm animals. "For your mum," he said. "Bet she'll think you've both grown a lot. Don't move."

"Let me take one of you," she begged when he'd finished. He looked so handsome in his uniform.

"You don't want me," he said.

"Please." How much more confident she felt now that she'd written the letter. She could see the white top of the envelope sticking out from the top of his jacket pocket. He hadn't noticed it yet. She pictured him opening it on the train, or perhaps sitting on his bunk at the training depot, reading her words and knowing that, whatever happened, Evie would be waiting for him, as loyal as one of the ladies in the stories of the knights he'd told them at night.

"All right. Where do you want me to stand?"

She made him walk to the blood-red roses by the front door. "I feel like a Royal," he said. "Or a film star."

Evie clicked the shutter down and caught his image for ever. When she handed back the camera she noticed

Martha standing on the side of the lawn observing. Perhaps she should have offered to take Martha's photograph too for Robert to keep. But she couldn't bring herself to suggest this.

That night, as she switched off the little lamp between her bed and Charlie's, Evie thought she heard the back door open. Voices murmured in the kitchen. She turned over but sleep wouldn't come. Who was Robert talking to? He'd never told them not to come downstairs once they'd gone to bed but Evie hadn't liked to get out of bed. It was how Mum had brought them up: good children stay in bed.

Another door opened. Robert and his guest were going into the parlour, unused since the war had started. Evie sat up, wide awake. Her feet seemed to find their own path across the floor. She hovered at the top of the stairs. She heard more movement downstairs, a man's deep baritone and a lighter, fluting voice.

She crept downstairs and across the carpeted hallway to the parlour. The door hadn't been closed completely. Evie peeped through.

Robert and Martha lay on the sofa. He had his hand down the girl's blouse. She was weaving her hands around in the front of his trousers. Every now and then he'd mutter something and stretch out his back, like the farm cat when you stroked it.

Evie took a step back. She couldn't understand what she was seeing but it scared her. She took another step away and another. The couple didn't seem to have noticed her. She couldn't draw her eyes away from the

**120**

pair on the sofa. Robert was pulling down his trousers now and Martha had slipped her legs from underneath him to remove her stockings and underpants and hoist her skirt up so that the bits of her that should be private were visible. Evie put a fist to her mouth. She'd only been months on this farm but already she knew things she hadn't known in London about male and female animals and what they did. Animals, but not *people*, not *Robert*. He lay down on top of Martha and now Evie could only see his firm, rounded behind and Martha's naked legs, covered with fine hairs, crossed above it. Robert was grunting now, as though he was hurt. One of Martha's hands dangled down from the sofa, curling and uncurling.

Evie looked back at the door to the parlour. Perhaps if she made a noise, coughed really loudly or dropped a book . . . She didn't know why she wanted to stop *this* but it seemed imperative that it be halted. Then she remembered Fly, the dog. He wasn't allowed past the kitchen. On the few occasions when he'd managed to sneak into the rest of the house he'd burst through doors, fascinated by the forbidden territories. She tiptoed to the kitchen and called to him. From his basket he raised an eyebrow. "Come on, boy." He looked uncertain. She grabbed a knife from the dresser and cut a tiny sliver from the ham joint sitting on the table.

He got out of the basket, ears pricked. *Will this get me into trouble?* still on his face.

"It's all right. In you go." She patted her legs and pushed open the kitchen door. "Go and find your

121

master." She led him out, managing to creep on up the stairs in front of him. He stopped outside the parlour door. Robert made some kind of muffled exclamation and Martha responded with something between a moan and a laugh. Fly sniffed at the door, tail wagging. "Go on!" she whispered. He put a paw to the door and scratched it. From the stairs Evie threw the sliver of ham. It landed a few feet inside the parlour and the dog sprang after it.

"What the devil?" Robert said. She heard the sofa springs squeak and the door open. "Fly? What are you doing here? Bad dog! Out." His leather belt clinked against the parlour floorboards. He must be picking up his trousers from the floor and putting them on.

Now was Evie's chance. She stood and came downstairs. "Robert? Is something wrong? I heard you calling."

He opened the door, fully dressed though his shirt was untucked. "Nothing. Just the dog. I must have dozed off. Go back to bed, Evie."

"All right."

She paused at the top of the stairs, hearing him return to his companion. ". . . You should leave now, the children . . . awake . . ."

". . . come up to the cottage with me . . . your last night . . ."

". . . carried away . . . shouldn't do this again . . . always . . . friends . . . respect."

". . . just playing with me, Robert Winter."

The parlour door squeaked open and someone came out. There was a brief pause and Fly yelped in the kitchen. "Don't take it out on the dog," Robert called. "Here Fly, here boy."

Then there was the sound of the kitchen door slamming.

Evie peered through the banisters and saw Robert, face pale, shivering, though it wasn't a cold night. For a moment he looked quite unlike the person he was when he was showing them how to do jobs on the farm. He looked lost.

Evie tiptoed back to bed and fell almost instantly asleep.

# Part Four

# CHAPTER
# FIFTEEN

**Evie**
**The night of the Golden Jubilee party, June 2002.**

The chairman of the parish council placed the lighted taper against one of the twists of newspaper on the beacon. A small blue flame ran up the twist, looking too anaemic to achieve what was required of it. But the beacon-builders had done their job well. The flames multiplied and crackled as they found more twists of newspaper and dry kindling to consume. And the fire took form, hissing as it found new food.

Evie stood apart from the others, hands folded in front of her, feeling chilled inside despite the growing heat of the flames. It was a mistake to come this evening. She'd fooled herself into thinking she'd recovered from the party in the afternoon. She'd been keen for people to see that she could manage the Jubilee celebrations. Her pride had overrun her common sense.

A couple of children beside her giggled at one another, already restless, probably wishing there were fireworks to go with the bonfire. Evie strained her eyes to look out for other beacons to the north, on the

Cotswold or Chiltern hills, but couldn't see them. It wasn't quite dark yet. These June days stretched on and on until she almost begged for darkness.

At this time of year the green of the grass and trees was almost too much to be true, as though it had been assembled for a Hollywood film set. The warmth of the bonfire stroked her back and she moved her head to the left so that she was looking west towards the sun's embers. Back at the time of the Silver Jubilee she'd have regarded the night sky with a farmer's eye, thinking of her livestock, planning ahead. She wished she still had them to preoccupy her but there were no animals left at Winter's Copse except for the dog, Pilot. Perhaps she should buy some more animals, chickens, possibly. But she'd only be trying to fill a gap which was impossible to fill. She recoiled, too, from the prospect of becoming an elderly lady who was too fond of animals.

She was the last left of the Winters — for however long she might last. The Queen still sat on her throne, though, with her dogs and horses and her ill-married children and vigorous, Germanic-looking grandchildren all around her. Some people didn't like the Royals, Evie wasn't sure about all of them but viewed the Queen in the same way she did the Silver Jubilee tree on the village green, almost fizzing with new growth now but withered and naked in the winter storms that blew in from the west. The Queen, the tree and Evie herself were survivors; they just kept on going.

But she wasn't entirely alone, she reminded herself. There was Rachel, dearest niece anyone could have

128

wished for. But Rachel was young and had her own life and shouldn't be over burdened. Especially as something had obviously gone wrong recently. Until about a month ago Evie had noticed a liveliness to her niece's voice when they'd talked on the telephone, a buoyancy. That bounce had vanished in recent weeks. Setbacks with the longed-for baby, perhaps. How well she could sympathize.

As the last of the sun's rays dissolved, the bonfire light played kindly on the faces of those standing round it, making everyone glow rosily. Lines were smoothed out and eyes sparkled from the blaze. Evie thought of the centuries during which the drovers had herded sheep and cattle along the Ridgeway. They must have lit fires at night and sat round them, singing perhaps. Or telling stories. She glanced up at the shadowy ridge above the beacon. Some people said they saw the ghosts of the drovers and their animals up there. On a night like this, it was almost possible to imagine the brightness of the fire drawing them down from the white pathway. Or perhaps the flames would attract those who'd lived up here long before the drovers had, back in the Bronze Age. This area had been continuously inhabited for thousands of years before Christ was born.

Evie looked into the flames again until the brightness made her eyes ache and she glanced away. A figure disentangled itself from the shadows and stood at the other side of the fire. Martha. The flickering light gave her face no rosy hue; she looked as though she'd been carved out of stone. For seconds the two women looked at one another. Still this animosity — that was the wrong word because nothing was ever said — this sense of something unresolved between them. And yet it had been Martha who'd provided the strangest but strongest reason for Evie to carry on. Some mornings, flattened by longing for her daughter, Evie had sat at the kitchen table asking herself if she could be bothered to go out to the cattle or up the hill to the sheep. Martha had appeared in the farmyard, fork in hand, or with a can of oil needed for the tractor. Her presence had been like a challenge, a suggestion to Evie that she should prove herself a true native, someone who'd stick it out on this hillside, even if there was no point because there was no surviving Winter. She'd pull on overalls and boots and go to join the woman, silently helping her to hitch the trailer to the tractor or to move livestock from one field to another. Martha's quiet presence became something that marked the days and weeks, something that stopped her from sitting in that chair by the range, even though the other woman had never once said anything about the loss of Jessamy. Perhaps because of that. Evie thought back to that evening more than half a century ago when she'd discovered Robert and Martha together on the parlour sofa and wondered whether Martha had ever suspected that it had been she who'd let the dog out and disturbed the lovers. Perhaps that was where the dislike had originated. And it had never faded. Even on sludge-grey days when depression wanted to clamp Evie to her bed she'd forced herself out to meet

Martha's unfathomable stare. *Here I am. Still here. Despite everything.*

Evie turned now so that the warmth of the flames bathed her back, resting her eyes on the darkening vale beneath them.

". . . drinks in the Packhorse," someone said. Tonight there'd be drinking and singing. The troubles of the previous year, the burning pyres of animals just miles from the village, needed excising. The Jubilee was the time to forget about foot and mouth. But Evie didn't want to follow them down to the pub. Freya Barnes lingered when the others walked on down the hill.

"Coming, Evie?" But the tone of her question made it clear Freya knew the answer would be negative.

"I've got things to do." Excuses, and Freya would know this. But she wasn't one to press a point.

"Look after yourself." Her soft eyes looked sorrowfully at Evie before she joined the others trooping down the steep lane towards the car park.

Evie lingered in the shadows of the trees to give them time to get ahead, wrapping her silk scarf more tightly around her neck. She followed the lane down the steep hill and then struck out across the fields, not needing to stick to footpaths and barely requiring her torch to avoid young crops because she knew each one of these acres and what grew in them as well as she knew herself. As she descended she could almost feel the difference in the soil, the downland chalk turning to sticky clay beneath her soles. She reached a stile and crossed the field of thoroughbreds shaking their heads in enjoyment of the freedom and whinnying softly as they spotted her. The grass squeaked beneath her thick shoes and she could smell the juices at each footstep. Once she'd welcomed early summer with an almost animal relish. But now she longed for autumn and its gold-tinted afternoons and evenings, with the wind wailing round the roof, the heat and gentle light in the kitchen like an embrace on her return from the village shop or a walk with Pilot. The long nights could safely contain all those unanswerable but necessary questions she needed to ask herself. In the summer brightness she'd be forced to re-examine them.

A single lantern burned bright in the western sky. Venus. She hadn't known anything about the planets until Robert Winter had taught her their names and where to spot them. One day, Evie Winter and her hopes and fears would just be a speck of dust on a small planet. She'd curl up in the sweet-smelling soil beside Matthew and rest in his quiet presence for eternity.

She'd reached the field in front of the house, in sight of the trees sheltering the farm. The oaks were becoming too tall. But she couldn't bear to call in the tree surgeon and have him cut them. She had an almost supernatural fear that the chainsaw would somehow cut into her own body. Her eyes fixed on the gilded boughs of the largest oak. She ought to leave this place while she still possessed the strength to start again somewhere else, a small cottage on the Dorset coast, perhaps. But she couldn't. Not just because Jessamy, assuming she still lived, mightn't be able to find her if she left the village; anyone could find anyone these

**132**

days, using the internet. That is, if they wanted to be found.

No, she couldn't leave because, for all the bitterness nights like this inflicted on her, the first stars in the clear evening light and the smell of the blossoming year still held her in their grip. Even though the farm was becoming too much for her and she had been forced to close up rooms upstairs as the attempt to heat and maintain them defeated her. Once this place had employed half a dozen men to work the land and two girls to help in the house and dairy. And Martha. Always Martha up there on the down, watching the sheep. Watching the farm. Now it was just Evie and two afternoons of Slovakian cleaner.

She lengthened her stride, suddenly anxious to make the farm before the shadows grew any deeper. The house was now only a minute away if she kept to the fields and climbed the stile. The bottom plank swayed as it took her weight. Evie made a mental note to find hammer and nails in the morning, feeling her shoulders hunch at the prospect of yet another chore. How cheerfully she could have fixed a loose plank if her daughter had still been in her life. "I had to mend that stile again," she'd have said in the course of their weekly telephone catch-up call with Jess. "Damn nuisance."

"Can't you get someone to do it for you?" Jessamy would have replied, impatient at this imposition on her mother. "Or leave it for me to do when I come up next week." Because, of course, her daughter and her young family would be regular weekend visitors.

133

"I need more biscuits," she'd announce in the village shop. "And some boxes of cereal. The grandchildren will be here tomorrow and you know how much they eat." And all the old women and young mothers standing in the queue would roll their eyes and laugh indulgently.

Or would Jessamy have perhaps been living at Winter's Copse by now? If so, the responsibility for the stile would have been hers. Or her husband's. Jessamy would have brought a strong, handsome, kindly man to live on the farm. The grandchildren would be living here, running down the lane to the village school each morning and bringing their friends back to play on the bales, just as she and Charlie had all those years ago. She, Evie, would have converted one of the farm cottages as a home for herself; on hand in case she were needed to help with the animals or grandchildren, but at a discreet distance.

Evie gave herself a mental shake and felt for the torch she always carried in her pocket so she could see to undo the lock on the gate. If she let herself she could fall into a familiar trap: she'd imagine that Jessamy was striding out just ahead of her, just yards away, reachable if only Evie could quicken her pace. She forced herself to slow down, not to play the game with its inevitable painful ending.

She could make out the chimney pots and the swaying outline of the first roses on the trellis above the garden gate. Pilot would be pacing up and down behind the door, anxious about his supper, anxious to have her back with him.

134

"Evie." The figure stepped out from behind the cherry tree and her heart shot into her mouth.

She clutched at the torch.

"Didn't mean to frighten you."

"You gave me a shock." She barely managed to utter the words.

"Sometimes I think she's come back." Martha's voice was a whisper. "I think I'll see her playing in the garden. Especially on nights like this."

"She'd be a grown woman now, like Rachel."

The idea seemed to shock Martha. "Grown?" She swallowed. "I suppose so."

"You never give up hope she'll come back one day, do you, Martha?"

The idea seemed to freeze Martha. Her face was immobile when she spoke again. "The child's life was never the same after her father died."

Evie's fingers curled. But it was pointless to defend herself against whatever accusation was being made. Hadn't she gone over the afternoon of the Silver Jubilee and the preceding weeks again and again in her mind, trying to pinpoint any possible blame she should attribute to herself? There'd been a time when even finding something for which she could blame herself would have been a relief. "Night, Martha."

"Good night." It was the longest conversation she'd had with Martha for years, since most of the fields had been contracted out and Evie no longer had need of extra help. Martha was too old to work now, anyway. God knows what she did with her days: she always seemed to be walking around outside, refusing to join in with the Afternoon Club or the WI like everyone else her age. Sometimes Evie would come across a fresh nail in a fence plank and know that the other woman still walked around the farm with that shepherd's crook of hers, checking on things. It might have made her angry once but not any longer.

She went inside, into the drawing room. Not quite cold enough for a fire, though she yearned for the comfort of yellow flames. She switched on the television, to see the roundup of Jubilee celebrations. All round the country people were huddling round beacons.

"Jubilees and Coronations are always cold," the pretty presenter said, with the air of someone reading an official verdict. "But Coronation Day was supposed to be sunny, that's why they chose the date." Evie remembered Richard Dimbleby saying something similar when she'd watched the Coronation coverage. She and Matthew had laughed. The weather here in Oxfordshire, or Berkshire, as it had been back then, had been terrible too. She remembered running out of the house and up the hill, the wet seeping down the back of her cardigan and turning her dress into a soggy dishcloth. Then she remembered Jessamy'd been wearing that thin cardigan over her cotton frock at the Silver Jubilee party.

Unable to settle, Evie switched off the television and stood. Above her on the mantelpiece stood the photo of the Winter brothers, taken in the camp in 1943. Something had happened out there in the East, something that was more than just the quotidian horror

**136**

and deprivation of those Japanese camps. It had left a mark on the brothers. It had been on her mind lately, even though she kept telling herself that it was old history, distinct from the mystery of Jessamy's disappearance.

Pilot whined to be let out and she roused herself.

# CHAPTER
# SIXTEEN

**Robert**
**Kanburi Camp, ? March 1943**

Dear Evie,

I wish I knew the exact date. I think it's March now. The turn of the year, Dad used to call it. You can start to see signs of winter ending at home. Mothering Sunday. Lent, Lady Day. What's happening on the farm now? How's the farm manager getting on? Drilling. Lambing almost done. Perhaps a few days that feel like spring. Aconites and crocuses in the garden and the daffodils just starting. I wonder if you pick them and put them in a vase for Mum. She loves those first flowers the most.

I know roughly where we are now: to the north/north-west of the last camp. I don't know if knowing makes it better or not. Matthew needs quinine. He's weak, weaker than I am. Beriberi, dysentery and several more bouts of malaria. We need medicines. The hospital hut is really just somewhere they lay out the dying men. In the last camp the Japs let us trade with the local Thais. At this one the Koreans who guard us push us away from the trading barges with the butts of their guns. On one of them sat a little girl of about your age, watching as the Koreans shoved us off. A pretty thing, just like you.

I dream of home every night. I dream that I come back to Winter's Copse but nobody recognizes me. I keep saying it's me, it's Robert. Eventually you all agree that it's me. Then I try to tell you what has happened to us out here but you won't believe me. "Don't lie to me," Mother says. "Remember your commandments, Robert."

## Two days later

I promised you I would fight the dark, didn't I? Something good has happened and I will tell you about it. We were allowed to go to the village to buy from the traders with the baht we've earned. I had a list of things I needed: rice, eggs, soap. And medicine.

When we reached the village some guards came out and waved their guns at us, making it clear we couldn't proceed. Macgregor tried to reason with them but got his answer in the form of a bloody nose from a swung rifle.

As we trudged back to the camp I felt someone tap me on the back. When I turned I couldn't see her at first: the child from the barge. She was tiny, shorter than you, Evie, though her face appeared about the same age. She held up something: a small bag of rice. I glanced over my shoulder, the guards were lashing out at some poor Australian who wasn't walking quickly enough. They weren't looking in my direction. "One baht," she said in English. I was so surprised I couldn't even work out whether she was overcharging me. All I could think was that Matthew could have boiled rice tonight. She opened the bag and showed me the rice, gleaming grains, not like the dirty stuff we have in the camp with its weevils and insects. I gave her the money and she seemed to pocket it and hand me the rice in the same movement, vanishing into the trees on her shoeless feet.

# CHAPTER
# SEVENTEEN

**Evie**
**A week after the Golden Jubilee party, June 2002**

Evie couldn't get the Thai jungle out of her mind. She kept recalling the men coming back from the East, returning to the village, trying to pick up the threads of their pre-war lives.

"Matthew didn't seem as changed by the camp as Robert," she told Freya Barnes the day after the Golden Jubilee. "But he'd never eat a complete meal. I found half-slices of bread in drawers and apples behind books for years after we married. He could never bear to finish it all." She looked round at the loaded fruit bowls on Freya's kitchen dresser, the cake tins, biscuit barrels. "Eventually he stopped doing it."

"You gave him what he needed, Evie. He knew he was safe with you."

"I didn't do more than any other woman would have."

"That I doubt. Matthew was lucky to have you." Freya let out a sigh. "What those poor men went through."

Evie was sitting at the kitchen table, feeling, as she always did, comforted by the gleam of well-polished worktops and kitchen cabinets. While she was with Freya some kind of external benevolent power still seemed a possibility. But perhaps that was just the after-effects of good coffee and home-made shortbread. "I don't know why I keep thinking about those early years."

"Remembering the Coronation probably brought it all back. It was still raw then, wasn't it, the war in the Far East? I saw a programme saying they were the forgotten army. Most people had no idea what the prisoners went through."

"We had a prisoner of war on the farm ourselves. Carlo. From Italy. At first we were a bit suspicious of him but after a month or so he felt like one of the family. Then he just vanished." The same day that Robert had died in the barn fire. But she didn't tell Freya that.

Freya glanced at her. "Did you ever meet Matthew before he went away to fight?"

"Just once, briefly, when he came back before he was posted. He was only home for a few days, though, and most of that time was spent discussing the farm and the manager they were to employ when Robert joined up too."

"Wasn't farming a reserved occupation?"

Evie nodded. "The authorities tried to persuade Matthew and Robert that the country needed food as badly as it needed men in uniform. But they thought they should fight. Plenty of less able-bodied men could manage the farm, especially with land girls and POWs to help out."

"And yet it meant so much to them."

"The Winters have always fought for their country, that's what Robert said. And they were so pleased that they could stick together. The war against Japan hadn't started then. Nobody could have imagined what would happen to them in Singapore."

She fell silent.

"I'll make you some coffee in a moment. And there are some scones and whipped cream." One of Freya's hands wove its way through her dark curls while the other tapped on the keyboard. She was writing her weekly column on household and rural matters for a small e-zine. She let out a sigh and leaned back. "Give me some ideas for what to do with all the Jubilee party left-overs."

"Best to throw them away." Someone kind had brought Evie a plate of Jubilee fairy cakes, decorated with sugar flowers and pink icing and she couldn't bear to look at them.

Freya eyed her. "Jessamy's haunting you again, isn't she?"

Evie looked away. Sometimes her friend saw more than was comfortable. "She's on my mind most of the time at the moment."

"You want to talk about it?"

Evie shook her head. "It just makes the sadness spread if I talk about it too much. If I can keep it inside me it feels controllable."

"And that's better?"

"At least when it's just inside me I don't feel overwhelmed by it."

Evie gave a shiver, remembering how once, years ago, the anger had filled her whole body, making her shake and her stomach flip within her. She'd banged her head on the wall by the piano in the drawing room, trying to force out the rage before it consumed her. The dog, not Pilot but his grandmother, had risen from her bed, hackles rising, whining. It was only the sight of the animal's scared black eyes that had made Evie stop. Before she'd only thought of herself as sad, anxious, preoccupied, obsessed. Now the full force of her rage hit her again. She felt the rank unfairness as a bitter taste in her mouth and took a mouthful of coffee to counter it. Her Jessamy ought not to have been taken from her. It went against all that was natural and just in the world. She'd already lost Matthew. And Robert. And her mother.

Freya nodded. "Well, you know you've always got a listener here when you need one."

"Just being here in your house with you helps." She touched Freya's arm, warm under the olive-green linen shirt. "Sorry for being such a bore."

"There is no need for sorry." Freya turned the pile of papers beside her and waved the printout of an email at Evie. "I'm already getting the nutters asking me about crop circles." She rolled her eyes. "That's the thing about this part of the world, you attract all the fools."

"You're still thinking of Midsummer Eve last year?" Despite herself Evie felt her lips twitch.

144

"You think I'd forget a horde of hippies streaming through my back garden on the way up to Wayland's Smithy?"

"They certainly won't forget you." Clad in her nightdress and waving a dishcloth, Freya had chased them off her lawn. Evie laughed for the first time in days.

"I wouldn't mind if they tidied up after themselves, Evie. If they had a respect for the land."

"You probably know more about this place and all the old myths and legends than any of the New Agers."

Beneath Freya's dark skin lay a repository of stories concerning the pale Norsemen and their myths.

"My father certainly loved the old stories. And he taught me to love them too." Freya laughed. "Strange for a man who never even saw snow his whole life." She switched off the laptop. "We should go for a walk up there one sunny afternoon, Evie. Do us good."

Evie was remembering her own night up at Wayland's Smithy, right at the end of the war. She'd never been back to the place in the nearly sixty years that had passed since the barn fire. As she walked home she thought again about Wayland's Smithy and Robert's return from the POW camp.

For years she'd been waiting for him to reappear. She and Charlie had stayed at the farm under the supervision of old Mrs Winter and Mr Edwards, the new farm manager, and she'd crossed the days off the calendar, knowing that she was coming nearer and nearer to . . . what? No correspondence had arrived from the Far East, just the original cards he and

Matthew had sent saying they'd been taken prisoner, and something from the Red Cross in 1942, briefly describing the brothers' removal to Siam, or Thailand, as it was called now. Evie had read the telegram to Mrs Winter. "Milk," she'd said. "To build them up." And Evie had agreed that they should be given milk on their return. Then there'd been silence for over two years.

By the summer of 1945 she'd been fifteen, old enough for the crush to have taken on an even more passionate drive. She'd sat in the hayloft with the land girls and listened to them chatting about men, and admired the photographs of their boyfriends in their various uniforms. And she'd felt a kinship with these older girls with their Coty lipsticks and waved hairdos. One afternoon they'd been sitting there and talking about one of these trivial things when Mr Edwards had rushed in. Clasped in his hand was a telegram. "I've taken it straight up to Mrs Winter and she already knows, but it's good news!"

Evie jumped down from the ladder where she perched. "What?"

"Both the Winter brothers are safe. Matthew was liberated from a camp in Siam. Robert was found back at Changi in Singapore. We don't know why they were separated."

"When will they come home? How long will it take them?" She was gabbling questions while her startled mind tried to make sense of it all: they were coming back, Robert and Matthew.

"The telegram doesn't say. I imagine they'll send them by train to Rangoon, I expect. And on by ship to

146

Bombay and from there to Cape Town. It could all take some time."

"Robert's coming back?" Evie hadn't heard Martha approach. Beneath the turban she wore over her hair while she worked her face was flushed. "Let me see that." She pulled the telegram from Mr Edwards's fingers. He tried to retain it.

"It's really Mrs Winter's telegram."

"Robert would want me to know." Martha frowned at it. "Doesn't say much, does it?"

"It's a telegram." Evie heard the acid in her own voice. "I expect they'll write."

"Robert will want me to know what's happening." Martha stuffed the telegram back at Mr Edwards, with a glare at Evie.

Evie sat on her bed that evening and examined Robert's photograph. She must have dropped the frame at some stage because a small screw at the back was loose. In the morning she took it into the workshop out in the barn to find a screwdriver. She placed the picture on the workbench while she searched the little drawers of nuts, bolts and screws on top of the cupboard. A shadow passed over the doorway as Evie found the right-sized screwdriver. She turned to see Martha standing there. "Morning," she said to the older girl.

"Morning." Martha examined her with those curious light eyes of her. "Whose photo is that?"

Evie picked up the frame. Not quickly enough.

"It's Robert."

147

She started tightening the little screw on the back as Martha came closer.

"Why've you got his photo?" There was a sharp note to her question.

Evie shrugged. "To remember him while he was away."

"You wanted to remember him?" Martha gave a short laugh. "And why would that be? He's not going to be thinking about *you*, Eve Parr, is he? You're just a kid."

She cast the photograph a passing look of scorn and walked out.

Evie examined Robert's face again. "She's waiting for you," she told him. "And so am I."

# CHAPTER
# EIGHTEEN

**Robert**
**Kanburi Camp, end of March 1943**

Dear Evie,

The little Thai girl's name is Noi. She came up to me again this evening as we marched back to camp. In her hands were two duck eggs, a pale blue like a winter sky at home. I thought of you collecting eggs in the farmyard, coming in triumphant when you found them all. I handed Noi the coins and once again she took the money and passed me the food in one single graceful movement. "Noi," she said, pointing at herself. "Robert," I said, pointing at my tatty shirt. I put the eggs in my pocket and made a gesture to suggest we should both sit down. I rested my back against a tree and put up a hand to push aside a slim swaying branch by my face. She called out and her face was white. I'd been about to brush aside a snake! I had the quickest impression of a browny/greeny form that hissed at me before I rolled onto my side and away from its fangs.

Noi's terror was replaced with laughter. She made one fist into a snake's head and pretended to bite her other hand. Then she stopped laughing and said something in

Thai that sounded more serious, even in the melodious sing-song tones that Siamese women use to speak their language. I knew she was telling me to be more careful where I put my hands.

Matthew and I had the eggs for our supper. It is wonderful how even a small amount of protein makes you feel stronger again. I used to like my eggs scrambled with butter, all yellow and creamy. Here they are plain boiled, eaten with salt if we can get it.

I wonder if young Noi will be able to find us more food. Or medicines.

# Part Five

# CHAPTER
# NINETEEN

**Evie**
**September 1945**

Into Evie's dream moved a dried-out husk the size of a tree. But the husk had a face. Evie woke. She caught sight of a face at her door then it was gone.

She rolled over on her side and pulled the sheet over her shoulders, closing her eyes and willing sleep to return. But the face was on her mind. She probably had imagined it but just in case she was going to close the door. She rose and walked towards it, her hand reaching for the handle, when a shadow passed across it.

Evie opened her mouth to cry out but found herself speechless. The figure must be a ghost. It looked like Robert Winter, but it was thin, its face lined like an older man's. Under her pillow Evie kept the photo of Robert in his uniform, taken at the rose-trailed farmhouse door the day before he left to go to war. This apparition in the doorway with its skeletal face and lined skin was a pastiche of that man.

Perspiration beaded her forehead. She heard her breath coming fast.

"Hello, Evie."

"It is you." She could speak again but her voice sounded as if it belonged to someone else. She rubbed her eyes. But he still stood in front of her with his gaunt face and huge eyes. He didn't look like the boy whose picture she'd kept in her mind for all those years. He didn't look like the handsome hero she'd imagined who'd return to fall in love with her as soon as she was old enough to be worthy of this privilege. For the last year, since her mother had died in one of the final bombing raids, anticipation of Robert's return had kept Evie going through long schooldays and evenings spent helping with the milking or trying to rustle up meals for Charlie and Mr Edwards.

"Back again. At long last."

She forced her lips to work. "I missed you so much." She'd rehearsed these words a thousand times. "And Charlie did too."

"Did you?"

"We wrote to you. Did you get the letters?" She had to keep on talking, nervous of what the silences might expose.

He shook his head. "We had nothing. In the end all I had was that letter you wrote me before I left the farm. Do you remember, Evie?"

"Yes." She took a few steps backwards until she reached her bed, where she sat. Her fingers picked at a loose thread on the eiderdown.

"Most of it disintegrated but I could still read the important bits."

What exactly had she said? She could remember writing the letter but not the words she'd used.

"It really kept me going, knowing that there was someone back here rooting for me. Got me through some bad times, I can tell you."

"I'm glad."

"I wrote to you, too, Evie."

"Did you? We never had the letters."

"I lost some of them in Singapore. But I kept on writing even though they'd never have let me send them. So I hid them. In all kinds of places. Matthew kept them safe for me."

"I'd like to have read them." But she knew she wouldn't have been able to bear it.

"Did you hear about what the Japs did to us, Evie?" He came into the room and sat on her bed. She willed herself not to flinch from him as he passed her. Even the smell of him was different: metallic and dry, like a road in hot sun. He'd once smelled of new grass and warm cotton. "Did Matthew tell you? Perhaps he thought a young girl like you oughtn't to know those things."

"He hasn't come back here yet. He's still in hospital."

"They told me that they'd had to amputate part of his foot. It rotted."

She heard the rasp of her drawn breath.

"He had a skin abscess and it went down to the bone. No penicillin out there to treat infections. And the heat and humidity made it worse. You could smell it from yards away."

"Poor Matthew."

"He had beriberi, too. And we all had dysentery and malaria. But the foot was the worst thing."

"It must have been dreadful." She sounded like a stuffed doll, mouthing tired old phrases.

"My health wasn't bad until towards the end when they . . ." He swallowed hard. "But Matthew'll come back here." He didn't seem able to speak for a moment. "We'll look after him, you and I. He can have our milk to drink: best thing for him."

"We kept the herd going," she said. "Only lost two in all the years you were away. One had milk fever and the vet couldn't work out what was wrong with the other. But no TB."

"You did so well, Evie. I'm so proud of you. I always said you'd make a farmer." If she closed her eyes and just listened to his voice it might have been the old Robert talking to her.

"And you should see the pigs. We've chosen the one to slaughter. He's a beauty."

"So we'll have pork chops this autumn." His voice was warm. "It's going to be just like it was before I went away, Evie, just like you wrote in your letter. And I'll forget everything. It'll be just as though it never happened." He sounded dreamy now. "Perhaps we just imagined the whole thing."

She wondered if he ever saw his own reflection in the mirror. Surely that would tell him that his imprisonment had been no bad dream? All round the village there'd been talk of the atrocities, the hunger.

156

He ran a finger over the ridges on her candlewick bedspread. "I was worried you and Charlie might have gone back to London by now."

"Our house was bombed last year. Mum died. We're still waiting for our dad to be demobbed but he won't have a home for us." Evie could list these events almost without feeling them now. Her mother was becoming just a memory. She'd seen her father briefly when he'd visited the farm for a few days in 1943. It had been like receiving a visit from a favourite uncle.

"So it looks like you two'll be here a while longer." He got up. "That's just as it should be. I should get to bed now. Night, Evie." For a second as he wished her goodnight it was as though she'd flipped back three or four years; there was a glimpse of the boy she remembered with his ready smile. Then the haggard man reappeared, moving stiffly towards the door. Evie waited until he'd crossed the landing to his own room and jumped up to lock her bedroom. She'd never locked the door before. When they'd turned twelve Charlie had moved to the little box room next to this one at the suggestion of Mrs Winter in one of her rare lucid periods.

"Making yourselves very comfortable," Martha had said, observing them moving clothes and books.

Back then Evie had taken this as reassuring evidence that they were both to stay in the farmhouse and of her own increased maturity and stature. Now she wished her brother was still sleeping in the bed beside her. But this was Robert she was worrying about: Robert Winter, who'd given her the best raspberries to eat and shown her where the farm cat kept her kittens. Robert, her knight.

During the day Robert was absent. He seemed to do little on the farm, but that was all right because there were still Mr Edwards, Martha and the two land girls, who'd been joined eighteen months earlier by an Italian POW, who came up to the farm from a small nearby camp every day. Mr Edwards had moved into Matthew's bedroom and had his meals with the children. A nurse had been employed to come in twice a day to look after Mrs Winter. Occasionally Evie's form teacher would express uncertainty as to the propriety of these arrangements. "You live with an incapacitated elderly lady and a man you barely know?" She frowned and the spectacles on her nose made her eyes look like blue pebbles.

"The land girls often come in for meals."

"They'll be going home soon." She paused. "And in my experience, many of those young women are very far from setting a good example to girls of your age."

"Mr Edwards is very kind." Evie cast desperately about in her mind. "He helps with homework. He can cook, too. And he plays Scrabble and Monopoly with us." And didn't even mind that Charlie always won.

"I'm sure he's respectable. But I'll be relieved when the Winter brothers are back home again. This arrangement doesn't seem proper for a young girl."

"There's Martha, too. She lives up the lane but she comes in every day."

For the first time Evie felt grateful to have Martha around.

And now here was Robert Winter, back to take care of them. Only he wasn't the same Robert he'd been before he'd left. Gone was the quick smile. Gone was the gentleness with animals. Evie had seen him slap Fly on the head when he failed to respond quickly enough to a command.

The smell of spirits on his breath was becoming harder to ignore. Where Robert acquired the spirits, heavily rationed, was anyone's guess. Mr Edwards, coming in from the cowshed to scrub up under the kitchen taps, wrinkled his nose. Robert saw the expression on his face. "You got something stuck up your arse?" The toffee-coloured eyes were hard like dirty windowpanes.

Evie stared hard at the history homework laid out on the kitchen table.

"Sorry, old chap." Mr Edwards shrugged. "Just seemed a little . . . early."

When he wasn't drinking Robert Winter retired to the barn with an old Norton motorbike he'd bought from one of the regulars in the Packhorse, taking it to bits and cleaning and oiling each part before reassembling it. Evie hoped the new interest might wean him from the bottle. Martha came down to the farm one evening, wearing a dress Evie didn't recognize. She must have been saving it for the homecoming.

"I could cook for you, Robert." She leant against the range. "Like old times. What do you fancy?"

"What if he says he wants lobster?" Charlie asked. She ignored him.

"Hens are still laying well. I could make a soufflé. I've got some cheddar. Bet it's years since you had one of those."

He gave a non-committal smile.

"And all those blackberries would make a good crumble."

"Evie wants them," he muttered. "For jam."

"Oh, Evie wants them, does she?" Martha tapped her long fingers on the edge of the range. "Hope she won't waste them: jam's a tricky thing. Well, have a think." She stood straight. "Or perhaps you'd fancy a stroll up the hill to look at the sheep?"

"I went out earlier. They're all fine."

Martha pursed her lips. "I'll be off then." Still she hovered. "If you're sure there's nothing I can do for you."

He shook his head. "Thanks for coming down, Martha." As she left the kitchen Fly cowered against the wall, even though it was years since Martha had kicked him.

Robert spent hours with Carlo, the Italian prisoner of war, talking and smoking with him, sometimes consulting him about the motorbike. Perhaps he felt a particular bond with Carlo on account of their both having been prisoners in a foreign land. Robert even gave the Italian some of his clothes, saying that they didn't fit him any more. One afternoon Evie brought them out their mugs of tea to find Robert handing over a pair of boots to the Italian. "Even my damn feet shrank in that place."

"*Grazie*, signor." Carlo's dark eyes shone. "They are nearly as good as Italian leather."

"According to you everything in Italy's better than everything here," Robert said. Evie looked at him quickly to see whether he was about to grow angry but his expression was relaxed.

"Not everything. Not politics." Carlo grinned. "And your girls are good. Take the land girls. Or Miss Evie, nobody better than her between Sicily and the Dolomites."

"Couldn't agree with you more." Robert's smile had a flintiness to it. "But don't mention Evie in the same breath as the land girls, old man."

Carlo glanced from one of them to the other. "*Scusi.*"

"Our Evie's special, Carlo."

"Yes."

"What about Martha?" Evie asked cautiously. "Would you say that she was beautiful?" Surely men would be impressed by that thick dark hair and that willowy shape.

The sudden tension felt like it did in church when the organist played a wrong note.

"Unusual eyes," Carlo said, in a buoyant tone she didn't recognize. "And she have good figure."

Robert said nothing but narrowed his eyes and stared across the farmyard. Evie cursed herself as a fool and cast around for a distraction. "You'll be repatriated soon enough," she told Carlo.

"Not sure I want to go back there, anyway. Italy is a very poor country, even more so because of the war."

"But you're always saying you don't like England and the damp and you can't wait to leave," she said.

"Perhaps I go to America. Sometimes people get to Ireland and go on from there. So I hear."

"By people I assume you mean POWs who escape," Robert said.

Carlo made what Evie could only describe as a Latin gesture, shrugging with his palms turned upwards.

"You could probably do it if you really wanted. Plenty of places you could hide out in." Robert shuddered. "Someone in the Packhorse was talking about German spies hiding in the Sarsens up at Wayland's Smithy on the Ridgeway."

"Do you think they did?" Evie asked.

"Good luck to them, if they did. Place is supposed to be haunted. No way you'd get me squeezing myself into a small space in the dark like that. When I was a lad I might have done it for a lark but not now, not since . . ." He broke off.

"If I escape I'll find a nice woman to hide me." Carlo's eyes twinkled.

The pig was ready for slaughtering. Evie helped Mr Edwards pull the measuring tape round the animal. He nodded. "Nice job, Evie, he's fattened up well." They walked back to the house.

"I can send for someone to do it," Mr Edwards said over breakfast. During the war they'd used a slaughterman from the village who came up with his sharpened blades wrapped up in a canvas pouch. Evie'd watched once or twice but preferred to absent herself when it was an animal she knew well.

"I'll do it." Robert sounded calm, controlled. He looked around the kitchen table. Evie made her shoulders relax and put a bit of toast into her mouth, where it sat like a slab of concrete. Mr Edwards stared hard at the teacup in front of him.

"If you prefer."

Evie rose and started piling plates and saucers to take to the sink; pieces of crockery crashed together as she stacked them. "Careful with the china, Noi," Robert said.

She stared at him.

"Evie, I mean."

"Who's Noi?"

He pushed his plate away. "Just watch what you're doing."

"Sorry." She plunged the plug into the sink and ran the taps so hard that all the crumbs shot off the plates and were lost in the suds. For the first time in months she was relieved to go into school, even though it was double Latin this morning.

When she walked back into the farmyard that afternoon a trail of bloodspots led from the barn towards the track up to the Downs. "Hello, Evie." Robert leant against the stable wall, watching her.

"What's happened?" He shook his head. "Where's the pig?"

His body seemed to stiffen. "He's still alive. For now, anyway."

She looked from him to the bloodstains on the ground. "I don't understand."

"They look like rubies, don't they?" She realized he was looking at the stains, too. "Almost beautiful. I started to do it, Evie, but I couldn't." The words were almost hissed at her. "He got up and ran out. Edwards had to go after him with the shotgun."

Evie put a hand to her own neck, as though she could feel the prick of the blade that hadn't gone far enough into the artery. The one unforgivable sin, to leave an animal half dead, suffering. Before he'd gone off to war she'd seen Robert pursue a fox he'd taken aim at and left with a smashed shoulder. He'd chased it for an hour and a half before he could finish it off.

And this pig was valuable. They'd given him scraps that could hardly be spared. He was supposed to last all autumn and well into winter. Bits of him had been promised to neighbours in exchange for sugar and tractor parts.

She heard the tramp of boots across the yard and Mr Edwards and Carlo came in, both bloodstained. "It's all right," Carlo said. "He didn't go far. Just the orchard. He is greedy for those apples. We finish him there."

"Can we . . . ?" She felt bile in her mouth. She'd been going to ask if they could still use the meat in such circumstances, if it had been spoiled by the pig's death in the orchard, but she had to run to the kitchen sink.

Robert burst into the kitchen one Saturday lunchtime when she and Mr Edwards were frying lambs' kidneys.

"Throw me a bottle of beer, Evie."

She sensed Mr Edwards stiffening as he turned the kidneys in the frying pan. She looked down at the crate beside the stove. Empty.

"They've all gone."

"There was one there last night." He glared at Mr Edwards. "Did you take it, Edwards?"

"I did. The first I've had for some weeks, I might add."

Robert moved closer. "Meaning?"

"Meaning that I drank the last bottle of beer, yes." Mr Edwards nodded towards the table. "I think we're ready, Evie. Let's call Charlie in and serve up."

"Don't try and brush me off." Robert was standing so close to him now that they looked like a pair of angry rams, sizing one another up. "This is still my home, you know, Edwards."

"I do know that. I appreciate I'm really in the way here. In fact, my time at Winter's Copse is coming to an end." Mr Edwards took the frying pan off the stove. "I've heard from the ministry about my next posting. Now you're back there's no need for me to stay. I'd like to spend some time with my father, too. He's getting on. And your brother's starting to recover, isn't he?" A letter had come from Matthew in hospital, saying he could now walk on crutches. They hadn't had to amputate his infected left foot, a souvenir from the Japanese camp.

Evie felt panic wash over her. Mr Edwards might be dull, pompous at times, but he was kindly. He'd locked the back door every night and if the fox got into the chicken house he'd get up with the shotgun and shoot

**165**

it. She'd felt safe while he was at Winter's Copse and the land girls came up every day. As though reading her mind he glanced at her as he handed her a plate. "When does Matthew leave hospital, Eve?"

"He'll never be right again." Robert picked up a fork and stabbed at the wooden table. "Those fevers, those diseases. But I should have forgotten about the quinine. It was a bad idea, Noi."

"We don't know what you mean." Evie heard her voice sounding like a taut length of wire. "We don't know who Noi is."

His eyes were wide, pupils constricted. "Sorry." He forced a sickly smile. "Look at me. Scaring a good kid like you, Evie. Who'd have thought I'd come to that?"

"Eat your lunch, old chap." Mr Edwards spoke softly. "We don't always know what to say to you. Or how to act. Be patient with us. Tell us how we can help."

"Sometime I feel as though I'm still out there. I can't shake it off." He sounded very young, almost like Charlie. "I think they're still here: the other prisoners, the guards, the . . ." He'd picked up his fork and was driving the prongs into the wooden table.

Mr Edwards placed a plate of kidneys and boiled potato in front of him. "It'll pass. I know that's precious little to say, but every day takes you further away from that camp."

"I wish I could cut out the bit of my memory that keeps throwing it back at me." As he always did since his return, Robert stared at the dinner plate. He caught Evie looking at him. "Can't get used to seeing so much food. And I know it's not as much as we used to eat before the war, but compared with what they gave us out there . . ."

"Who's Noi?" Evie asked again.

She thought he'd ignore the question.

"A girl about your age in Thailand."

"Try not to dwell on the past." Mr Edwards handed him the dish of carrots with a frown at Evie. "Get some of these on your plate. Vitamin C."

"You grew those here?" Robert gave an approving nod. "Carrots are hard on this soil. You must have added sand?"

"We did. Carlo and I mixed it in. Helped with the drainage."

"I noticed today that you'd got him to thin out the woods."

Mr Edwards's hands tightened on the vegetable dish. "Nice job."

How easily Robert could make a person beam. Even an ordinarily serious adult like Mr Edwards. There was still enough of the movie star charm in him to make you overlook the rapid changes of mood.

Robert picked up his cutlery and stared at the knife and fork. "We used to eat squatting down, like natives. I even wore a loin cloth." He blushed. "Sorry, Evie."

"That's all right," she said.

"And I used my fingers to scoop up the grains of rice from the bowl."

The days following that lunchtime were quiet. The last of the harvest came in. Robert spent his days out in the farthest fields. Checking fences, he said. The land girls tripped up the lane in the high heels and dresses they'd swapped for their breeches and boots and kissed Evie goodbye, promising to write. She sat on the gate and waved at them until they'd turned the bend.

Mr Edwards took the children aside one evening after school. "I don't think you should stay here after I've gone." He spoke quietly and intensely. "Young Robert's suffering from some nervous disorder. Not surprising really. Conditions in those Jap camps were grim. Don't know exactly what went on out there, but he's obviously been through something terrible."

"Robert would never ever hurt us," Evie said.

"I don't think he would do so intentionally. But he's not right in his head at the moment."

"Where would we go if we left here?" Charlie asked.

"If your father hasn't got a home for you I expect they'd find you something temporary."

"You mean a children's home, don't you?" Evie stared at him. She'd heard about these places. Girls at school whispered about what happened to children who'd been orphaned and had no families to take them in. Children's homes were cold, bleak places. Usually they split up the boys and girls, made them leave school as soon as they legally could and sent them out to work.

Mr Edwards blushed. "It wouldn't be for long."

"No." Evie walked to the parlour window. She could make out the apples on the trees in the orchard. "This is our home. We can't leave." A couple of leaves whirled down very slowly. She clutched the windowsill.

"Robert is a sick man, Evie."

"It's not his fault," Charlie said. "It was what the Nips did to them out there on that railway. They're war criminals. They should all be hanged, Martha says."

"Martha?" Evie felt her mouth curl as she spoke the name.

"She spends a lot of time with Robert up in the field with the sheep."

"Indeed." Mr Edwards sounded dry.

If Evie and Charlie left the farm Martha would be left alone with Robert. Another reason to refuse to leave Winter's Copse. Why she felt Robert and Martha should not be left alone Evie could not say. It was almost as though the two of them were two chemicals that would ignite one another if left together in the same test tube. She turned from the window. "It's kind of you to be worried about us, Mr Edwards. But we'll be fine."

"We'll talk again," he said. "Before I leave. I can't just leave you like this."

"Matthew will be home soon, anyway," Evie added.

Just saying the older Winter brother's name made her feel happier. She'd met Matthew just once when he'd come back on leave before his posting to the East. She remembered a quiet man, less handsome and vivacious than his brother had been, but kind.

They never had the talk with Mr Edwards because he left suddenly the next day while they were at school. "His father had a bad fall," Robert told them. "Insisted on going back to his bombed-out house in Portsmouth and fell through the floorboards or something. He's

**169**

very elderly. Edwards had to make a dash for the train. I took him to the station on my bike."

He put a hand round Evie's shoulders. "So it's just us three now."

"And Martha," Charlie said. Evie felt her cheeks heat. She hadn't ever told her brother about that long-ago discovery of Martha and Robert together in the parlour.

"I expect we'll muddle along fine enough," Robert said.

And fine they were for the first week or so they were in Robert Winter's charge. Evie didn't think he was drinking as much; at least there were fewer bottles stacked in the back of the barn. He'd finished the work on the motorbike and spent most of his time bartering vegetables and eggs for petrol. Martha came down to the house, always with lipstick on. Robert seemed to treat her with no particular interest. Sometimes Evie spotted her on the down, or examining the field of turnips where the sheep would be folded in the winter. Often Martha would stand completely still, a hand over her eyes, gazing down at the farmhouse.

Looking out for Robert, Evie thought. So she could spring out at him.

Charlie now spent most of his free time out of doors, taking sandwiches with him. He preferred to avoid mealtimes with Robert, when conversations could suddenly dry up in the middle of a discussion of the hens' laying habits and Robert would stare out through the dining room window into nothing and they knew he

**170**

was back in the camp again. She offered to play Monopoly with Charlie and not to mind when he filled up Park Lane with hotels but he said it was no fun with just two. "Everyone knows the whole city's bombed, anyway. When I leave here I'm going to get a job building everything up again."

"Real hotels, not little red wooden ones?"

"Why not?" Charlie waved a hand towards the down behind them. "I'm getting sick of all this open space. Spaces should be filled. I want to build places where people go to have a good time."

Released from the watch of Mr Edwards Carlo worked less intensely. Evie came across him enjoying an extended break in the October sunshine, cap pulled over his eyes, back against the warm barn wall beside a pile of empty food sacks and the milk cans waiting to be scrubbed. He gave a start at her approach.

"Hey, *bella*. Where's Mr Robert?" He moved up so that she could sit next to him.

"I don't know. Shouldn't you be doing something?"

"I'm taking a break. It's allowed, no?" He took his lighter out of a pocket.

"I suppose so."

"Mr Robert, he's more relaxed than Mr Edwards."

"Is that good?"

Carlo shrugged. "He is . . . what you call it . . . not right here." He tapped his head. "He stays away from Martha, though. That is good."

"Why?" She wondered whether he'd think the same as her, that the two were somehow unstable together.

171

"She is also not right up here."

"Oh."

"For her, I think, it has always been so. But she encourages him to see things in the wrong way." He gave another half-shrug. "But he is a good man really. He give me these, remember." He pointed at his boots, which he'd polished so they shone like new conkers. "My old ones leak but not these." The cigarette lighter wasn't working. Carlo muttered something in Italian and replaced it in his pocket. "Mr Robert says I can borrow his lighter."

"Won't he need it himself?"

"He hardly smoke these days."

It was true; Evie couldn't remember seeing him with a cigarette since his return; even that means of relaxation seemed to have failed him. She tasted a sour flavour in her mouth. "He was so different before he went off to war." She remembered how he'd shown her how to feed the calves. He'd been patient with her and when she'd finally got the hang of it and the calves' tongues were slurping milk from between her fingers he'd smiled as though he was as pleased as she'd been.

Carlo stubbed out his cigarette. "You learn a lot about a country by the way it treat its POWs. Whatever happened to him out there must have been very bad."

"We haven't been cruel to you in this country, have we, Carlo?" She couldn't bear the thought.

He shook his head. "Little boys throw stones at us once when we were working alongside a railway. And the food in the camp is terrible but here Mr Edwards and Mr Robert give me good food and decent tools and I don't work if I am ill."

"And you can have your little naps."

He winked. "Farming is hard work. And you, little Evie, you and your brother give me plums and apples and are kind. You almost make up for the dreadful weather." He stood and stretched.

"Carlo?"

"Hmmn?"

"Do you think Robert still loves Martha?"

His eyes rolled. "Love? He never love that one."

"But . . ." She couldn't bring herself to tell him about what she'd seen that night before Robert had left for the war.

"She is . . ." His hands described a woman's curves in the air. "But that's all it will be, all it should be, for Robert."

"Why? What's wrong with Martha?" Evie asked, feeling a shameful enjoyment of the implied criticism.

He was silent for a moment. "She keeps him in the camp," he said. "She should listen to him, yes, is good to listen. But not always ask him questions, questions, questions. Perhaps a good friend would help him look forward again."

Something rustled in the empty food sacks behind them. "Damn rats," Carlo said. Then his eyes narrowed.

"What is it?"

"Thought I saw someone. But perhaps not."

Evie looked but could see nothing.

Carlo gave a yawn. "Back to work now." His face grew dreamy. "One day I'll run away, Evie."

"Even though we're so kind to you?"

"I want to be free again, free to smoke all morning if I want. Or free to earn lots of money. I want to go to America."

"Oh America, America!" she teased. "What's so great about America?"

For a second he looked almost serious. "I think my life would start again out there, Evie. I really do."

Robert seemed like the old Robert: teasing her about her frumpy old school uniform and her love of running races against her classmates. "How'll a boy ever catch you if you run that fast, Evie?" They were standing up on the down and she was holding a fence post steady for him while he hammered in nails.

She smiled and wondered about throwing in a quick question of her own but before she could someone called over the brow of the hill, "Robert?"

"Hello, Martha." His eyes were on the post.

"Haven't seen you for a few days. Thought I'd check you were getting on all right." Martha spoke with apparent casualness as she approached but Evie could hear the tension in each word.

"Everything's fine, thanks." He kept his eyes on the nail. "Just busy."

"How's your mother?"

"The doctor found a nursing home for her on the coast. Thought the change of air would do her good for a week."

174

"Mrs Winter's at the coast? Nobody told me." Martha sounded put out. "You coming down to the Packhorse tonight?" She clenched her hands in front of her.

"Probably stay in and have an early night." He raised the hammer to strike the nail and Evie stared down at the post. The hammer fell and when she turned her head, Martha had gone. Gloom had veiled Robert's features as though someone had lowered a blackout over his face.

That night they sat round the table with their tea. "I used to dream of this when I was in the camps along the railway out in Siam," Robert said.

Charlie's face lit. He'd been longing to ask about the railway. "I looked it up on the map. It's amazing to think of the Japs building a railway. Even our British engineers never managed it."

"Amazing," Robert repeated as though he didn't know the meaning of the word. "Yes, it was amazing, I suppose. Amazing and appalling, with the river curling through the mountains and the treacherous currents. And the insects and snakes."

Evie shuddered.

"There were gibbons and macaques, though. I used to like them, although sometimes . . ." He broke off.

Sometimes they'd eaten them, she guessed. Robert took a sip of tea. "We had tea with our evening meal but it was just leaves floating in dirty water and I'd close my eyes and think of tea made properly, with our own milk, in a china cup. And sometimes the only source of protein in a whole day would be whatever

**175**

weevils we found in the rice. Think of that, Evie, we ate feed we wouldn't give our livestock here."

"I wish we'd seen your letters," Evie said. "To know what you suffered."

"It's in the past now." He stirred his tea and stared down at it. "And it doesn't show me very well, Evie."

"What do you mean?"

He shrugged. "I told you, it was different out there. Things happened."

"I don't understand."

"Perhaps I'll explain, one day. I've got the letters back now. Matthew sent them on to me from the hospital. Perhaps after I marry you and I know you've got to stay here with me."

Evie's tea spilled over the rim of the cup onto her fingers and the scalding liquid made her wince. A couple of months ago this suggestion of future marriage to Robert Winter would have been her dream-come-true. She tried to muster a smile. That foolish, foolish letter she'd written.

"Not much of a prospect, eh, Evie?" He shook his head. "But I'm fattening up, aren't I?" His eyes had taken on the hard, glassy expression which meant he was somewhere else; not sitting in the Berkshire farmhouse but out in the East. "I'm becoming more the kind of man who'd catch a girl's eye?"

"I'm a bit young to marry," she said at last, trying to sound calm.

"I'd wait for you to grow up." His eyes were still staring out at something she couldn't see. "In the meantime I'm going to take such good care of you."

**176**

She glanced at her watch. Nine. Thank God. She caught Charlie's eye and pointed at the dial. "We should go up."

"Time for a half in the Packhorse," Robert said as they left the kitchen. "Night, you two."

Evie'd been up early every morning this week to help with the milking and there'd been games at school this afternoon. She heard the purr of the motorbike taking Robert down the hill before sleep claimed her.

# CHAPTER
# TWENTY

**Robert**
**Kanburi Camp, ? June 1943**

Dear Evie,

Not sure about the date for this letter. Lost track of time again. Been working out on the next patch of ground to be cleared for the railway, breaking stones and clearing trees. Not much food.

"Why do you write all these letters you'll never post?" Macgregor asked me yesterday. "What's the point?"

It was hard to explain. But somehow when everything's written down it feels more controllable.

You'll remember my friend, Noi? I have been able to repay her for saving me from snakebite last month. She and I were sitting at the edge of the market stalls in town. I'd bought some sweet potatoes from her. You may think it strange that we're allowed to go into the settlements and openly barter with people. But the Japs know we won't escape. Where would we go? We're surrounded by dense forest and mountains. I suppose someone could smuggle themselves onto a barge, but these are regularly inspected. Even if you managed to make it to the coast, this is controlled by the Japanese, too. A white man is an obvious fugitive.

I drew Noi some pictures in the dust of my home: Mum, Matthew, you and Charlie. It was hard to explain who everyone was — she thought you were my wife! I also drew some cows, which interested her greatly. They don't have cows in this part of the world. Pigs and chickens were less interesting for her as she sees them here. She liked the horses, though.

Then she drew her barge and herself, parents and baby brother. Her mother called to her, presumably warning that they were about to leave. I looked up and saw why: a guard was staggering around, drunk out of his head, armed with a club. Noi jumped up and ran towards her mother, who was standing at the far side of the marketplace, baby strapped to her back, gesturing at her to hurry. Something about the girl seemed to grab the guard's attention: he staggered towards her, waving the club, muttering something. Noi seemed to shrink while her eyes grew big with fright.

Already everyone was rushing from the marketplace. A drunk camp guard with a gun is enough to clear a town. A pile of metal cooking pots sat beside an abandoned stall. The guard swung around Noi, waving his gun, shouting; his back was momentarily to me. I ran to the pots and kicked them a passing blow. They crashed to the ground like cymbals but I was already sprinting to the cover of the teak trees. The guard jumped round, gun in hand, and saw only a heap of fallen pots. He shouted into thin air. I peered out from my hiding place. In the seconds that he'd switched his attention from her, Noi had run to her mother and the two of them had dissolved into one of the backstreets fanning out from the marketplace. The guard spat into the dust and wobbled away.

For days I didn't go anywhere near the traders. But I spent some time in the workshop with some pieces of discarded wood. At home I was a fair carver and I managed to use our few blunted tools to fashion a doll for Noi. It took some time: my hands are so sore from the splinters and blisters. I even found some old tins of paint, used to mark the sleepers, and drew on a red mouth and black hair, eyes and nose, using a bamboo splint as a kind of quill pen. The poor doll was naked and I am no seamstress but I managed to cajole old Macgregor into helping out. You remember I said he'd been a tailor before the war. He said he'd made doll's clothes for his own daughters. The finished doll wore a fine cotton dress, made from a shirt I'd discarded. When I saw Noi the following day I threw the doll behind my back and winked at her. I heard her quick, light steps and a chirp of joy, like a bird trilling, as she picked up the toy.

## July 1943

Quite a break since I last wrote. Things have been happening. There are other radios in the camp now. What happened before has not put people off making them. It's quite ingenious how they produce them from strips of wire and off-cuts of metals scrounged from the workshops. I pretend I haven't noticed. What's on my mind is quinine. I know there is some along this section of the river. But the guards are taking more of an interest in our dealings with the traders now. Often they'll seize bags of rice from us or smash eggs on the ground. Sometimes I see Noi in the road but she looks away. Frightened. But I see the little doll I made her tucked into her belt.

Matthew and I both had a fever the same night. I thought we were at home again and kept shouting at him to come and have a dip in the brook now we'd finished haymaking. In between my bouts I don't feel too bad, weak, but I can stand. Matthew is feeble. He can't get up. The guards come and shout at him. I fear that hospital hut. I've heard the guards sometimes come in and finish off those they know won't work again. It's not looking good, Evie. I keep trying to stay on top of things, to keep my spirits up but I feel weighed down and helpless. The guards seem to be waiting for something. They laugh at us and their eyes are calculating.

I try to cling on to Robert Winter of Winter's Copse in the county of Berkshire, but Robert Winter, prisoner, seems to have taken me over.

# CHAPTER
# TWENTY-ONE

**Evie**
**Autumn 1945**

Evie woke knowing something had happened. It took seconds for her sleepy brain to work out that the change was to the light. The bedroom door was open and moonlight streamed in from the window halfway up the stairs. She glanced at her wristwatch. Midnight.

She lay back and tried to calm her mind. Sleep, she told herself. Just go to sleep. He'll be better in the morning. She forced her eyelids down. A floorboard on the landing creaked.

A shadow passed back over the moonlight. "Don't be scared," Robert whispered. "It's the guards. They've come for us. But this time I'm ready for them. They won't hurt you." He moved and she saw that he was carrying a stick.

"The guards?" Her voice was high. "What do you mean?" The blood pulsed round her veins in icy waves. He moved again and she saw that the stick in his hand was a shotgun. Evie's mouth opened in a soundless scream. She pushed herself out of bed.

"Keep quite still and they won't see you." Robert took another step into the room.

"There's nobody here but us." She made for the desk, back to the wall, keeping her eyes on the man. She could use the chair, if she had to.

"Stay still," he hissed. "They're here, in the trees." He raised the gun so that it pointed over her shoulder.

Using all her force she lifted the chair and pushed him with it. He grunted and stepped back, doubled over, onto the landing. Evie ran out of the room, skirting him. "No, no," he shouted. Charlie was asleep in the next room. It had a lock. She shoved open the door, slamming it behind her and turning the key. Charlie murmured something. She shook her brother by the shoulders. "Wake up." Terror made her rough. "He's going to kill us." Charlie put his hands out like a supplicant to stop her.

She let him sit up.

"Whatchermean?"

"Robert. He wants to kill us." Her voice was high, panicked. "He's got the shotgun."

Charlie's eyes went from her to the locked door. Robert pounded on the wood. "No!"

Charlie pulled back the covers and jumped out of bed. From the chest of drawers he pulled out two jumpers and threw one at her. "Let's get out of here."

"I haven't got any shoes on," she hissed. A silly thing to remember at a time like this.

"Boots in the cowshed." He prised open the window sash.

Robert shook the locked door handle.

"Evie! Let me in," He was half shouting and half pleading. "I need to help you."

They'd climbed out of the window and down the drainpipe so many times for dares under the benign rule of Mr Edwards that they could escape without making a sound. Outside the night was moonlit, clear, the dew on the grass cold under Evie's bare feet. In the cowshed she found boots, too big, but welcome. "We need to hide from him." She peered out of the door. "He's mad tonight."

Charlie looked out at the farmyard, bathed in creamy light. "He'll find us easily anywhere out here."

"Where shall we go? To find the constable in the village?"

"We wouldn't get there before he did, not if Robert's on his bike."

The farmhouse door squeaked. "You kids out there? Don't be scared. I think they've gone now." Footsteps crossed the far side of the farmyard. Evie and Charlie clutched one another, frozen like statues. The Norton's engine rumbled into life.

He knew every inch of the village. There was nowhere down there they could hide. Evie felt her legs pin themselves to the ground at the same time as her heart pumped cold fear round her body. Charlie tapped her on the arm, pointing at the open window at the rear. They were up and out in seconds, running towards the field which ascended sharply towards the top of the down. Evie prayed the slope would be too much for the motorbike. To the left was the track leading to Martha's

184

blacked-out cottage. Charlie glanced at its shadowy square outline.

"No!" she hissed. "Not there. She . . ." The gasp of air she needed to keep up with her brother swallowed the end of the thought.

"The Ridgeway, then," he whispered. "I know a place along there we can hide."

Thank God they were fit. Charlie was the fastest boy in his class; nobody could beat him. But she was falling behind. He slowed for a second and grabbed her arm. "Come on."

Below them she heard the motorbike purr through the farmyard. The engine throbbed intensely and then there was silence. Had he stopped so he could listen out for their footsteps? Charlie surged forward, fear seeming to propel him up the incline. "We need to get up there before he works out where we've gone."

But once on the white surface of the Ridgeway they'd be visible like black chess pieces on white squares. Evie could hear the motorbike again. He'd be cruising the lanes, stopping at each alley. Perhaps he'd think they were hiding out in a barn or shed; there were probably scores of them down there in gardens and allotments; it would take him all night to search them all. The moon passed behind a cloud and Evie uttered silent thanks.

Charlie was slowing, unable to maintain the pace now that the hill curved upwards into a convex. To their left was Dragon Hill, where the mythical beast was said to have been slain. Above them, somewhere, the strange chalk White Horse ran across the hillside, still

**185**

camouflaged from the war. Evie was tired. They could conceal themselves in one of the hollows dotting the springy turf, like sheep in treacherous weather. But if he came up there he'd find them easily. Robert knew each bump in the ground up here and the moon still shone.

Her knees jarred with each step she took and each breath of cool autumn air felt as if it was bruising the insides of her lungs. She pulled at Charlie's sleeve. "I can't run any further." She doubled over.

"We'll walk for a moment." They were above the White Horse now. Charlie pointed out the stile beyond which the white ribbon of the Ridgeway curled east and west. "Here we go."

"Noi," she said when she'd drawn breath. "That's what he was shouting to me back there. Not 'No, no.' I wish I knew who Noi was."

"I couldn't care less. Whoever she is she's certainly made him go mental."

She winced. The moon came out from behind a cloud and she could see her brother's face, pale like a pearl. She looked down at her white and blue pyjama trousers. Robert would be able to spot them. He'd come up here on his motorcycle and he'd pursue them.

They were crossing a track running straight up the hill. Charlie glanced down it. Somewhere in the vale the motorbike engine purred, audible in the cloudless night. "It's him. We need to run again."

"We could still take shelter somewhere in the village. The vicar —"

"Robert Winter's from an old village family. We're incomers. Who're they going to believe, Evie, him or us?" Charlie sounded bitter as he pulled her into a run. He'd never felt at home in the village the same way she had. The local boys had fought him when they'd attended the village school and he'd been relieved to move on to grammar school in town.

"Of course they'd believe us if we tell them he's running around with a gun."

"It's just under a mile now, Evie, you can do it. In the morning we'll ask for help."

She dropped her head and ran beside him. She'd never been this far west along the track before, preferring the grassy slopes above the village for walks. Beech trees each side of the track waved at her, their clumps containing shadowy pools. "Couldn't we just hide here?"

Charlie raised a hand to silence her. She heard it too, the purr of the engine now much nearer, perhaps just a quarter of a mile behind them.

"It's not far now." Charlie was almost dragging her down the track. Her legs throbbed. They must have run nearly two miles already. He slowed for an instance and then shot right, pulling her through a gap in the beeches. "He'll never come in here, never."

Evie made out four pale shapes ahead of her. Ghosts. She shrank back.

"They're just the Sarsen stones, silly." Charlie sounded proud. "They guard the entrance."

He pushed her towards a gap between the two middle Sarsens. "Climb up and then you'll see the opening."

They were standing outside what appeared to be a cave. Waves of panic rippled through her. "I can't, not in there." She sounded shrill.

Charlie shook her. "He's close now. Hurry." Evie closed her eyes and let her brother push her up into the entrance and through into a chamber behind. She could see nothing. The cave smelled of dead leaves and damp stone.

The motorbike engine purred outside. Then there was silence. "If he finds us in here there's no way out," she whispered.

"He won't come in here."

She remembered the conversation about spies hiding in here and what Robert had said.

Feet trampled through leaves and swished through long grass. Robert coughed once. She held her breath. The flicker of a torch beam shot across the chamber entrance.

"Evie!" he shouted. "Sweetheart, are you in there? You can't stay in there all night. Not in a hole." His voice shook on the last word. "The guards have gone." His voice sounded thin and tired, somehow more frightening than it had done when he'd been shouting at them. "I promise I won't let them hurt you."

Her mouth felt bone-dry. She couldn't have answered him even if she'd wanted.

"Come out!" he called again. "Please, Noi." Something calm and despairing in his tone now. She opened her mouth to respond but Charlie's fist dug into her ribs and she said nothing. Seconds passed. Dead leaves crackled as he trudged back to the Norton.

The engine fired and the bike hummed away. Evie's heart quietened its pace. She squinted at the shadows.

"What did they do in this place, Charlie?" she whispered. "Was it something to do with horses?"

He was silent.

"Tell me."

"You must have heard the rumours."

"Not really."

He hesitated. "It's a burial mound," he said at last.

She put a hand to her mouth. He held her back as she lurched towards the entrance. "We're in a tomb?" She lurched towards the entrance.

"The bodies will be below us." He grabbed her arm and shook her. "Listen, Evie, there's nothing to be scared of."

"I want to get out!"

"It's fine. I come here all the time."

So this was where he disappeared to with his sandwiches. He was still holding her tight.

"Robert Winter's listened to too many old wives' tales in the Packhorse. Or to Martha. She probably thinks that Wayland lives here with his apprentice."

She remembered the old legend about the ghostly blacksmith, a Saxon god or something similar, who hurled boulders when angered.

"Martha says the White Horse gallops over here from its hill once a century to be shod." Charlie snorted. "If it can escape from the camouflage, that is. And she believes that Wayland and his apprentice go drinking in the Packhorse once a century or so. She doesn't know the difference between legend and real history."

**189**

Evie stared at the shadows, which could contain anything.

"It's just an interesting historical site, that's all. And Martha's a peasant who talks rubbish," Charlie said. She closed her eyes so that the shadows wouldn't worry her and leant back against the stone walls of the chamber. He explained about Neolithic people, their burial habits, about the later-coming Saxons and the blacksmith legends they'd learned from the Danes. To distract herself from what was outside, Evie let him talk on and on until her head bowed down to her chest.

In the morning she woke with a stiff neck. She winced as she straightened it. Charlie had fallen asleep with his head in her lap and stirred as she moved. He yawned, stretching out a hand to look at his watch. "Seven. The drink will have worn off by now. We should get back. But just in case . . ." He put a hand into his pyjama pocket and pulled out a coin. "That's lucky."

"What is?"

"I've got a sixpence." Feeble light penetrated the chamber. Evie saw her brother push the coin against the stone wall and scoop earth over it. "That should keep him happy."

"Who?"

"Wayland."

"The mythical blacksmith? The one you don't believe in."

"It's like church, Evie, you keep going just in case there's something in it. And donating the coin is like Roman Catholics lighting candles for their intentions."

He shifted position, grimacing. "I've got pins and needles." Then his brow creased. "Robert's never been as bad as that before. He must have drunk a lot."

"He thinks we're suffering."

"So he wants to put us out of our misery or something?" He sounded scornful.

"It was that camp. It did something to his head." In the chilly dawn it suddenly seemed impossible that Robert Winter would have tried to kill them. Hysteria. That was what Evie's form teacher called it when the girls were overcome by extreme emotion. Had she and Charlie been hysterical last night? Perhaps Robert had just been badly drunk, ranting. But then she saw the image of the shotgun in his hand.

Charlie grimaced as he stood. "C'mon."

She followed him out into the light. She saw that what they'd spent the night in appeared to be little more than a cave. "He could have come in here and dragged us out. He didn't want to hurt us, you know."

"The poor devil," Charlie said, making for the track. She followed, looking out for the motorbike, ears straining for sounds of its engine.

"Charlie . . ."

"What?"

"I think we've made it all worse. We should have talked to him."

He halted. "You think you could reason with a man waving a loaded gun? What else did he have to do, Evie? Fire it?"

"All the same . . ."

He gave an angry shrug and marched off. Evie followed him, wincing as the blood returned to her cold limbs.

They headed east, sunlight in their eyes. Still there was nothing. Charlie kept a brisk pace, almost a run, and in less than twenty minutes they were skimming the top of White Horse Hill. No sign of Robert. Sheep bleated in the fields beside them. They were within sight of the farm, spread out beneath them like a child's toy, trees sheltering the house, horses in the paddock, pigs in one field, hovering round their food troughs. Evie looked for Carlo, who should be feeding the pigs by now, having already done the milking. She could hear the cows mooing. They shouldn't be clustering round the gate like that. Foreboding gripped her.

They climbed the stile into the top field above the farm-house. From here they could see the duck pond. Charlie sniffed the air. "Can you smell that?"

She picked out the burning aroma just as a horse neighed: a high-pitched, panicked sound. "It's the barn."

The barn was full of hay, tinder-box dry.

"C'mon!" And they were hurtling down the hill, risking ankles in rabbit holes and sending sheep flying from their path towards the smoke beginning to curl up from the roof of the barn.

# Part Six

# CHAPTER
# TWENTY-TWO

**Rachel**
**March 2003**

On this clear early spring afternoon the Vale was almost flattened by the light, spread out below me in detail in shades of green and brown. I thought I could detect the faintest hint of the new season — an electric-green tint to the edges of branches, a softness to the contours of slopes. While I cursed myself for my soppiness I couldn't prevent myself from admiring the lambs in the field, which belonged to Winter's Copse and was rented out now. Once these would have been Evie's lambs. How she'd loved this time of year. It had been a sadness to her when she'd had to admit that it made no sense for her to continue with the sheep and it would be better for her to rent out the grazing. She should be with me on this walk, showing me the fences she'd repaired, commenting on ewes, pointing out a pair of red kites riding the air currents.

The scene was one of fertile promise. How unlike me. I couldn't resist a dry laugh. Despite my attempts to forget the vocabulary of the last years — follicles, ovaries, hormones, drugs — my dreams last night had

**195**

been haunted by images of baskets left outside Evie's kitchen door. I'd thought they would contain babies but when I looked inside I found they were empty. A powerful symbol to tell me my dreams of becoming a mother were dead.

Then the little lead knight in the Coronation mug climbed down from the dresser and took on full size and I saw that he was in fact King Arthur, but with long-dead Uncle Matthew's features, locked into an expression of sorrow.

I shook these dreams — closer to nightmares — out of my mind. I noted that my toes ached and wondered whether Evie's boots were too small for me. But they felt roomy enough. My head felt unusually heavy, too. I walked a few more paces and realized what the cause of these ailments was: I was hunched over, weight too far forward. *Sit up straight, Rachel*, I heard Evie call across the years. I was nine again, riding Jessamy's pony, practising for the handy pony competition at the gymkhana held every year alongside the agricultural show. My depression had literally bowed me over. I swallowed hard and forced myself to walk with a straight back and head up, concentrating on the landscape ahead.

I could pick out every hedgerow, every copse, the silver ribbon of a road running east-west, cars and lorries moving silently along it. A train heading west to Wales slunk past. Along the pale blue sky the twisted branches of oaks and elms spelled out secret words. It was where I belonged. "I belong," I told Pilot. He

**196**

pricked up his ears. "But I shouldn't still be here. I should be back in London."

It wouldn't take me long to sort out my aunt's affairs and rent out the house. Several letting agents had expressed interest. There was a shortage of good-sized family houses in this part of the world and, as crocuses and snowdrops and aconites flowered in its gardens, Winter's Copse would certainly elicit plenty of interest. I could have finished all the business and returned to London within a day or two, but I found myself lingering over the task, needing to stay in this village, close to Evie.

The dog gave a gentle bark, as though trying to prevent me from maudlin sentiment. I did what I'd once done at boarding school on glum Sunday evenings: cast around for distraction. But my eyes lit on the faint, brown rectangle on the grass below where the old barn had stood before it burned down. Pilot decided that more direct methods were needed to propel me forward and barked once, politely.

"Sorry." It was supposed to be his walk, after all. He was young and young creatures needed movement. Strange how I kept on differentiating myself from the young. "I'm thirty-five, not fifty-five, that's young," I said crossly, out loud. "There's still time for me . . ." What? Time for what? Time to recover from the disappointment Luke and I had suffered?

The dog nudged my calf as though to tell me to get a grip. I laughed. "Let's go." We walked briskly eastwards. The white track led uphill so that we left the White Horse behind us. Not that it resembled anything like a horse from any angle I could find. As a child I'd complained about this: "It's more like a kangaroo than anything."

Jessamy had narrowed her eyes at me. "Don't come here and criticize our horse," she'd told me, reminding me that I was just a visitor and not a full-time inhabitant of Craven.

Martha had been with us. "It's a very old symbol, Rachel," she'd told me, reproof darkening her eyes. "Older than Christ himself."

I'd blushed. "The White Horse has all kinds of powers," she went on. "Some of the stories we used to hear when we were youngsters —" She stopped abruptly as Evie came up towards us.

As we climbed we passed a couple of other walkers and their dogs or infants in buggies, making the best of the promising weather. They threw a quick greeting or nod our way. I tried not to look at the small children. Perhaps the next few years would be spent in avoiding them. Presumably, after a certain period, the worst of the longing would pass. I wondered if I had the words Unfulfilled Neurotic Woman stamped on my head but those we saw simply smiled or nodded a greeting. Pilot and I were part of the landscape. Ordinary.

That was a word that had sprung to mind each time I'd run through the events of that Jubilee party twenty-five years ago. Everything that afternoon had seemed so safe and . . . ordinary. If anyone had drawn up a list of places in the world where something as appalling as the abduction of a child were to occur, safe, quiet little Craven would have been bottom of the list.

Every time I replayed my memories of that day I came up with images of children running around and their parents eating and drinking and chatting. I couldn't recall a single jarring scene at the party except for Jessamy being annoyed at me for dropping the baton in the relay.

As we walked down the lane to Winter's Copse I groped again for any otherwise unnoteworthy detail that I had stored away mentally and couldn't retrieve. Between making calls to the bank and solicitor and signing papers I racked my memory. But the harder I tried to focus on the details of the days before the Jubilee the more blurred the images became. "I know something," I told Pilot. "I just can't pull it out of my mind." He gave a wag of his tail. It was comforting to have an animal around me again. Coming to the farm as a child and throwing myself into the routine of the cows and sheep and the pigs Evie had kept when I was younger had always been a thrill. I'd loved the hens, too. Hens. I was remembering something. Hens the fox had taken. And something else the same week, something more serious, something to do with the cows. They'd had some disease which had meant they'd had to be destroyed. TB. That had all happened just before the party. Evie must have been beside herself; she'd always worked so hard, and so successfully, to keep the farm going. Only the year before last there'd been the foot and mouth outbreak and I'd been so relieved Evie no longer kept livestock. But this had nothing to do with Jessamy vanishing.

Something moved behind me in the lane and I turned. Nothing. Just a deer or even a hare, dashing for the shelter of the hedge.

That night, about to drift into sleep, the image I had sought flashed back into my mind. I sat up and concentrated. Jessamy. On her way back to the house very early one morning. She never had told me where she'd been that morning. Even as I concentrated on her image with its bruised legs the details began to splinter.

I clawed at the fragments in desperation, trying to pull them back, but it was like trying to reassemble a kaleidoscope image. I banged my arms against the covers in frustration. Perhaps she'd just been seeing to her pony, as she'd said at the time. But then she'd muttered something at the Jubilee party about not knowing "what to think" any more. Had she been meeting someone outside the house? Martha, perhaps? But Martha could have had no responsibility for what had happened to Jess. She'd been at the Jubilee party right until the very end. And she couldn't drive so she'd have had no way of removing a child from the village in haste. I reminded myself that I still hadn't managed to get up the hill to see Martha. It was something I needed to do before the funeral; she'd been such a constant presence in my childhood, standing beside me while I picked blackberries or fed calves, patient with me when I was clumsy, only ever cross if she thought I hadn't shown a proper respect for local ways and customs. I'd been remiss in not paying her a visit.

I couldn't stay in bed any longer. Pilot whimpered gently. I hadn't meant him to follow me upstairs when I'd gone to bed but hadn't had the heart to send him down. I stood by the window and looked out. The clear afternoon had preceded a frosty night, a sudden return to winter. Moonlight streamed across the meadows and over the hills above the village. The window was open an inch and I heard a rustle in the bushes bordering Evie's garden. A fox slunk over the white lawn, bathed for an instant in silvery light. As a child I must have shared this room with my cousin. Did we talk much after lights out? I remembered midnight feasts. Evie must surely have known about them: she couldn't have missed the Mars bar and Wotsit wrappers in the wastepaper bin the morning after. Once or twice she'd left a plateful of fairy cakes out on the kitchen table and not commented when they'd vanished overnight. But there'd been a time when Martha had brought up a fruit cake. "For the littl'uns." She gave her mirthless laugh. "I see their light on some nights. Very late."

"You're always watching, Martha," Jessamy said, reaching for the cake.

"Indeed," Evie had said drily. And Martha's eyes had shone with that strange intensity.

"Young girls need their sleep."

What did we discuss at these midnight feasts? We were very young, I had still to turn ten at the time of Jessamy's disappearance and she had only just passed this landmark; we weren't even pre-pubescent. We

**201**

talked, I seemed to remember, about ponies and pop stars, our friends at school, giggling when we discussed any boys we knew. I couldn't remember her telling me anything which might have led me to believe she planned to run away. "Jessamy," I found myself whispering. "Where did you go? What happened to you?"

And for a moment I swear I felt her near me. I swung round, half expecting to see her standing beside me. Pilot, asleep by the wardrobe, whimpered briefly.

# CHAPTER
# TWENTY-THREE

By the following afternoon there was little left for me to do at Winter's Copse. The undertaker, vicar and crematorium had all been briefed. I'd invited just about everyone I could think of who needed inviting to the funeral in the church the following Monday and back to the farm for refreshments after. A caterer had been booked to provide sandwiches and cake. "I'll be back either tomorrow or Sunday," I told Luke's mobile answer phone. "I'll let you know later on. We need to talk. I'll cancel next week's blood tests but I need to speak to you first. Hope you're OK. And Luke . . ." I felt an apology coming on but wasn't even quite sure what I was sorry for. *Sorry for not being a proper woman.* "I'm really, really looking forward to seeing you." Suddenly I longed for my husband in a way I couldn't remember having done for years, since before we'd been thinking about children.

I decided to take a look at the garden, washed in pale late-winter sunlight. Pilot shot past me as I opened the back door, tearing across the lawn. The snowdrops were past their dazzling whitest best but a fresh crop of narcissi seemed to have appeared overnight. I noticed that someone had cleared last year's dead geraniums from Evie's terracotta pots. The shrubs rustled and I called to the dog but he had already dashed off somewhere else. Probably sniffing around in the barns.

I couldn't help but think of this garden in summer and how the colours graduated across the flowerbeds: reds and oranges by the kitchen door, cooling to blues and purples and from there to soft yellows, silvers and whites at the bottom by the hedge fringing the lane. Evie'd created a garden that looked as though it had designed itself but which anyone who knew anything about horticulture would recognize as the product of a talented mind. I hoped that whoever rented Winter's Copse would be a gardener too. The thought of seeing the shrubs and flowerbeds covered in bindweed and dandelions made a lump form in my throat. I went inside, slipping off Evie's wellington boots on the kitchen doorstep.

On the kitchen table sat the cardboard box I'd filled with the photo albums and scrapbooks. The photos drew me to them. Me, a small figure with a mop of curls riding a Shetland and sitting on the tractor with Matthew, grinning. Uncle Matthew, a man I barely remembered except for his slow smile, slight limp and quiet presence around the farm. I think my uncle must have been one of a breed of Englishman, gentle and strong, not quick tongued but deep thinking and feeling, who've gone out of fashion these days. A bit like Luke. I focused my attention on a picture of Jessamy dressed in a pinafore, face covered in cake batter, waving a whisk. Martha stood beside her in the bright oblong that was the open kitchen door. The woman's face wore an expression of extreme concentration as she watched the child.

I picked up an older album, its leather edges starting to wear. It contained black and white pictures of Matthew and his brother as children, raking hay into triangular-shaped stooks, feeding lambs and holding up piglets with proud grins. Someone had had money for a camera to capture these informal moments. But the Winters had always been prosperous. I thought I could make out Jessamy's cheekbones in both her father and uncle as small children. Matthew was always an inch or two taller and Robert's eyes were often turned towards Matthew. He must have been fond of his big brother. Impossible to think of these healthy, glowing boys growing up to spend those years in prison camps.

From 1941 there were few photos. Both Winter brothers were away. But someone had photographed a teenage Evie and my father on top of a hay wagon smiling down at a man in an unfamiliar uniform. This must have been the Italian POW, Carlo, whom Evie had remembered with such affection. "Carlo was always smiling," she'd told me. "It was wonderful having him on the farm. He kept us going."

What a contrast to Robert when he'd returned, so wrecked that he'd self-destructed, Evie said: spending time in the Pack-horse drinking whatever he could buy, talking about people who weren't there as though he could see them in the house. Then he'd burned to death in the autumn of 1945, having consumed a quantity of alcohol and taken shelter in the barn. "He'd been in the Packhorse and he'd already scared us out of our wits that night," Evie had told me during one of our long conversations tidying up the garden back last autumn. "He must have gone to sleep it off in the barn. And lit a cigarette and dropped off before he noticed that it had set the straw alight."

She paused. "I haven't really talked much about that morning."

"It sounded traumatic."

She gave a shiver even though the afternoon was warm. "It was."

# CHAPTER
# TWENTY-FOUR

**Evie**
**1945**

"Ring for the fire engine!" Charlie screamed as they ran towards the barn. His face was the colour of chalk-stone.

Her legs still ached from last night's sprint and the smoke scorched her chest but Evie found new strength that sent her hurtling towards the house. Thank God Winter's Copse had its own telephone and she hadn't had to run into the village to summon the engine. By the time she'd given the details and was tearing out towards the barn, the smoke was thick. In the yard, Charlie was filling a bucket. "Find another one," he yelled. "Fill it and bring it to me." He pushed past her with the water.

Then someone was pulling the bucket away from him. "Let me, you find the hose." A man from the village, the father of a girl at school. There were other people in the farmyard now. Thank God. She helped Charlie locate the hose in the cowshed and pushed the end into the tap. The fire engine bell clanged as they turned on the water. Men jumped off and pulled their pump and thick hose off the engine. "Take it to the pond!" one of them shouted. A lighter ringing of bells marked the arrival of the ambulance. "Stand back, kids, we'll sort it from here." Evie and Charlie shrank against the cow-shed wall and watched them race past. Evie's legs shook and she let herself flop to the ground. Still the smoke rose from the barn.

She heard a shout and voices raised in response.

Then there was only the hissing of the firemen's hose against the barn wall.

Evie felt the farmyard spinning round her. She let herself fly around. Perhaps she'd died, too. Her cheek felt the coolness of the cobbles underneath it seconds before her brain registered the fact that she'd fallen.

Charlie was shaking her. "Evie."

He pulled her to her feet. She looked at him, rubbing straw from her face. "Was he in there? Was Robert in the barn?"

Charlie didn't return her stare.

"Charlie, tell me."

He shook his head. "They found a body."

Evie's stomach heaved and she leant over. Nothing seemed to come up. Too long since her last meal.

Charlie's shoulders were rising and falling. "Why did this happen? Why did he have to die?"

"He wouldn't have suffered," a woman said. The smoke lifted a little and Evie saw Martha was standing next to them. "The firemen think that the smoke would have made him pass out quickly." Martha spoke in gasps, as though she'd been running.

"What will they do with him?"

Martha's eyes suddenly gained focus. "What'ye mean?"

"With his body?"

It was as if the full horror of what had happened had only now struck Martha. "I don't know . . ." she swallowed. "God's sake, Evie, I don't know. The ambulance is taking him away. I expect there'll be a, what do they call it, a post-something?"

"A post-mortem," Charlie said. "Or an inquest. But I'm not sure. It's up to the coroner."

"Can I see him?" Why was she saying this? She couldn't quite believe Robert had gone.

"Of course you can't." Martha sounded furious. "Do you think he'd want that, Evie? Do you think he'd want that to be your last sight of him?"

Impossible to explain that what Evie imagined Robert's appearance to be in his burned and ruined state would probably be far worse than the reality. She felt her stomach lurch again.

"Take your sister inside, Charlie." Martha spoke more softly now. "Let them finish their work."

As they walked across the yard towards the house the ambulance men were carrying out the stretcher. Something long lay beneath a blanket.

Martha stuffed a hand into her mouth. She looked at the children and removed the hand. "You played your part in this." The green lamp eyes were lit so they looked right through Evie.

"We had to run away from him last night," Evie said. "He wasn't . . . right."

"Not right." Martha gave a strange laugh. "It's you, Evie, that isn't right."

"Shut up!" Charlie turned on her. "Leave us alone."

"Where's Carlo?" Evie looked back. "I wish he'd come in." She needed Carlo's smile, his warmth.

"I don't know," Martha said. "Why do you want that lazy Eyetie at a time like this?"

"Oh no." Evie put a fist to her mouth.

"What?" Martha was watching her. "What's the matter, Evie?" She looked wary. Or perhaps it was just grief, making her face close up.

"Carlo's run away. He was always talking about it and he's chosen today of all days to make for Ireland." Her shoulders crumpled.

"You may be right." Martha nodded. Evie had the feeling something she'd said had reassured the older girl. "Yes, I think you probably are. Carlo's made a dash for one of the ports."

Her expression suddenly altered. A fireman was coming towards them, wheeling Robert's motorbike. "Found this in the lane leading up to the down." He looked at Martha. "You must have passed it on your way here?"

She shook her head. "I came through the field."

Which was odd, as there'd been no sign of Martha up on the hillside when Evie and Charlie had spotted the fire. Not that they'd been paying attention to anything else apart from the smouldering barn.

"Poor young fellow." The fireman shook his head over the bike. "All the time and attention he gave to this machine, if only he could have looked after himself like that."

# CHAPTER
# TWENTY-FIVE

**Rachel**
**2003**

Despite my declarations that I was going to leave the past alone now I was still mesmerized by the photograph albums and diaries. I stared at a photo of Evie, Matthew and Jessamy, taken when Jess was a baby. They were sitting on bales in the farmyard and sunlight bathed their three smiling faces. Perhaps it had been a blessing for Matthew to die before his only daughter had vanished. A blessing for him; a further wound for Evie.

Matthew had been older than Evie. When Jessamy had been born he'd have been forty-six or so, quite old for a first-time father. Evie herself had been nearly thirty-seven, probably considered elderly back then in 1967. They must both have been ecstatic when the miracle finally occurred. But I was heading towards dangerous territory. Don't think about pregnancies, I told myself. Move on. Just do the job: tidy up the loose ends, check the printers are going to send you proofs of the order of service today, as they promised. Then get the hell out. Fighting words. Words I wasn't sure I could live up to.

In the garden below Pilot barked at something I couldn't see. Probably another dog walking down the lane. He needed a walk. It was time to finish here for the day.

I went down and found his lead and we set off for the green again. I noticed that my feet didn't hurt as much today and my neck felt less stiff. I checked my posture. Not too bad. I could see my aunt's approving smile. "That's right, Rachel, nice and straight." My mobile gave a trill. A text message from Luke. I read it. "R U sure about clinic?" "Yes, luv R," I texted back.

"Hello."

I turned to see an elderly West Indian woman beaming at me. "Freya!" I said with delight, and fell into her rib-crushing hug.

"I'm sorry I haven't been up to the farm while you've been here. I've been in bed with a bug. But they told me in the shop that your lovely car had been spotted in the village." She pointed at the cluster of modern houses at the far side of the common. "I wondered whether you'd like a glass of wine." A pause. "Or a cup of tea if you think it's too early for wine." The tone of her voice made it clear that she didn't think this was the case. I'd become so used to avoiding alcohol that it took me a moment to remember that I could drink anything I wanted now.

"I'd love that." But I wondered what to do about Pilot. "He can sit in the conservatory." Freya was following my gaze. "He's used to it. Evie often used to bring him round."

I could tell from the near smile on the dog's face that he was only too pleased to visit Freya. So was I.

I sipped my Sauvignon and looked round at the photographs arranged on shelves and tables in the sitting room of Freya's large brood of nephews and nieces.

"It was a shock when Evie died," Freya said. "She always seemed so strong."

"I'm wondering whether she had some kind of virus she didn't take seriously enough which weakened her heart muscles. But the doctor doesn't have anything in her notes about it."

"I saw her the day before she died and she had just finished baking four Victoria sandwiches for a church fundraiser."

We were both silent for a moment. "I know you always looked out for Evie," I said at last. "Thank you. Even the way you tied her scarf after she died — she'd have appreciated that."

"Her scarf?" Freya's brow wrinkled. "That wasn't me. I came to the hospital when you rang me to tell me they'd brought her in. She was already wearing the scarf when I . . . saw her there."

When Evie's body was lying in the side room, she meant.

Strange. We lapsed once again into silence, companionable and comforting. "I'm glad she wasn't bitterly unhappy," I said. "I tried to see her whenever I could. I tried to fill the gap. I . . ." I shook my head, unable to express exactly what it was I'd attempted through the years of Jessamy's absence.

Freya ran a hand across her eyes. "Thank God she still had you."

"I was just a niece, though. I could never be as close as her own daughter."

"Close enough." Freya nodded, as though remembering. "She talked about you a lot. She was proud of you, of your work. Sometimes we'd see one of your ads on the television and she'd point it out. 'That's one of Rachel's,' she'd say."

Before I'd turned myself into a freelance copywriter and general marketing oddjob person I'd worked as a creative for a West End ad agency. I'd given it up to adopt a more balanced lifestyle, one which would be compatible with bringing up children. Evie had nodded with approval when I'd explained the decision to her. "Sounds sensible. But make sure the work's interesting and demanding enough for you, Rachel. It's important to love what you do."

My loss suddenly hit me again. I focused hard on the pewter coaster under my wine glass. While Evie was alive there'd always been someone who was delighted to hear from me, to know my news, to ruminate over career decisions, to commiserate with my failures and celebrate my successes. Of course there was still Luke, but that was different. Evie had loved me since my childhood.

"I just don't know why . . ." I didn't know how to phrase what was on my mind and toyed with my glass.

"Why she died when she did. Her lifestyle was healthy: all that gardening and dog-walking. She didn't drink much and she never smoked. It seems so strange that it happened out of the blue like that."

She sighed. "I can't come to terms with it, either. But I suppose Evie might have preferred it to cancer or Alzheimer's or another disease which slowly strips you of your body or mind."

Freya was probably right. Evie would have hated the gradual reduction of mobility and independence serious illness would have brought her.

"I wish I'd been with her when she died." The words came blurting out. I sounded like a schoolgirl, me, the capable Rachel, the one who was good at managing.

Freya rested a hand on mine. "Sometimes it's like that, honey."

"To die alone, with just medical staff, I would never have wanted that for her." I rested my head on my hands and blinked hard.

"But she wasn't alone when they took her into hospital."

I frowned. "What?"

"Someone was with her when she came to the hospital in the ambulance."

"Nobody told me this when I came in."

"The shifts may have changed by then. Amy Jackson told me."

Amy Jackson. One of the traveller kids.

"I don't know how Amy knew, though," Freya continued. "Perhaps she saw the ambulance coming to the house."

"She didn't have a name for this companion?"

"No. Could it have been the cleaning lady?"

"She comes in the afternoons."

"Martha?"

"It would be unusual for her to come to the house," I said. "And she certainly wasn't at the hospital when I arrived. But perhaps that's who it was." Poor Martha. Perhaps that's why she'd been staying away from me. It must have been a terrible thing for her to have witnessed Evie's heart attack. "I haven't seen Martha yet."

"She'll be feeling Evie's loss."

"They never seemed to get on." I could clearly remember the tension when they were together. Yet Evie never said a word against Martha.

"No. But they worked on the farm together for more than half a century. They were part of one another's lives. In some ways . . ."

"In some ways, what?"

Freya seemed to consider her answer. "In some ways Martha was one of the family. At least, that's how she saw herself. Now, after all those centuries of Winters and Stourtons working together with the stock, she's the only one left on the hillside."

From the conservatory Pilot gave a whine. "He'll be expecting his supper." I put down my glass. "It's taken him a few days to break me into the routine but now I know what's expected."

"That's a nice dog. I'd have taken him in myself but Lionel, my husband, has allergies."

216

"Oh, I'm going to take him back to London when I go." I blinked. Where had that plan come from? The thought of the large dog in the warehouse conversion was an interesting one. And I hadn't asked Luke what he thought. I stood up.

Freya rose too. "Hang on a moment. I think I've got something you'd like to see. Now where did I put it?" She pulled a newspaper from a pile on a dining room chair. "Look, Evie giving out the prizes at the flower and produce show last autumn." She folded the sheet so that the picture was on top and placed it over my mobile. I stared down at my aunt, smiling a radiant smile as she handed a small boy a cup. Moisture blurred my vision. I knotted my scarf.

At the doorway Freya took my hand and squeezed it. "Will you sell the farm, Rachel?"

"I'm only an executor." I could have clung to Freya's hand all evening. "Along with Evie's solicitor. If Jessamy doesn't reappear within the next twenty-five years, I'm at liberty to sell. Or keep the house myself. Either way money has to be put into a trust for any of her children or grandchildren." It wasn't like me to be so open about such private financial matters.

I forced myself to release her warm, soft hand. "Make sure you take care of yourself, Rachel."

My eyes threatened to let me down. "I could never take the pain away." It had lurked in the depths like a shark in dark waters, ready to grab my aunt and pull her down. "I could never make up for Jessamy."

"Not completely. But think how much worse it would have been if she hadn't had you." She looked over my shoulder at the trees blowing in the wind. "Will you be all right walking home in this?"

"It's only a five-minute dash." Pilot pricked up his ears, probably anticipating his supper.

"Storms are forecast for later." Freya shivered. "I hope it doesn't flood again — I've got my Pilates class in Faringdon."

Pilot and I ran past the green and down the lane. The first drops of rain were starting to fall as we reached Winter's Copse. I fed him and couldn't think of anything else to do with myself. So I sat at the kitchen table with Evie's scrap-book and the photograph albums. I felt most at home here by the solid metal range, sitting in Evie's old chair. The faded gingham cushion she wedged between her and the wooden back was still in place and I took comfort from its saggy presence.

The first pages, those covering the years before Jessamy's disappearance, seemed to relate to events long ago: maypole dancing on the green, agricultural shows, village fetes. I flicked through to the later cuttings: Jessamy on her pony winning the egg-and-spoon race at the West Berkshire hunt gymkhana in 1975. Jessamy's school netball team winning a local tournament. Jessamy receiving a Parker fountain pen from the mayor of Wantage after she'd come second in a handwriting competition. Perfect, perfect Jessamy.

I found myself thinking about the shadow in the DVD film of Jessamy's acrobatics on the lawn all those years ago. Who had cast that greyness over the grass? Again I thought of a shark in dark waters, restless,

**218**

prowling, constantly watching for prey. Probably the shadow had merely been cast by a neighbour visiting the farm to borrow a tool or by the vicar's wife coming with the flower-arranging rota. It might even have been my own shadow or that of my father, coming down here to drop me off for a weekend. He never stayed at Winter's Copse himself. Nor did my mother. I couldn't ever remember them setting foot inside the house. Yet they'd been happy enough to deposit me here while they went off to look at holiday apartments in the south of France or Majorca.

Evie and Dad had been close as children, cast off together during the war, finding a home here. They'd stayed on because their old family life in London had crumbled away, following the death of my grandmother in a bombing raid and of my grandfather during the Great Floods of 1947 in East Anglia. The twins had been through a lot together. My father had never said much about his time on the farm, intimating that he'd been relieved to grow up and carry out his National Service. I thought of the rectangular outline on the grass where the barn had once stood and wondered whether Robert Winter's awful death had prompted Dad's desire to leave the farm. Or perhaps he'd just had enough of the grinding hard work: up early in the mornings before school to help with the milking on days when the frost gripped the hillside like an iron hand.

I pulled a photo album towards me and found a picture of my father and Evie as small children in happier times, helping with the haymaking, each clasping a pitchfork and grinning at the camera. This must have been taken before Robert had gone off to fight.

No shadows fell on this idyllic scene; I could almost hear the creak of the wheels of the hay wagon and the thump of the horses' hooves as they moved forward, could almost feel the dust tickling my nose. Nothing here, nothing at all to predict the tragedy of what happened to Robert and his brother in the war, and to Jessamy a generation later.

"If only you could have stayed at Winter's Copse," I whispered to the young man who'd died in that fire all those years ago. "If only you'd never had to go away."

# CHAPTER
# TWENTY-SIX

**Robert**
**Kanburi Camp, July 1943**

Dear Evie,

Do you ever go into the chemist's in Wantage? Do you breathe in that smell of eucalyptus, TCP and Dettol, so clean you can almost feel it killing the germs? Evie, I long for that scent, for doctors in white coats, and nurses to help us.

I must get hold of Noi. Matthew won't survive another night like the one he's just had: he shivered and sweated by turns and called out to Mum and to Dad, as well, even though Dad's been dead for years. He didn't recognize me. He was so strong before we came out here, we both were.

We need medicine. Quinine most urgently, but anything else Noi can find for us. Disinfectant. Aspirin. Surely those barges with their painted eyes must trade up and down the river? Anything can be bought, they say, if you have the money.

Evie, if you think of us, say a prayer for us now.

# CHAPTER
# TWENTY-SEVEN

**Rachel**
**2003**

I woke next morning to the rattle of a window. Dimly I remembered Freya's warnings about the weather changing. As I went to close the catch I saw how grey clouds were already bunching behind the medieval church tower.

I wanted to stay on another day. I felt ready to find Martha. Again I felt ashamed that I hadn't already been to see her. Something had held me back. My relationship with Martha had never been quite the same after Jess's disappearance. If I saw her it was by chance, coming across her leaning over a gate and gazing downhill. Sometimes she'd rise from a hollow as I walked up the hill, making me jump. Our conversation was limited to the barest basics: Martha would point to a ewe needing attention, or tell me to tell my aunt that there was a big dog fox hanging around the sheep.

Evie had sensed disapproval on Martha's part. "She thinks I was careless with my child," she'd told me on one occasion when I was staying with her as a teenager in the early eighties. "Once she told me that I hadn't looked after Jessamy properly. I don't know why she said that, Rachel."

Nor did I. "Why do you let her stay here?" I'd asked. "That cottage of hers belongs to the farm, doesn't it?"

"Where would she go, dear? She's known no other life than this and has no skills outside farming. Agricultural jobs are growing rarer and rarer."

Remembering Martha's comment still made me angry, even today. I remembered Evie's vigilance. When she let us out to play she was careful to point out the limits of our freedom. "No further than the top of the hill . . . Don't take the pony out of the field by yourselves, he's still not good with cars. If you go to anyone's house to play, you must ring me and tell me where you are . . ." Her warning words rang through my ears and made me think of my husband. He needed to know I wouldn't be coming back today. I went to pull out my mobile from my jeans pocket. It wasn't there. I'd taken it out at Freya's yesterday evening while we were talking. Then she'd laid the local newspaper on top of it to show me the story about Evie presenting prizes at the flower and produce show.

I plugged my laptop into the landline socket. "I'm staying on till tomorrow. More to sort out than I thought yesterday," I emailed him. "Lots of love." Again I felt like a guilty addict, denying a drink or drug problem. Then I grabbed my coat and went out.

As I climbed the lane to Martha's cottage, Pilot at my heels, the wind caught my right cheek with a rasp. The sheep in the field were huddled in the hollows and there were no walkers out this morning. It would have been so easy to turn round and return to the dreamy warmth of the kitchen at Winter's Copse. But I'd promised myself that I'd see Martha. And I would.

The curtains were half drawn over her front windows. I rapped on the door. No one in. Martha used to keep chickens, I remembered, so instead of letting myself escape I walked round to the back of the house. Someone was sitting on the rough garden bench beside the chicken run. She stood up. Amy Jackson. I felt the familiar mixture of awkwardness and guilt I'd felt ever since the Jacksons had been accused of taking Jess.

"Er, hi." She brushed down her jeans, looking furtive. Presumably she was supposed to be at school, probably the big comprehensive in Wantage to where most of the children were bussed. Like most of the traveller kids, she'd probably given up going to school once she'd finished at the village primary school. It was said that the travellers didn't like their children educated past the point of basic literacy.

Pilot tore over to her and rubbed his head against her jeans. "Hiya, boy!" She patted his head. "I used to take him for walks if Mrs Winter was away for the day."

"Were you waiting for Martha, Amy?"

"My mum wanted eggs." Amy shivered. "I hate coming up here. Martha's out, anyway, and I can't be bothered to wait any more. It's cold." As though to confirm this, the wind rattled the corrugated roof over the chicken house.

"Let's walk down together."

The breeze blew her hair over her face. "I miss Mrs Winter. She gave me jobs to do."

"You used to see my aunt fairly regularly then?"

"I'd do a few odd jobs, take her letters to be posted, help her pick fruit in the summer or rake leaves in the autumn." She slowed. "Why did you want to see Martha?" She rolled her eyes. "Sorry, that was nosy. I hate it when people ask me questions like why aren't I at school." She gave me a sharp look.

I blushed.

"I'm a diabetic," she said simply, brushing the hair from her face. "I've got a doctor's appointment in about an hour so it wasn't worth going in to school first. Mum'll drive me in later. She doesn't like me missing lessons."

We'd almost reached Winter's Copse. I was still silent, sensing that the girl would talk, wanted to talk, but that too many questions would scare her off. I waited.

"I looked in on Mrs Winter just before she died," she said as we reached the gate. "To see if I could take the dog out for her. I had another doctor's appointment so I wasn't at school." She gave a scowl, as though to emphasize that she didn't expect any praise or thanks for her visit. "She had someone with her."

"Was it Martha?"

"No. Dunno who it was." She gave me a sidelong glance and I sensed there was something she wasn't sure she should reveal. "Mrs Winter was shouting."

I stopped. "What?"

"Shouting. I was almost . . ."

"What?"

"Almost scared." Amy spoke the words as though she couldn't quite believe them. "I didn't bother knocking. I just left."

"And you didn't see who was with my aunt?"

She shook her head. "I couldn't make out the voice."

"Was it a man or a woman?"

She shrugged. "Sorry. I was so surprised to hear Mrs Winter raise her voice I wasn't really paying attention. I kind of felt I shouldn't be there. So I ran past the house." We stood in silence for a moment. "Hope you find her, then." Amy started to walk on, suddenly halting, as she passed the drive and saw my convertible. She turned back. "By the way, nice car." There was a slightly mocking glint in her eyes. She was probably daring me to think the un-liberal and worry that one of her rougher cousins would creep up here at night and steal the hub caps.

"Thanks." I went inside and sat in the kitchen alone, suddenly longing for company, wishing I'd thought to ask Amy in for a quick cup of tea. It seemed as though the past was very close this morning. I decided to drive into Wantage and restock the fridge and post the letters I'd written in my executor's role. As I drove up to the main road which cut along the edge of the Downs I thought of Jessamy aged ten, getting into a car. A stranger's car? Perhaps someone had told her something needed collecting for the Jubilee party; Jessamy was an obliging child when it suited her.

She'd have been anxious to get back to receive the longed-for Silver Jubilee mug and to watch the cake being cut. *Oh, we'll be back in ten minutes, don't worry about that.* How long was it before it dawned on her that she wasn't going back to the party? Was she speeding away in the car by then; hurtling along the M4, still quite a new motorway back in 1977, having been opened just five years earlier? *Where are we going? You said you'd take me back to the party.* I pictured her rising panic and indignation as she realized that she'd been tricked and I shuddered. *Let me go! I'll scream until someone finds a policeman.* How had he — I was certain it was a he — silenced her screams? I felt the old familiar terror grab me, so that it was almost as though I had been abducted, too. My skin felt damp and I took shallow breaths. This was the nightmare of my childhood. Night after night I woke, heart pounding, convinced that the kidnapper stood in my room.

Just remember, Evie had once told me, Jessamy only went through this once. You keep on reliving it again and again for her. You don't need to punish yourself like this, Rachel, it won't help Jessamy.

But in this savage mood I did indeed need to punish myself and I let the deep minor chord play over and over again in my imagination. I indulged all the fears I'd tried to keep bricked up over the years. Perhaps my cousin had been intrigued by the thought of a secret getaway, a big adventure for which she'd been singled out. Perhaps she was pleased to have been taken off somewhere where her cousin wouldn't be. *Can we really have steak and chips in a Berni Inn? And go to the pictures afterwards? Just me?* Perhaps she resented my stays at the farm each holiday.

I reached the supermarket car park, the poison of these thoughts still burning through my veins. Perhaps this was what was meant by a haunting: an inability to rid yourself of the sadness and guilt of loss.

It was time to let it all go. Evie's death should have drawn a line under the past. But my imagination was still grasping at small fragments of the past and trying to stick them together to form a narrative. "It's too long ago." I must have spoken aloud because a startled elderly man in the supermarket's fruit aisle widened his eyes at me.

I pulled apples, bananas, bacon, bread and juice off shelves and forced myself to concentrate on choosing a piece of fish for my supper. When I'd finished buying the food I felt quite peculiar: a strange taste in my mouth. Probably the taint of the past. I went into the chemist and had a word with the pharmacist. She told me that a stomach virus was doing the rounds. Just what I needed. I was still thinking about Evie and Martha, how they'd spent all those years working together in polite dislike. I wasn't really paying attention to the pharmacist as she advised me to drink lots of fluids. I handed over my credit card and took the white paper bag. Then, as I was pushing the door open, I thought more clearly about my ailments, standing motionless in the shop doorway until someone coughed politely behind me. "Sorry." I let an old lady through the door. Then I turned and went back into the chemist's again.

★   ★   ★

At the house I opened the fridge to put the supplies in. Evie's white glistening shelves stared back at me. I should eat but couldn't face more than a banana. As I ate it I read the white board on which Evie made shopping lists. *Bonios, washing powder, vitamin tablets, library books, order Churchill biography.* Death had come so unexpectedly that morning.

"Don't brood," I heard Evie tell me. "What about your work, dear? You should get back to London and get busy." She'd always encouraged my career. And the voice in my head was right: I had work to do. My clients would be wanting their finished copy. I had a VAT return to complete. At the very least I could answer some emails today and preserve the fine thread still binding me to my job, my security, my life. And Luke. I wanted to speak to Luke, hear his voice, get his maddeningly logical response to all that was going on here. Tomorrow I'd be on my way, with a large dog spilling out of the back seat of my convertible, to return just once more to Craven for the funeral and the light lunch afterwards I'd organized back at Winter's Copse for Evie's friends and neighbours. And then perhaps not again for some time. "Perhaps it's as well," I told myself.

But now I could almost feel the past spilling out of the old farmhouse walls. I could almost hear the conversations of fifty years ago; whispered endearments and warnings; the voice of the long-lost Jessamy explaining how she left the Jubilee party. And there were other voices, too, whispering of jealousy and regret. It was impossible for me to wrench myself away from this house and back into the world of work and logic and emails. The stone walls and fields and trees and the lives of those who'd lived here had bound themselves to me.

The photo albums I'd placed on the kitchen table drew me back to them. I'd just have a quick look before I logged on to email. I felt the addict's rush of adrenalin as I flicked through the pages: 1951 — Evie as a bride on Matthew's arm. He wore an expression of pride on his face. She looked calm and serene. How long had she been in love with Matthew before she married him? Surely at first he must have regarded her as his little sister, or even a daughter, not a potential lover. "It took a while," Evie said once. "At first we were like polite strangers: Charlie, Matthew and I. We hardly knew Matthew, after all, we'd been children when he returned to the farm on that one occasion. When he came home from the hospital we thought he might want to send us away. Why would he want a pair of youngsters hanging around? But old Mrs Winter had grown fond of us, you see, even though she was hardly talking by that stage. She was in and out of the cottage hospital but when she was at Winter's Copse she liked me to read the newspaper to her. And I'd go down to the shop and pick up all the village gossip and come up to her room and tell her. I think Matthew must have realized this."

"Was Matthew disturbed in the same way as Robert?"

She shook her head. "He'd seen bad things in the East but I don't think he'd been through what his

**230**

brother had. Matthew just slipped back into civilian life, although his foot injury must have caused him some problems. He didn't say strange things like Robert did or see people in the house who weren't there." A smile lit her face. "I can remember the afternoon he came home as though it was yesterday."

# CHAPTER
# TWENTY-EIGHT

**Evie**
**December 1945**

Mrs Winter had made it clear that she wanted to be downstairs when her older son came home. The district nurse and Evie helped her out of bed and into the woollen dress she hadn't worn for years. Evie had brushed her hair and found a pot of powder and an ancient lipstick in the dressing-table drawer. The old lady smiled at her reflection in the mirror, her face serene. Hard to know if she even remembered that her younger son had died in the barn two months earlier.

When she'd returned to Winter's Copse a week after the fire for the funeral Mrs Winter had sat silently through the service. Only when they were wheeling her out of the church had she spoken. "Robert was always careful with his cigarettes," she said, quite clearly. Martha, walking just ahead of her in the aisle, had made a choking sound. After that Mrs Winter had retreated into speechlessness again.

Martha had stayed away from the farmhouse, working outdoors without coming in for the usual cups of tea or to eat her sandwiches by the warmth of the

232

range. Evie had cooked for herself and Charlie and tried to keep the house clean. The nurse had come in twice a day to tend to Mrs Winter. Two more POWs, Austrians this time, had been sent to help Martha, directed by a friendly neighbouring farmer as a temporary measure until Matthew was fit to come home.

Charlie and one of the Austrians carried her down in her chair. "Good thing these stairs are so wide and you are so light as a bird, Mrs Winter," the Austrian joked. They were going to carry her into the parlour but the old woman made an exclamation of distress and put out a wrinkled hand. They set her down. "What's the matter?" Charlie asked Mrs Winter.

"The kitchen," Evie said. "She wants to be in the kitchen when he comes back." Perhaps she wanted to link herself with the woman she'd been in the past: the nurturer of growing boys, the provider of food.

"No." Martha put out an arm to prevent them from turning round and making for the kitchen. "The parlour is where the Winters always receive their guests."

"I'm not a guest."

The voice was deep and quiet but it made them all jump. A man stood in the passageway, duffel bag over his shoulder, crutches under each arm. His eyes seemed to stare at them across a wide, wide space. "Matthew," Evie breathed, suddenly shy. She'd only seen him once before, briefly, in 1941.

Mrs Winter struggled in her chair. "Hold on, Mother." He walked round so that she could see him.

For seconds they gazed at one another. Then he slipped to his knees and buried his head in her lap. "Oh Mum," Evie heard him whisper. One of her gnarled old hands stroked his hair.

Evie looked at Charlie. They tiptoed away into the kitchen. "When did you get to the station, Matthew?" Martha was saying. "Did you have a good trip? What would you like to eat?"

"Why doesn't she just leave them alone?" Charlie snapped.

"She's part of the family, really." Evie filled the earthenware teapot from the kettle. "I suppose she's like a sister to Matthew."

"Sister, my foot."

"What do you mean?"

"She couldn't get Robert so she's set her cap at his brother now."

"Charlie!" But then she remembered the night she'd caught Robert and Martha in the parlour and let in the dog to disturb them. Was this what Martha wanted from Robert's brother too? The thought made something tighten inside her chest.

He sniffed. "Didn't you notice how she's stayed away until now? None of the Winter men to chase." He glowered. "Now Matthew's back things will change round here, Evie." He straightened a teaspoon on a saucer. "He may not want us to stay on."

"I know." Where would they go? So much had hung on Robert, she realized. He'd been the one to choose them and bring them to live here. There was no reason for his brother to feel bound by the same obligations.

234

Matthew was coming into the kitchen. "I wanted to thank you," he said, putting his duffel bag down on the chair.

"Thank us?" Evie's eyes widened.

"For keeping things going through the war. And while Robert was so . . . ill. It must have been hard."

Evie felt her eyes prickle. "We couldn't save him," she whispered. "I think we made it worse for him. I think we — I — reminded him of something bad."

He took a step towards her. "That wasn't your fault," he said sternly. "They tortured him. His mind was gone by the time he came back here. He could never have settled to normal life again. While I was in hospital I talked to some men who'd come across him in the last months of the war. They were wrecks, too. We don't know what happened to Robert, but it must have been bad."

"Matthew?" Martha stood behind him. "Shall we have tea in the parlour now? Your mother's waiting."

"We'll bring her in here." Matthew grinned at Charlie. "Let's ask that young Austrian fellow to help you move her again." He waved a crutch. "As you can see, I'm not much good at lifting at the moment."

Martha stayed in the kitchen, watching Evie as she cut the fruit cake she'd made with precious sugar, dried fruit and butter. "I expect you'll be moving on soon, won't you, Evie?"

Evie stopped and looked up. "I haven't finished school yet."

"You won't want to intrude now Matthew's back."

The arrival of Mrs Winter in her chair stopped Evie from needing to reply.

"Here we are." Matthew smiled at Evie. "You'd better be mother, Evie." He laid down his crutches and pulled out the chair at the head of the table for her.

She glanced at the older girl. Martha bit her lip.

"I expect Martha's got time for a quick cup of tea before she needs to go off to do the milking, haven't you, Martha?"

Martha nodded, reaching across the table for the teapot.

"Probably easier for Evie to do the pouring, isn't it?" Matthew said.

Martha's hand scuttled back like a startled crab. Her eyes showed no emotion but Evie shivered.

# CHAPTER
# TWENTY-NINE

**Rachel**
**2003**

The sun had made its last attempt to come out. I lifted my head from time to time to watch how the light altered the outline of the Downs above the village and tinted the fields and trees with a watery silver.

A window rattled and it was as though my conscience was reminding me that I still hadn't done any work, still hadn't even thought about my work or my clients, hadn't checked my email. The photographs and press cuttings could wait until later. The breeze coming into the kitchen was colder now and the rain was falling. The view over the garden was of scowling skies, and the dog towel I had pegged to Evie's washing line waved like a warning flag. I remembered the hints of storms. Well, I'd be cosy enough in this kitchen with its Aga and the warm mass of the dog lying on the floor at my feet. "We'll be fine," I told Pilot. "I'll just get on with these emails now." He pricked his ears and whined gently as though expressing polite uncertainty.

I flipped open the laptop and switched it on. The screen flickered into life for a second before dying. The battery needed charging. I dug around in the laptop bag and found the mains cable, which I plugged into a socket underneath the kitchen table. Nothing. "A power cut," I told Pilot. "A little inconvenient, but never mind." I seemed to have fallen into a state of catatonia. All I wanted to do was sit in the dark and look at the old photographs. But I could hardly see them now.

How black the countryside was when there was no sun and no electricity. It must have been like this for generations until fairly recently. They'd all have to come indoors when the weather turned bad. Oil lamps wouldn't have been much use outdoors in winds like this. Perhaps there were candles somewhere in this kitchen; almost bound to be, knowing my efficient aunt. In a moment, before it was completely dark, I'd get up from this chair and look for them. I felt as though the chair had grown straps and bound me to itself. The thought of moving seemed too much of an effort to contemplate.

There must be something useful I could do, something which would . . .

I thought I heard a noise above my head, but before I could be sure the wind crashed against the windows again. This was going to be quite a storm. I was still staring at Matthew's photograph, the one showing him examining his tractor. For all his apparently easeful appearance in the photographs I wondered whether the stress of his captivity had taken a physical toll on him. He'd died of lung cancer though, having, like most men, smoked in those days. So perhaps his captivity hadn't made any difference to his longevity.

My subconscious was wittering on, trying to distract me from something that was happening above me, something I could no longer ignore.

Upstairs something was still creaking. The wind was shaking this old house, releasing all the old memories, the old joys and sorrows. I could hear the movement even above the howling of the wind and dashing of rain against brick and shingles. Pilot whined gently. I stooped to pat him. "If you weren't here, I might feel just a bit nervous now." Nervous didn't begin to express it. I was almost starting to worry that all my rummaging around in old scrapbooks and photo albums had somehow conjured up ghosts. Or unhinged me so that I could even believe in them.

No more creaks from upstairs but the rain whipped the walls and windows as though it were trying to wash all the old sins out of the village. "Leave us clean and bright again," I muttered to myself. Where had that thought come from? This place was starting to prey on my nerves. It had a seductive power to pull you back into the past and make you brood. To snap myself out of this, I forced myself to think. I might not have a laptop or electricity but I still had my mobile. I could ring people. Check text messages. Explain about my lack of internet connectivity. Enquire about my projects, make it seem as though I were still thinking about work, still keen to return, still the busy, successful marketing consultant they'd all wanted writing their adverts and brochure copy. This would take my mind off the groaning of the old house and the lashing of the rain against the windows. And the rest of it.

I reached for my jeans pocket and again felt the rectangular-shaped absence. Damn. If any of my clients had tried to call me this morning my name would be mud. No point in trying to retrieve the mobile now; I'd be soaked before I even reached the lane. Luke would assume I just didn't want to talk to him. And I did. Suddenly I wanted him badly.

"I'll just have to find those candles," I told Pilot, trying to shake myself out of my longing. "Where do you think your mistress kept them? In a drawer? Or out in the utility room?" He let out a sigh and dropped his head so that it rested on my foot, a welcome warmth. In a moment I'd make myself go upstairs and shut the window I must have failed to close properly this morning so that the wind couldn't keep blowing it back and forth, each movement resulting in a deep creak. Curious how reluctant I felt to leave the kitchen with its stove and friendly dog. Perhaps I could persuade Pilot to come upstairs with me, but it wasn't really fair if I was trying to train him not to come up at night with me. Consistency was important where dogs were concerned . . . I was wittering again. I could ring Luke on the landline.

But, of course, the telephone line always came down in bad storms. This recollection made me want to curl up on the floor beside the dog.

Why aren't you here now, Evie, I raged silently at her. Why did you leave me? I don't even know where the candles are kept. See how utterly hopeless I am? Why did I never make a note of where you kept them?

I rose and walked towards the telephone, just to check it really was dead. When I picked up the receiver the emptiness on the line came as no surprise. I flopped back down at the table, trying to work out what I should do. Check all the windows were closed, for starters. Which would mean going upstairs. I didn't want to go upstairs.

Pilot whined and stared up at the ceiling.

An even louder creak made me sit bolt upright in my chair. It wasn't the wind. Someone was moving up there: it sounded as though they were walking out of one of the bedrooms. The cleaner. It would be her cleaning upstairs. But I knew full well that today wasn't one of her afternoons. Now I could hear foot-steps. Pilot rose and padded over to the kitchen door. He stood there looking upstairs, whining gently, tail wagging. I eyed the back door. The sensible course was to pull on my boots and the waxed jacket and run for the village shop, assuming it was still open in this downpour.

Stop blathering on and get out of here. But I couldn't. My feet seemed to take root in the stone flags. Whoever was upstairs I would meet in this kitchen, with its creamy-yellow walls and gingham curtains. Courage seemed to reach me at last and I pulled a knife out of the wooden block on the worktop. "Who are you?" I called.

A long shadow reached down the stairs. Pilot gave a single bark and now his tail was a windmill. "Steady, boy," a woman's voice said. "I'm coming down now. No need to be frightened, I'm not a burglar and I won't hurt you."

A strong, confident voice with an Australian accent. "What the hell are you doing here?" I shouted.

Now she was coming into view. A slight, slim woman of about my age with dark hair and grey eyes that met mine without a blink. Her skin was clear but there were lines around the eyes, as though she'd lived in a warm climate.

I knew this face.

# CHAPTER
# THIRTY

I was going to collapse. My hands flailed around and caught the edge of the table. I clung to the oak, feeling my mouth opening on unspoken words, heart in spasm. Still I stared at her, half expecting that she would dissolve. I must be imagining this. Thunder crashed overhead; the storm was very close now. I looked down at the table, staring at the grain to reassure myself that what was happening was real. Then I looked up again. Still she stood in front of me. I was not dreaming this: Jessamy was here.

"Rachel . . .?" She sounded scared. "Is it really you?"

I nodded my head, incapable of speaking.

"I'm Jessamy. I've come back." She was trembling.

The woman who'd gone with Evie in the ambulance. The terracotta pots which someone had tidied. The neatly arranged scarf. All falling into place. Evie, my aunt, my bereaved and stoic aunt, you died knowing she was still alive. I slumped into a chair, my own weight suddenly too much for me.

She came towards me and I almost shrank from her, part of my subconscious still screaming at me that she must be a phantom. The electric light flashed back on and I heard the reassuring hum of the refrigerator. "You look as though you're in shock," she said. "And so am I." The light showed me that her arms were thin and beneath the T-shirt her skin was goose-pimpled. She'd been slight as a girl. That hadn't changed. She carried a small leather rucksack in one hand.

"How long have you been here?" In my disturbed state I could almost imagine that she'd been lying upstairs for the last twenty-five years like the Sleeping Beauty.

"An hour or so. The car was gone and I thought you'd left. But the door wasn't locked." Old habits. Evie had never locked it so I hadn't either when I'd gone shopping.

"I couldn't resist coming in to take a look at the house."

Why shouldn't she? It was hers now, after all. She was the last of the Winters.

"I went upstairs to look at my old bedroom again. Sat on the bed in my old room just looking at it, remembering how it had been when I was a child. I must have fallen asleep." She gave an apologetic shrug. "I woke up when it thundered. Heard you down here. Wasn't sure what to do." The clipped words made me think that Jessamy, too, was frightened: of me. The lights flickered off and on once more, showing me Jessamy's face in illumination, her skin slightly weathered, her eyes sharp.

She took another step towards me and I found myself shrinking from her again. She must have noticed because she came to a halt. "This must be a huge shock for you, I'm sorry."

I nodded. "I'll be all right in a moment." I took another deep breath and forced control onto myself. "Jessamy, won't you sit down?"

Bit presumptuous, really, as the house belonged to her.

She perched on a chair diagonally opposite me as though she expected me to interrogate her. But all the questions I had built up inside myself for the last quarter-century seemed to muddle themselves up into something so huge it couldn't be expressed. "It is really you, Jess, isn't it?" I said at last. "I'm not dreaming this?" I blinked several times.

She nodded. "I didn't know you were still here when I came back this afternoon. I would never have done this to you. Oh God, Rachel, I didn't want to frighten you." She dropped her head in a gesture of despair which I certainly didn't remember in the bold girl she'd once been.

I got up and filled the already full kettle and put it on the range not because I had any desire for a hot drink but because I had to do something with my hands. "I kept feeling there was someone around," I said.

"I was staying at a B&B in the next village but I kept coming back here. Couldn't keep away. I let myself into the garden a few days ago and tidied up some of the terracotta pots in the garden." A note of apology in her voice. "I'm a plantswoman by trade, run a nursery just outside Sydney."

Her love of plants would have been inherited from her mother.

I was taking my time about finding mugs and teaspoons and milk, in part because I was so distracted and in part deliberately. I needed to keep my hands busy. For years I'd dreamed she'd come back. Now here she was. And I couldn't talk to her. I found the teapot and Evie's tea caddy but when I went to spoon the leaves into the pot my hand shook so much they spilled all over the worktop. I abandoned my efforts and sat down again. She was still there, my cousin. I stared at her, tracing the child's features in the woman's face. She was still dark-haired and her eyes were the same shade. Her skin was slightly wrinkled. "Oh, Jess." My eyes filled. "Oh, Jess. I . . ." I shook my head, not even sure what I wanted to say.

"Are you all right?" Her eyes swept my face anxiously.

"I'm fine." I rubbed my hand over my eyes and smiled at her. "It's just the surprise. You must think I'm behaving really oddly." I put out my hand and touched hers. She felt warm. She clutched at my fingers. Excitement started to fizz through me. My cousin was back. Jessamy was back.

"Where did you go?" The question burst from my lips. "We looked everywhere for you, all over the village. "Who took you, Jess? And why? Why?" Tears started to pour from my eyes. "Did they hurt you? What happened?"

I bit my lip to prevent more questions rushing out. I didn't even know which one I needed to her to answer first. I was worried I'd scare her off.

"I'll tell you, I'll tell you everything. But first —" she stroked my fingers — "I need to know that you're really all right, that you've recovered from the shock. That I haven't . . . hurt you by reappearing so suddenly."

At first I wasn't sure what she meant. But then it hit me with the force of a train. I moved my hand. "You were here with Evie that morning when her heart gave up, weren't you?"

She nodded. "I killed my own mother, Rachel."

# CHAPTER
# THIRTY-ONE

**Jessamy**
**A week earlier, 2003**

Jessamy drove into Craven and everything started to come into focus. She thought she might actually throw up. She remembered the village shop where surely she'd once bought lollies — sweets they were called in England, she corrected herself.

Instinct abandoned her. She had no idea which way to drive so headed towards the church tower ahead of her. The church and the school looked tiny, as though they'd shrunk in the intervening years, but were still recognizable. She'd played British bulldog with the boys in the playground and hide-and-seek among the gravestones in the churchyard.

She felt suddenly panicky again and had to resist turning the car and driving back to London. Anxiety had made her slow down. Two women walking along the pavement glanced her way. Suppose she wound down the window and told them who she was? Would they even remember Jessamy Winter so long gone?

She tried not to let herself think too much about the exact location of the house. Her instinct would guide

248

her. All she had to do was trust. But the village seemed altered from what she remembered from childhood, not quite real; a film-set version of what she'd built up in her memory.

Her first attempt to find the house drew her up a dead-end. She turned the car. Surely she should just go into the shop and say who she was and ask for help? That would be the reasonable thing to do? Damn it. How stupid it was not to know where her own home was. She glanced at the speedometer and saw that she was now breaking the speed limit and took her foot off the accelerator.

Yet again she asked herself what she was doing here. Her mother must surely have believed her dead by now. Otherwise she'd have tracked her down to the ends of the earth. Wasn't that what a parent would do? Wasn't that what she herself would do if one of her own children went missing? Misery had made Jessamy blind to the route she had chosen up a gently climbing lane. Something thumped in her chest. A large chestnut tree, a garden gate to her right. A tall house built of creamy stone, with soft red bricks picking out the door frames and windows.

Winter's Copse. Jessamy clutched at the steering wheel for support, concentrating on the pale walls of the house, then moving her gaze to the garden, to the apple tree in the corner, which she'd climbed as a child.

She wished she could take the Jubilee mug out of her rucksack and hold it up like a talisman in front of her.

She parked the car on the verge, reminding herself that today's excursion was for reconnaissance purposes only. But her hand stole towards the door handle and she found herself getting out of the car and walking to the garden gate. Just a quick look at the house; she wouldn't knock on the door. As she pushed open the gate a huge black dog ran to meet her, tail wagging. She prayed he wouldn't bark. He reminded her of the dog they'd had at the time of her disappearance. He let her come up the garden path to the front door.

Home. She touched the wood. Time to go back to the car and drive away. Find somewhere quiet to park up and phone her mother and try to break the news gently. Or, even more sensibly, write a letter to her or attempt to find an email address or something. But her finger stole towards the bell. Nobody came. Jessamy's legs screamed at her to leave. She thought she might actually be sick. Yet something made her push the door open, curiosity perhaps. They'd never locked the doors in her childhood. Usually people went round to the back door, though. Interesting that she'd chosen to come to the front like a stranger instead of making her way round to the back door opening into the farmyard. Still nobody came.

Even if her mother wasn't in the house, she could at least have a look at her old home. She was standing inside the hallway before she could stop herself. It seemed smaller than she remembered but otherwise unchanged. Possibly Evie had painted the walls a darker shade of green, but that might just have been her memory.

"Hello?" A woman's voice came from the kitchen and Jessamy stiffened. "Is someone there?" the voice asked, more sharply. Jessamy opened and closed her mouth, her leg muscles trying to force her into flight, her heart too stunned to allow this to happen.

A shadow fell on the parquet floor. Too late to run away now. Jessamy was trembling. "Who is it?" The woman was speaking more softly now. She came into view, carrying a basket of laundry. She must have been taking it in from the washing line. In her early seventies. Evie had always favoured fresh air for drying clothes, even at the end of winter. She stood very straight, her figure still slender. Her face was wrinkled, the face of a countrywoman, but there was no mistaking those still beautiful features: that straight nose, those well-shaped lips.

"Mum?" Jessamy said. "It's . . ." And the words rose in her throat and choked her. "I . . ."

"Jessamy?" Jessamy could hardly hear her. The woman seemed to shrink back against the banisters, looking suddenly smaller and frailer. The laundry basket fell from her arms.

Jessamy found herself stooping to retrieve blouses and towels. She tried to pick up a drying-up cloth and it fell out of her fingers so she stood up. "I'm not normally like this," she burbled. "I'm not clumsy." As though it mattered. The blood was rushing to her head now and for a second she thought she might fall over. She screwed up her fists, holding on to an invisible wire to support herself. Now the woman was coming forward, taking her by the arm. "My Jessamy?" She still sounded doubtful.

"It is me." Jessamy thought of the childhood nightmare she'd had many times in Australia: that she'd somehow managed to return to the mother who was dead only for Evie to doubt her, to send her away. *You are not my daughter.* "It's me," she said again, feeling the hysteria rising inside her. "I went off at the party. I'm back now." She laughed, a harsh sound. It was so funny to say it like that: as though she'd merely ambled off for an hour or so. "I'm really sorry," she went on, still in her ten-year-old persona. "For everything. I . . ." Her throat had tightened, making further speech impossible.

The woman — Evie, her mother — was holding her by the shoulders, eyes boring into her face as though the secrets of the missing years were written on it. Then she removed a hand and put a finger on Jessamy's cheek, as though to reassure herself that what she saw was flesh and blood.

"Jessamy!" It came out like a scream, as though seeing her again was painful. Jessamy grabbed at her as she started to shake. "Kitchen," her mother mumbled. "Need to sit down." Jessamy led her into the back of the house, a reversal of all those times she'd fallen off her pony as a child or hurt herself playing a game with Rachel, and her mother had brought her into the kitchen to patch her up. The kitchen. Scrubbed oak table. Ancient cream-coloured range. The dresser with the Coronation mugs arranged on it. Still there, all of it.

Evie seemed to recover her strength and staggered towards a chair. Jessamy stood over her. Evie's eyes were still like two lasers probing Jessamy's soul. "I'm so sorry!" Jessamy cried. "I'd have come back years ago but I thought you were dead."

"Dead? Me?" Her mother's face had already blanched at the sight of Jessamy but now it seemed to take on a shade even paler than white, as though all the blood had seeped out of her, as though she was becoming a ghost. Perhaps Evie was really a ghost after all, perhaps all this was something Jessamy's imagination was weaving out of old memories and hopes. "Why? Why did you think I was dead? Who told you that?"

Jessamy put a hand to her throat, trying to let out the words. She flopped on a chair and let out a wild cry, like an animal trapped and desperate. The black dog, who'd followed them in, whimpered and ran to Evie, placing his head on her lap and giving half-wags of his tail, trying to steady his mistress.

"Every day," Evie whispered. "Every day I missed you. First thing in the morning and last thing at night. And during the day, too. If I saw someone you'd been at school with my heart would give a jolt. Whenever I passed your bedroom door. Every time Rachel came to stay, I'd half expect her to run in and say she'd found you somewhere out on the farm, it had just been a joke, one of your pranks, and you were coming inside now." She paused, as though letting herself recover from what she was recalling. "Every time the telephone rang I thought it might be the police saying they found you. We came back from the Jubilee party and there in the field was the new chestnut pony I'd bought for you. A surprise. Standing there, with his head over the gate, waiting for you. And you never came back." She was half sobbing, half shouting now.

"Did you look for me?" Jessamy flushed. She'd never intended to let that one out, that nasty little suspicion that her mother hadn't tried hard enough to find her. That she hadn't been missed. That Rachel had filled the gap. For God's sake, she was an adult, a mother herself. Grow up, Jess.

"I gave TV and radio interviews. I put out ads in the press. And in France and Holland too. Every night the dog and I would go out with a . . ."

With a long stick, Jessamy guessed. To poke around for a child's body in a ditch.

"Every time the police told me they'd found a child's body my heart stopped. Then, when they said it wasn't you, I would —" she swallowed — "I'd feel a wild joy. Then I'd think of the child's poor parents. And I'd understand that I'd have to go on living with it, every day, every week, every month." Her voice was rising. "Stretching on ahead of me, for the rest of my life. Sometimes I prayed that I could die and not have to feel it every day. Charlie used to send Rachel to me. I think he did it because he knew I wouldn't kill myself if the child was here. Oh God, Jessamy."

Her hand was stealing across the wooden table now, in search of Jessamy's. They held one another in a grip so tight white marks formed on their hands. Her mother's hands showed the wrinkles and spots exposure to all kinds of weather had caused. But they felt delicate, too. "I used to go to the graveyard and

254

stand by your father's grave and tell him how sorry I was that I hadn't taken proper care of you. I always thought that you wouldn't have vanished if he'd still be alive."

"You did take care of me." And now Jessamy left her chair. She collapsed on the floor in front of her mother and buried her head in Evie's soft wool jumper. The dog sprang out of the way, continuing to whine. And for all her slenderness Evie's embrace was as fierce and strong as it had been when Jessamy's father had died and her mother had hugged her after the funeral, telling her, wordlessly, that she would be all right.

"Who?" Evie said. "Who took you, my darling? Who did this to us?"

Jessamy said nothing but raised her eyes so she could look at her mother.

"I have to know!" Evie's eyes were shining but her face was grey. Perspiration beaded her forehead and Jessamy could hear her breath, quick and shallow. "For decades I've lived this moment, I've planned how it would be and it was always perfect. But it feels . . ."

"What's wrong, Mum?"

"I feel so strange." She put a hand to her upper chest. Jessamy moved back, still watching her all the time. "As if I'm breaking up inside. I need to know what happened, Jessamy."

Jessamy sprang up. "You don't look very good." She rummaged through cupboards looking for glasses and pulled out a tumbler and filled it with water. "Here."

"Tell . . . me . . ." her mother panted. "Who . . .?"

"Just drink this first. You've had a shock. Take some breaths. When you're feeling better I'll tell you everything."

Her fault. She'd done exactly what she'd told herself not to do: turned up unannounced. "How could I have been so stupid?" she muttered. "I should have written to you first. I'm just so bad with writing things. And I hate the phone."

"Not stupid," her mother gasped. She made a movement for the glass, missed it and slumped forward in the chair. "My chest . . . Can't breathe . . ."

"Mum!"

"My heart . . ."

Jessamy ran towards the phone. How the hell did you dial for an ambulance in England? Was it still 999?

"Don't . . . leave me . . . again."

"I'll never leave you again."

"Who . . . ?" her mother was still trying to ask the questions that needed asking. "Who, Jessamy . . ."

"Which emergency service do you require?" the voice on the telephone asked.

# CHAPTER
# THIRTY-TWO

**Rachel**
**2003**

"But she had already lost consciousness before I could tell her," Jessamy said. "The ambulance arrived and I went with her. They asked if I lived with her and I just said no, without thinking. I just couldn't tell them who I was, I felt too . . ."

I could imagine her terror and confusion.

"When we got to the hospital I sat outside while they tried to revive her. They asked me if they should ring anyone and I said you. I didn't know your number so I went through Evie's mobile — I'd thought to take it with me — and gave them yours. Then they came out of the room one last time and I knew it was because . . ." She dropped her head. "Because she was dead. My fault. I killed her. Should have written first."

The shock. The terrible and wonderful shock. Evie was a strong, fit woman, but years of suffering the loss of her child must have weakened her. And then that child had reappeared, without warning. Dreams come true can be deadly.

"And when she died I just . . . panicked. I went and hid in the ladies. I'd sprung my surprise visit on her after all those years and she'd had this attack." She put a hand to her mouth then continued. "It felt like my worst nightmare, only even more terrible. And I'd imagined quite a few appalling scenarios, I can tell you. They took her into a side room and I stole in to see her. Nobody noticed me, there'd been a big pile-up on the M4 and they were bringing in lots of casualties. I kissed her and took out my brush to do her hair."

"You put her scarf back round her neck, just as she liked it."

"Yes." Jessamy swallowed. "I'd always remembered how particular she was. Then I said goodbye and left the hospital. I must have wandered around in the car park for about an hour. I don't remember much about it at all."

"You were in shock."

"Must have been. After a while I found myself sitting outside A&E. I went inside and rang for a taxi to take me back to the B&B. I think I felt . . ." She seemed to struggle for the right words. "That if I went away quietly I might just wake up and find it had all been a bad dream, I'd never seen her, never made her heart give up."

"And you didn't want to speak to me yourself?"

She bowed her head. "I was just beside myself. Didn't know what I was doing. But I couldn't face ringing you and telling you I'd killed her. What would you have said to me then?"

"You weren't to know she'd respond like this."

"I was terrified by then that you'd see me. I went back to the B&B and hid out for the next two days, told them I had a bug." She drew a breath.

"And then I wondered exactly what good telling you I was here would achieve. I assumed that Mum would have left you the house so it just seemed best to fade back to Australia and out of your way. Cowardly, I know. But then —" she took a breath — "I went to buy a few bits in the shop in the next village for the flight home and heard them talking about Mum's funeral. My mother was being buried in Craven churchyard. I had to be there at the service. He wasn't going to take that from me, too. I started feeling bolder and came back here. I was just in the garden then. And the farmyard. And then I came back again this afternoon."

"Who's the 'he', Jess?" I asked. "Who took you? You still haven't said."

She looked at me as though I was mad. "Robert Winter, of course."

# Part Seven

# CHAPTER
# THIRTY-THREE

**Jessamy**
**A few days before the Silver Jubilee party, 1977**

"I haven't been back here since I left in 1945, Jessamy," Robert said.

"So why are you back now?"

He looked past her, down the hill towards the village. "It's the Jubilee coming up. It's reminded me of home, of the way things are done here: the party, the bunting, the cakes and mugs." For a moment he looked younger than he had done at first, as though he was a boy reliving it all. "I missed it all so much all the time I was away. But you won't tell your mother I'm here, will you?" His eyes held hers, refusing to let her doubt the seriousness of what he said. They were sitting with Martha in a hollow on the hillside very early in the morning, sheltered from the wind and from anyone who might wish them ill.

"Why not?"

A film seemed to pass over Robert's eyes. "It's just better for her not to know."

She wanted to ask why this was but she didn't. He was her Uncle Robert, after all. She'd seen the photographs of him. Mum had always told her that it had been Uncle Robert who'd brought her and her brother to live on the farm.

"Mum thinks you died in the barn when it burned down."

"It wasn't me."

"Who was it?"

"Never mind that now," said Martha.

Jessamy decided to ignore the old woman. "Mum gets really sad every time she talks about you, Uncle Robert. She told me how you chose her and Uncle Charlie to come and live on the farm."

A snort from Martha.

"You really care about your mother, don't you?" His eyes were soft.

She nodded.

"Even if she's angry with you sometimes?"

"She doesn't get that angry."

"Angry enough." Martha stared at the bruise on Jessamy's eye. "You need to know what's been going on here," she told Robert. "I mentioned the cows —"

"You should get back now, Jessamy." Robert spoke gently. "I'll see you again soon. I've been wanting to meet you for a long time. I've heard a lot about you." He and Martha exchanged another glance.

She rose. "I'm glad I've met you at last," she said. "I've seen your photos in the house. It wasn't you they found in the barn when it burned down, so who was it?"

He started to answer but Martha cut through. "We don't know, child. Might have been that Eyetie — Italian."

264

"Carlo." Jessamy remembered the name. "Mum liked him too. She used to give him apples."

Martha's face grew more set.

"I'm glad I've seen you, too, Noi." Robert stood and placed his arms around her shoulders.

She wanted to ask him why he called her that but Martha got up as well. "I'll walk part of the way with you, Jess." They left Robert crouching in the hollow on the hillside and descended the steep track back to the farm.

"Robert Winter is a good man." Martha's voice shook slightly. "He is your father's brother and your father would have wanted you to do as Robert said."

"What does he want me to do?"

"You'll find out." Martha stopped. "Do as he tells you, Jess. And be ready. Trust me. I always make things nice for you, don't I?"

She nodded.

"Remember our little trip to Oxford?" They'd gone for the afternoon, had tea. Martha had taken her to a photographer's and had her portrait taken for a surprise. Jessamy hadn't seen the photo yet. Perhaps it was to be a present for Evie because Martha had told her not to tell her mother. Seemed unlikely though.

"Why don't you like my mother?" The question popped out of her mouth.

Martha's mouth opened and closed. "I never said I didn't like her," she said at last. "But there are some things that aren't right." She glanced at Jessamy. "Sometimes you have to be born in a place to really belong, Jess. To know how to deal with the beasts: the

265

sheep and the cows and their ailments. You need to be born to it."

"Like me."

"Like you." Martha put out a hand and gave her a gentle push. "You hurry along now before she wonders where you've been."

Be ready. The moment came when she wasn't expecting it. At the Jubilee party on the green. Martha came to stand beside her as she admired the mugs in their cardboard box again. "Where's your mother and Rachel?"

"Outside getting orange squash for Rachel, I think. Why?"

"Never mind. We've got something for you, Robert and me. Follow me."

It seemed a strange game to play.

"Oh, and we'll take this ahead of time." Martha pulled a mug off the top of the box. As they walked out of the tent Evie and Rachel were standing with their backs to them. Rachel would still be feeling bad about that dropped relay baton. It hadn't been her fault but Jessamy couldn't bring herself to tell her this yet. "Come on." Martha gave her a little nudge towards the fence. She squeezed herself through the planks, nimble as someone half her age. Jessamy followed.

"Where are we going? I don't want to miss the cake."

Martha pointed to a grey car in the lane, one she didn't recognize. "It's your uncle. He's got a surprise for you."

Of course, the surprise.

"Hello, Uncle Robert." She opened the door. "What's the surprise? Mum was talking about it."

"Was she?" For a second he looked flustered. Then he recovered. "It's a trip to Australia." He held out a piece of paper in his hand. "Here's your ticket."

"What about a passport?" Jessamy was on her mother's passport, obtained last summer so they could both go on holiday to Spain with Rachel and her parents.

"You won't need it."

"Oh. I thought —"

"We got you a brand-new one." Martha smiled. "Remember that lovely photo we took of you?"

"That trip to Oxford, the backstreet photographer's studio . . ."

"You need to hurry, child," Martha said.

"Where are we going? Australia?" He'd already told her about Australia, about the animals and hot sun, the long beaches. "I'm going to Australia? Really?" Nobody she knew had been to Australia. She'd be the first in the school.

"Yup."

"What about Mum? And Rachel?"

"Your mother knows. But she didn't want to make a fuss about it in front of your cousin. It wouldn't have been fair. I can't take Rachel with us. It's just you. You can see how much your mother's got on her plate. This will give her a bit of time for herself."

Mum always was very fussy about being fair. She'd been pleased when Jessamy had dropped out of that race so that Rachel would have a chance of winning.

She never liked Jess to go on about successes in front of Rachel in case she hurt her feelings. It seemed strange that Mum hadn't packed her stuff, though.

"What about my clothes?"

"We'll get new ones." He held up the teddy bear she always slept with. "Got this for you, though." She got into the car.

"Bye, Jessamy, be good for your Uncle Robert." Martha handed her the Jubilee mug and shut the car door. Jessamy still wasn't certain, but this was *Martha* telling her to go with him. Martha, who'd made clothes for her doll, taken her to look at the new lambs, shown her the right herbs to give to her pony so his coat would shine. Martha, who'd always time to listen to Jessamy, who was never too busy or tired or flustered for her. Martha, who'd watched over her, so she'd told Jessamy, from the day she was born.

"How long will it take to get to the airport?" She'd enjoyed the airport last year when she'd flown to Palma.

"An hour and a half." He started the engine.

She waved to Martha as they moved off. "And Mum will know where I've gone?"

"Yes."

"Will she be OK?" Jessamy bit her lip. "Can't she come with us now?"

"Not yet, sweetheart. She needs some time." He turned the key in the ignition. "You've got to be a brave girl, Noi."

# CHAPTER
# THIRTY-FOUR

**Rachel**
**2003**

Robert Winter. I still couldn't get my mind round it. More questions needed answering. They burned a hole in my tongue but still I managed to hold on to them. Even as a child you could never get much from Jessamy by questioning. You had to let the information drop out of her at her own pace; even if it was just something as simple as the location of a robin's nest or the first strawberries. And I felt physically weary.

"Perhaps I should leave you for now," she said, reading my mind. "It's been a lot for us both to take in, hasn't it? You'll need time to catch up on all of this."

I nodded. Then felt terrible. "This is your home, Jess. You don't have to leave it." I looked at the window, blind still open, revealing the grey, stormy evening. "You'll get soaked. How did you get here, anyway?"

"I walked. It's only about two miles. But I won't walk back. I'll call a taxi." She pulled a mobile out of her pocket.

"No." I put up a hand. "Stay here."

She shook her head. "We need some space, Rache." I saw how white her face was. She looked as though she needed to crash out. So did I.

"I'll drive you. If we go now we can probably get through."

The water in the lane seemed only a foot deep. To get to Jessamy's guest house I'd need to negotiate the dip under the railway bridge: a flood blackspot. As we drove through the village I could hear, above the beating of the windscreen wipers, the gurgling of water through drains. "Reminds me of floods we had in Queensland," Jessamy told me. "At least here you don't have to watch out for snakes being sucked up into the inside of the car as you drive through the water."

I shuddered. She grinned and for a second my ten-year-old cousin sat beside me, trying to wind me up. "I won't tell you about the crocodile we found in the garden one morning."

"Nice surprise." It was a relief to talk like this. But the mention of a surprise had brought my mind back to the method Robert and Martha had used to lure Jessamy away. "You thought taking you off on a trip to Australia was the same surprise Evie had mentioned earlier that Silver Jubilee day?"

She nodded. "Mum told me it was actually a new pony."

"She thought we'd have more fun riding with two ponies."

Her head drooped and I wished I hadn't told her that. She was probably picturing the two of us riding up

270

on the Ridgeway, picnics in rucksacks. "And Robert Winter whisked you straight to Australia?" I went on, to change the subject.

"Sydney first."

"With a new passport?"

She wrinkled her brow. "I don't know how he managed that. But there was no trouble at the airport."

I pulled the car up onto the bank as a large four-by-four approached. The driver gave me a thumbs-down. Looked like the road under the railway bridge wasn't going to be passable.

"I think we should turn round."

Jess nodded.

"We'll be fine together back at the farm." I laid a hand on her arm. "Anyway, I may need you if this rain carries on."

"The roof," she said. "Sometimes it leaks. And you have to make sure the drainage ditch in the lane doesn't get blocked." She smiled. "I remember, you see."

I turned the car round and headed back towards the village. "Tell me more," I said. "If you want to, that is."

It felt safe in the car. I kept my eyes on the road and couldn't see her face. Somehow it was less emotional that way.

"Whatever he'd done with my passport it worked. No computer records and electronic passport reading devices at airports back then, I suppose. And he relaxed once we'd got on the plane. I remember that bit. Once we were in Australia we took another flight in a small plane up to Queensland. Right into the outback, miles from everywhere, I couldn't even show you where it was on the map, that's how remote it was. That was the first year." Words tumbled out of her now.

A question was on my mind but it was one that even the warm security of the car's interior couldn't prompt me to ask.

"I know you're wondering why I didn't try and escape from him."

For a moment I was looking at her mother, sitting silent and white-faced by the stove, her dog beside her.

"You're thinking that I couldn't have missed my mother and my home very much if I didn't try and get back." She sounded angry.

"No, I'm not —"

"How could I not miss Mum? I couldn't work out why she hadn't written. I was worried that there might have been more cases of TB in the cows. It seemed like such a strange holiday for me: a dustbowl in the middle of nowhere."

"Jessamy, I know you must have wanted to come home, I —"

But she wasn't going to let me complete my sentence.

"I kept asking when I'd be going home again, when I'd hear from you and Mum. 'Not yet,' he kept saying. 'It's so wonderful for me to have you here, Jess.' But I kept asking when I'd come back to Craven. So then he told me . . ." She sounded choked up.

"What?"

For a second or so Jessamy couldn't speak. I lifted my foot from the accelerator and changed down a gear so that we were moving forward through the murky waters very, very slowly.

# CHAPTER
# THIRTY-FIVE

**Jessamy**
**Queensland, July 1977**

Evie was sick. It was the only reason why her mother would not have written to her. By the third week away from home Jessamy knew this as a certainty. Her mother was unwell, bed bound or in hospital. This was the only reason she'd let Jessamy go off without her. Could humans catch TB from cattle? She glanced over the breakfast table to Uncle Robert.

"Is my mother ill?"

The colour seemed to drain from his face. "Why do you say that?"

"She hasn't written. She hasn't even tried to telephone."

"It's hard to ring Australia from England," he said, quickly. She couldn't seem to get his eyes to stay on hers.

"Is it very serious?" She clenched her hands together so hard it hurt.

He swallowed. "Yes." He put down his cup of tea. "It was very bad, Jess. In fact . . ." he paused. "You need to prepare yourself for bad news, sweetheart. I'm afraid

274

she died. I only got the telegram after you'd gone to bed." His face was set, rigid. "I was going to tell you after breakfast. I'm sorry, Jess."

Her brain refused to accept what he'd said at first. Then the information started to percolate through the cells of her body, reaching the inside of her, her heart. She dropped her head to her hands. "She can't have died." The sobs were starting now, coming up from somewhere deep inside her. "She was fine when we left."

"It was an accident. On the farm. She slipped in the field and one of the heifers kicked her in the head. They must have been frightened. Perhaps a dog had got into the field."

Hadn't Mum always warned them about the heifers and dogs? "She can't be dead." Her crying shook her as though a giant was shaking her by the shoulders.

"She never wrote to me."

His hand reached out and touched her shoulder. "The letters may have got lost. And you're fine with me, aren't you, sweetheart? We get along, don't we?" He sounded upset himself.

"Will we go back now?" She looked up at him. The tears were flowing so fast now she could hardly make him out. "I want to go back to the farm."

"Listen, Jess, there's no family left there."

"There's Rachel."

He paused for a second. "Her father's taken her abroad. The farm's going to be sold. There's nobody to run it now. It's really just you and me, Jess."

No, she wanted to scream. She'd never have died without me knowing she'd gone. She wouldn't let that happen.

"I want to go to her funeral and see the grave." The tears were pouring so thickly now her shirt felt wet. "I want to see Rachel."

The hand tightened round her. "The funeral's been and gone and one day I'll take you back to see the grave. But not now. I'm going to look after you. I'm all the family you've got left now and I'm going to take such good care of you, Noi."

# CHAPTER
# THIRTY-SIX

**Rachel**
2003

Sickly yellow light bathed us. A car drove through the village towards us. "Robert was a bastard." I spat the words out. "What an utterly cruel thing to say."

"And yet he wasn't a cruel man. Not intentionally."

The wake from the oncoming car left a wave which rocked us. I clutched the wheel, suddenly on the edge of feeling nauseous, of wanting to pull over and open the door and abandon the car. And Jessamy. This realization shamed me. But it wasn't my cousin I found overwhelming. It was the revelations she brought with her, the emotions which churned like the dirty water under the wheels.

"I know, I know, it's a crazy thing to say about the person who ruined my life. But he didn't mean it cruelly." She tapped her fingers on her head. "Up here he was all broken."

"What happened then?"

"We carried on at the cattle station for a while longer." She shuddered. "I hated that place so much. There was nobody my age to play with and it was such

277

an arid, dusty place, you couldn't even go to school, it was all done by radio." She paused. "At night I'd cry and he'd come in and stroke my head and tell me he'd look after me. I believed him. He was so . . . tender." She made a quick movement with her hand over her eyes.

"That's it for today," the teacher said over the radio. "Complete exercise five on page twenty-eight and exercises six and seven and send them in. Well done, children, you've all worked hard."

Jessamy said goodbye, switched off the radio and hung up her earphones. At home in Craven they'd have spilled out into the playground at the end of school, asking one another home to play, or running down to the shop to buy sweets. Here she just had the dog to play with when she finished lessons. The small terrier gave a wag of his tail.

"It's too hot. We'll go out later." She could read, she supposed. A box of new books had arrived this morning. Robert liked her reading. But the pad of writing paper she kept on her desk drew her to it. She'd write another letter.

"If it's cool we can go riding later on," she told Rachel. Rachel never wrote back but Jessamy liked to keep sending the letters. Perhaps her cousin had moved house again. Robert took the letters off every week when he went to the post office. She'd asked if she could come with him and he'd promised she could, now she was feeling better about her mother. Now she was getting used to her new life.

"And we'll be moving on, too," he told her. "It's too hot for you out here. I'm trying to find something nearer the coast. You'd like the beaches, Jess."

The thought of the sea was almost enough to lift her out of the flatness she'd felt since he'd told her about her mother. "Can we take Drake?" The terrier pricked his ears as she mentioned his name.

"Of course." And Robert gave her a gentle smile. "And we might be able to sort out a school for you, too." Her heart gave another slight lift at the thought of being with other children. "If we can find somewhere safe," he went on.

"I would like to go to a proper school again," she wrote to her cousin. "It's not the same doing it over the radio. You can't play with the children at break time. I wish I had my pony here. Do you know what happened to him, Rachel? And all the other animals? There are cattle here but the dogs live out-doors and they growl if I go up to them. Except for Drake, my terrier. He's a nice dog."

There was something she really needed to ask Rachel. "Did my mum miss me when I left? She didn't write. Was she really, really busy on the farm? It was so strange to go off on holiday without saying goodbye to her and you. But Uncle Robert thought it was for the best. And Mum had told us there'd be a surprise after the party, hadn't she? So she must have known I was going to be all right. It's lucky I've got Uncle Robert to look after me now that Mum's dead. He's very kind, even if he does sometimes forget my name. Sometimes he says weird things and it's a bit frightening. But then he seems to go back to normal."

Even driving this slowly we'd reached Winter's Copse at last. The sight of its pale walls filled me with relief. Home again. Thank God the drive rose up steeply from the lane. The car would be safe from the floodwater overnight. Jess and I dashed for the door.

We flopped by the range. I thought of the bottle of whisky Evie kept on her drinks tray but the thought of alcohol made my stomach remember that it felt unusually delicate.

Before I could even suggest Jess might like a drink she started to talk again, words again seeming to flood from her like the rain from the skies.

# CHAPTER
# THIRTY-SEVEN

**Jessamy**
**Cardew sugar cane plantation, near Cairns,**
**Queensland, January 1979**

He'd lost more weight since she'd been away at school. It had only been twelve weeks since she'd seen him but he looked much thinner. His hand shook as he poured the tea. She suspected long nights in the hotel with his mates. "You'll have to show me that report of yours, Jess."

"You'll be impressed." She worked hard, always had done, ever since she'd started at the new school in Brisbane. The teachers had told her she was behind, she, Jessamy Winter, always top of the class back in Craven. She'd been so cross she'd put her head down and worked. The other girls had thought she was a swot until they'd seen her play netball. Then she'd won the sprint and the hurdles in a schools' championship and found herself a bit of a hero among her year. Strange, really, as she didn't give a damn about any of them.

"This house looks smaller." It had been a shock, coming back to the plantation. The girls' school in

Brisbane was an old Victorian building, with high ceilings and marbled floors.

"Places always do when you come back to them. Tell me about school." And he asked her scores of questions. Did she have the right clothes and sports equipment? Were they kind to her? She'd reassured him that she was fitting in well, crossing her fingers behind her back.

"How's the cane doing?"

"Should be a good year. It's nearly all in now."

She noticed the shadows under his eyes and the grey tint to his skin, even under the tanned skin. The cutting was dusty and noisy. Every year someone got injured or bitten by one of the snakes curling around the canes. "I'll be out in the fields with the men all day for the rest of the week, I'm afraid."

He looked exhausted. The climate didn't suit him, the doctor said. Robert had told the doctor that he knew all about the tropical jungle, thank you.

He came in at six and she cooked him some tea: chops and a pudding made with a locally grown pineapple, and sponge, which Mary, Robert's half-aboriginal housekeeper, had taught her to make before she'd gone off to school. Back in England pineapples were a treat: you got them once or twice a year, perhaps at Christmas. Up here they ate them whenever they wanted.

After they'd eaten they sat on the veranda, looking out over the trees to the west of the cane fields. The fields still to be cut were lined with the canes, now far taller than she was. Behind the bluey-green mountains rose up, steep and lined with forest. The landscape should have been beautiful, it was populated with birds and exotic-looking animals which still took her breath away. But things were only really beautiful if you felt them inside you. This lush landscape meant nothing to her. Sometimes Robert took her for walks in the forest. Once the trees had covered these fields and the house, too, before they'd cut them back.

What on earth was she to do with herself up here? Robert had designed a garden that flowered all year round. He'd redecorated her bedroom while she'd been away, buying her new blinds and a rug. There were flowers in a vase by her bed. He said he'd borrow a pony so she could ride.

There were few girls her age to play with. In the township a half-mile away there was a hotel, a bar, really, where the men drank, and a general stores. There was nothing else except for the elementary school. The nearest library was miles and miles away in Cairns.

It was past eight now but still the heat pushed down like a steam iron. All those weeks in Brisbane she'd longed to leave school and come back here. Now she was here the thought of the long Christmas holiday stretching out seemed to crush her like a python. Perhaps she'd catch the bus down to the town, to the beach. She'd have to go swimming just to keep cool, but not in the local pool with all those children who stared at her because she didn't fit in here. And not in one of the apparently inviting creeks. Only last year a child had been pulled from the bank by a croc. Jessamy shuddered, remembering. They'd found one of her hands on a muddy shore half a mile upstream.

Sometimes there were people to talk to in the town: hippies in their VWs peddling herbal soaps and flower oils. Robert had an almost animal aversion to their patchouli-oil-scented presence and would try to hurry her past the camps where they grew vegetables and plaited strips of leather with beads to make belts and necklaces to sell in the market. Sometimes boats went out from the town to look at the Great Barrier Reef. If Robert wasn't with her she could chat to the visitors. Some of them came from England. Robert wasn't keen on people from England. He wasn't keen on lots of people. "Best to be safe rather than sorry," he said whenever someone new appeared in the township. "You get odd sorts up here. Drifters."

Something rustled behind a clump of vivid blue agapanthus. "There he is again." Robert nodded and Jessamy saw the stubby-legged brown bandicoot with its long nose. "Sniffing around." They watched the creature, like a cross between a badger and a possum, Jessamy thought, but without the striped nose, or perhaps a badger and a rat, but more appealing. He scuffled around below them, before vanishing under the veranda. When they'd first moved here Robert had taken her out into the garden and clasped Jessamy's arm so tightly it had hurt. "Never ever go under that veranda." He pointed at the space beneath the stilts. "Even if you lose your best ball, even if Drake goes under there and you can't get him to budge. Just wait for me to sort it for you."

She already knew enough about this country to know there'd be snakes and spiders under the veranda.

Robert was good at sorting stuff for her. He was good around the bungalow, too. He'd already emptied her trunk of clothes and washed them all for her. Every morning she found her sandals outside her bedroom door, dusted and polished.

Nobody could have taken better care of her but at nights strange images swarmed in her mind. The space under the veranda had become a space in her head, populated by dark thoughts rather than snakes and centipedes and other creatures that bit or stung. Once or twice she dreamed that Martha had taken up residence under the veranda, but when she called to the woman, she turned into a lizard and scuttled away.

Drake growled at the bandicoot. "Stay here, boy." Robert put a hand on the dog's collar. "You'll get yourself into all kinds of trouble if you go chasing him."

Robert sniffed.

"What is it?"

"That jasmine smell." He sounded disgusted. "I'm going to have to pull that bush out."

Why? She added the question to all the other unspoken questions she'd accumulated over the last year and a half. "I like the smell."

"It's too sweet." Perspiration ran down his head. "Sickly. Think I'm going to have to get myself a beer at the hotel. Would you mind, love?"

"No." It would be a relief not to have him here for a while.

It was late when his friend dropped him back. "Come in!" Robert shouted. "Make yourself at home. Jess will have turned in. I'll make some coffee."

She turned in bed and tried to find a cool spot. She must have fallen back to sleep because for a while she was back at home, at Winter's Copse and it was cool and grey and her mother was telling her to hurry and get up because she was late for school.

Robert was talking loudly. "You try and save them, you do your best but then it all ends up bad. And you know it's your fault, that everyone blames you."

"You've done a grand job with the girl, mate." Another male voice. A local.

"I wasn't going to let anything happen to Jess, that's for sure. Not after I'd seen what they did to Noi." A pause. "It looked just like a ruby, you know. Pretty almost."

"What looked like a ruby, mate?" the friend asked.

"The mark on Noi."

Noi. When he'd first taken her on holiday he'd sometimes called her Noi by mistake. She'd asked him who Noi was but he'd stared at her with blank eyes and she hadn't liked to ask again. She fell back asleep and this time she dreamed of a child, a girl who lived under the veranda and came out at night to haunt them.

It took some weeks before she could persuade Robert to take her into Cairns so she could shop. Perhaps visit the library too. By now the school holidays were almost over. She dared not plead too much. He'd have to think it was his idea. Fortunately nature provided her with

286

another growth spurt and her clothes became unwearable.

He loathed the town, hated it, abhorred it. "You don't need to take me." She tried to sound casual. "I can go by myself on the bus."

"By yourself?" His eyes widened. "I'm not sure I'm keen on that idea, sweetheart."

"Mary could come with me. She likes looking at the shops and she can visit her niece." Mary had a European niece who worked in the hotel kitchen. Jessamy examined Robert. His head was lowered. One of his feet kicked against the kitchen table. Don't push it, she told herself. Don't drive him into a corner or he'll start talking about stuff you don't understand, weird stuff.

Jessamy rose and feigned a yawn. "Not sure I can really be bothered. I like my skirt short. Some of the girls say it's a bit daggy, though."

A bit risky; he hated her looking different from the others and the worry that she didn't look quite proper might send him into another black period. "You'll buy a new skirt. And shoes. I don't want you looking like, like . . . that."

"OK."

He handed her some notes. "Get whatever you need, honey." She could see that he was trying hard to calm himself. "Don't mind me, I just worry about you. There are people in this world you just wouldn't believe, Jess."

In the library she found the shelf of books about foreign countries. There were lots on England. Probably because so many Australians came from there. Most of them just had dull black and white photographs. But there was one that had coloured plates: *A walk through the Berkshire Downs*. She flicked through it. *Above the downland villages the Ridgeway crests the green wave of the hills*. There were photos of the White Horse taken from the air. Not at all like a kangaroo, Rachel. She flicked over and found a view looking north across the vale. Jessamy squinted at the villages, trying to work out which one might be Craven. She thought she could identify it by the square tower of the church, but couldn't be sure. If it was, her mother would be buried in the shadow of this very tower. She wanted this book but wasn't a member of the library.

Perhaps she could join. The librarian at the information desk assured her that she could. "We normally ask for a parent's signature on the application."

"Both my parents are dead."

The woman flushed. "Sorry, dear." Her eyes went to the book Jessamy had chosen. "Are you from those parts? My husband grew up in England."

"I lived there once." Something made Jessamy guard her tongue. "But I live here now."

"There are some more books you might like, then." She led Jessamy across the parquet floor to the geography section. "These are slightly less accessible but there's one about the geology of the Downs. You might find it interesting because there are some good photos." She reached over Jess's head. "Oh, and here's a good map of the area."

**288**

"Thanks." Jess's legs wanted to sprint to a desk so she could pull open the book covers but she made herself shuffle across the library parquet as though the heat had rendered her listless.

She opened the map. Wantage had been the nearest town to Winter's Copse. Jessamy remembered a market: boxes of cauliflowers and leeks, tangerines wrapped in bright tissue paper, the stallholders shouting greetings to her mother, their cheeks red in the frost. There was a statue of a king in that marketplace, crown on his head, holding something in his hand . . . Which monarch?

King Alfred.

But even looking at these books and the map made her feel guilty, as though she'd forgotten what she owed Robert, who'd looked after her with such care. She didn't understand why this should be. Why shouldn't she look at pictures of these places?

Something was knotting up in her head, pulling it tight. She mumbled a farewell to the librarian.

"Don't you want your books?" she called out after her.

Jessamy shook her head and ran for the door. The pain in her head pressed against her. She felt chilled and her legs shook.

# CHAPTER
# THIRTY-EIGHT

**Rachel**
**2003**

"I came down with something," Jessamy said. "It was bad. Still not sure what it was. Medical care wasn't exactly extensive out in that little township. I had some kind of weird fever, pains in my muscles, a rash. For days and days my temperature stayed up at 104. Robert didn't move from my side. He just let the men get on with the cane harvest. He sponged me down, changed my sheets and helped me to the bathroom." She nodded to herself, as though reliving the illness. "I had bad dreams, terrible nightmares."

"About being taken from here?"

She shook her head. "About monsters coming out from underneath the veranda and pulling me down there with them. They were snakes, swollen to six times their normal size. And the kookaburras flying in the sky were like pterodactyls." She grimaced. "I begged him not to leave me. He sat there every night holding my hand until I fell asleep. By the time I was better Robert Winter had become my protector. While he was with me nothing terrible could happen to me. If he even went out of the room to fetch me a drink I shouted at him to come back. I was so weak I couldn't go back to school for days after the holidays ended. I have to tell you, Rachel, I felt I owed him after that."

"You owed him nothing!" I spat. "OK, he'd mopped your brow when you were ill and made sure you had a decent education, but so what?"

"I loved Robert," she said in a low tone. "I couldn't let myself think badly of him. I was —" she seemed to hunt for the right words — "in torment, really. Whatever I did, someone would get hurt. And then Robert got sick again himself while I was back home for Easter, another bout of malaria — that seemed to be happening more and more frequently. And he was disturbed in his mind, going on about the jungle and the Thais he'd bartered with while they were out there. Something about the Thai trader's daughter —"

"The girl in the jungle."

She nodded. "The one he called Noi. Something had happened to her. I didn't understand what he was on about. All I wanted was to go back to school. Life was boring there but it felt safe and ordered and I had time to think."

I could imagine how reassuringly normal school must have seemed.

"Seeing me off to school on the plane to Brisbane was tough for him. He had his friends, men he drank with in the hotel. Many of them had been POWs in the East."

"Do you think he told them about what had happened to him? Perhaps it would have helped to talk to people who really understood what he'd been through."

She snorted. "They'd have understood all right. But they wouldn't necessarily have thanked him for bringing the subject up. Men of that generation, Australian ones, anyway, just kept it all buried." She settled back in her chair. "Today we think that's unhealthy, it all needs to come out. But Robert and his friends probably worried that once it started leaking out, the punishments, the executions, the hunger, it would take them over."

"Keeping quiet about what happened to him stopped Robert getting help for his nervous disorder, though," I pointed out. "Proper treatment might have stopped him believing you needed 'saving' from something terrible that was supposedly happening here." I sounded acid.

"Back in the seventies nobody'd heard of post-traumatic stress disorder." Jessamy flopped into a chair, pushing back her dark hair, looking suddenly as though whatever had been charging her batteries had abandoned her. For the first time she looked her age: thirty-five, like me.

"You felt responsible for Robert, didn't you?" I saw it all, the teenage girl alone in the tropics with the sick man.

"Yes."

"But what about the farm? And me?"

"He'd told me you'd moved abroad with your father. He didn't know the address. And the farm'd been sold."

And, of course, she'd had no way of finding out this was untrue. No internet back then, no easy way of checking things out.

"To be honest, I wasn't even sure you'd want to hear from me after some years had passed. I thought you'd just forgotten about me, moved on."

I opened my mouth to protest but didn't say anything. She couldn't have known any different, isolated as she was from reality.

"Perhaps you did readjust to my absence," Jessamy continued. "Perhaps you were perfectly happy."

There was a tiny nugget of truth in what she'd said. Hadn't I started to enjoy those holidays I'd spent here following Jessamy's disappearance? Sometimes I'd hardly wanted to return to my parents at the end of the visits. "Aren't you pleased to be home, darling?" my mother would ask, thrusting beautifully wrapped clothes from Riviera boutiques at me. "See what we bought you." And as I tried on another perfectly tailored dress in yet another gleaming executive home in Weybridge or an apartment in some Mediterranean resort, and said thank you, my heart would be back in Evie's kitchen. The two of us dressed in our oldest clothes making hot chocolate after a night out in the lambing shed.

A whole year had passed before I'd lost the habit of mentally recording events to replay to Jess in the holidays. *Did I tell you that we all had detention because someone blocked the loos . . .? You'll never guess what happened in French . . . Mummy wrote and told me she found a lizard in her slipper and she won't wear them ever again now.* Sometimes when I was riding one of the ponies in the field behind the barn I'd expect to see her running towards us. "Try the jumps, Rachel! You can do it." When I'd stayed at Winter's Copse I'd continued to sleep in the second twin bed in her room. Sometimes I'd sit on Jessamy's bed, holding one of her soft toys or flicking through the pages of one of her books and longing for her so strongly it made my insides ache. After two or three years had passed Evie had covered her bed with a blue candlewick cover and moved the toys into the cupboard.

And yet . . . My eyes lit on the laptop on the kitchen table, top of the range and new. Out in the drive, mercifully now clear of the floods, stood my equally shiny convertible. I'd made something of my life. With Jessamy gone perhaps parts of my personality had flourished. If she'd stayed at Winter's Copse I'd have retained my position as the natural second, the quieter one. I'd never have done all I'd achieved. But, a little voice whispered, perhaps I'd have chosen a less demanding and rewarding career. Married younger and had children by now, instead of leaving it until I was in my thirties to start trying. "If I'd seen you four years ago we'd have had a better chance," the consultant had told me.

Perhaps my long silence had worried Jessamy. She uncrossed an arm and reached across the expanse of oak table to pat my hand. I sensed that the gesture had cost her quite a bit so I forced myself to clear the thoughts from my mind. "I know you weren't really glad I was out of the way, Rachel."

**294**

"Tell me what happened after you went off to boarding school."

"My life went on, I did well at school, even though it was an old-fashioned kind of place. When I left I managed to get a scholarship to a college in the US. It was fun but I fell apart a bit out there, couldn't deal with all the freedom. Robert had kept me so sheltered. I got into drugs."

I looked at her.

"Fairly badly. They made it easier to deal with this." She pointed to her chest. "All the emptiness inside me. Then I got out of drugs. Married the first guy who looked decent and kind."

"Are you still together?" I couldn't see a ring on her hand.

"Nope. But we're still friends. Have to be to manage custody of our kids."

"Tell me about the children." Even now, even at this moment, I felt a pang.

She nodded. "Twins of eight, one of each. They're in the States at the moment, with their father and his parents. I miss them." Her face fell. "We're civilized about it but it's complicated because I'm in Sydney and he's in Spain most of the time." She gave a dismissive wave. "But don't let me work myself up about it." Then her face crumpled. "My mother will never see Marcus and Sophie. They ask me about my family and I've never been able to tell them very much." I reached out for her hand." I can't believe I saw her for just that little time, Rachel. And now she's gone. It's so cruel." We sat listening to the kitchen clock ticking while her tears fell

295

onto the wooden table. There was nothing I could say to console her; I could only hope that just sitting with her gave her some comfort.

"Tell me how you found out the truth, Jess," I said at last.

"It was only weeks ago. He'd been sick. Skin cancer to start with. All those years in the tropical heat in Thailand. Then sugar cane farming. It would have been surprising if he hadn't developed melanomas. I kept telling him to go to the doctor. But he didn't and the cancer spread and it was obvious he was dying. I went up to be with him."

Her voice dropped to a whisper and I guessed that she was no longer in the kitchen at Winter's Copse with me: she was back in tropical Queensland, sitting with the man who'd brought her up and looked after her, who'd stolen her and lied to her.

"There was one afternoon when he was resting. It was too hot to go out. I managed to get a reasonable dial-up connection on the laptop I'd brought with me. Something, some crazy whim, made me think of searching on Craven, on the farm's name, just to see who still lived there. I had no idea . . ." She choked on the last words.

# CHAPTER
# THIRTY-NINE

**Jessamy**
**February 2003**

She closed her eyes and opened them again. But it was still there on the screen. *Pictured here, children from Craven Primary School enjoy newborn lambs at Winter's Copse farm.* And there was the woman, standing almost out of the frame, smiling at the children, a scarf wrapped round her neck. Jessamy focused so hard on the face that it fragmented into a collection of coloured pixels, nothingness. Was she wrong? Her imagination was willing her mother to be there. She forced her eyes to look at the blinds on the windows and then switched them back to stare at the screen. Her mother was still there.

The dial-up internet service up here was so slow that she hardly dared to carry out an internet search on her mother's name in an attempt to find more information about her, in case she lost this picture for good and couldn't reopen the file. "Jess . . ." came the voice from the lounge.

She stood so abruptly that the chair fell over. Trying to compose herself she walked to him. Years of experience had taught her how to hide emotion from him. Even now she was able to push this into the recesses of her mind.

It had been a better day; he could sit up, which helped his lungs. "Do you need more water?" She filled his glass again, amazed at how she could still communicate normally, as though the certainties governing her world hadn't collapsed. "Nearly time for the drugs."

He watched her, eyes buried deep in the yellowing, papery skin. "What've you been doing?" There must have been something about her that he'd picked out. Her hands must be shaking. God, her mouth felt dry, too. Robert was sensitive to mood, even when cancer was sweeping his body.

"Just looking at some old newspapers on the internet." She was surprised she could actually speak.

"They have newspapers on the net?" He laughed. "I haven't ever looked. Haven't really got to grips with the thing yet. It seems to take for ever."

"I've heard they're laying cables up here. It'll be quicker then." She felt hot blood pulsing in her head. Calm down. Think. There had to be a mistake; she'd been hallucinating. The kookaburras outside seemed to shriek mockery at her.

"Too quick for me." He gave his rasping cough. "You can find out anything on the internet, I've heard."

"So they say." Suddenly her heart was thumping and she thought she might retch. She longed to dash from the room, which seemed to spin in front of her.

**298**

"Jess." He was struggling to straighten himself in the chair. "There's something you need to know." The words were spoken quickly, like beads dropping from a necklace. "I should have told you last time you came up here but you had the kids with you and everything."

She'd left the children with a friend in Sydney this time, not wanting them to see their Uncle Robert like this.

"I need to tell you now while I can see things straight. Sometimes I just can't, you know. Sometimes it all blurs together."

He'd explain. There'd be a reason for all this. She sat down on the sofa opposite him. She could see him still struggling to sit more upright and got up again to rearrange the cushions behind his back. "Thanks." His eyes were suddenly less glazed; he looked more alert. Probably because he was due more morphine. Over the years she'd noticed how the alcohol had kept him in his strange world. Now the painkilling drugs seemed to fulfil the same purpose. He'd be in pain now. "I'm not stupid, I know that I'm not going to be around much longer . . ." He coughed. "I also know that I should be seeing a priest or minister. Or a police officer. Because of what I've done. But I'll take my chances with my maker. The person I need to be honest with is you, Jess."

"She's not dead, is she?" She almost looked around to see who'd spoken the words; it didn't seem possible that she could have uttered them. She forced herself to concentrate on a loose thread on the sofa arm, to make

**299**

its frayed cream colour her focus. If she let go of the thread she'd be falling.

"No."

Again she concentrated on the cream thread, holding on to it for dear life, afraid of what would happen if she moved her eyes from it. Her mouth wanted to form itself into a scream.

"Why?"

"Why did I take you? Why did I lie to you?" He gave the rasping laugh again. "God, Jess, you must want to kill me. I wish you would, in fact. Then we'd be even. Perhaps this —" he pointed to the oxygen cylinder and mask in the corner of the room — "is punishment enough." He seemed to slump. "But you want answers. Of course."

"Of course I bloody want answers." The rage was starting to build now. She stood. "Why?" Her mother: baking her cakes, reading her stories, taking her into her own bed in the night when she'd had bad dreams to stroke her hair and talk gently to her, her mother, stolen from her. The farm. Rachel. The games in the farmyard. All taken away. Replaced with the year in the dusty outback with the growling farm dogs. The remains of her childhood spent in this humid, distant township and a stuffy boarding school.

"What were you thinking?" Her hands were clenched into fists. She could have smashed them into his face. The blood was steaming inside her head now. He didn't flinch.

"I don't know. I saw things. Perhaps they weren't there. I thought you were in danger."

300

"Who from?"

"Your mother."

She tried to speak and choked.

"I can't explain, Jess. It's as though I was possessed. And Martha told me you were in danger."

She was shaking now. "You thought my mother would harm me? Why in God's name did you believe that bitch?"

"It's a funny thing, Jess, but the pain clears my head. It's like a probe which forces me to see what's true. I can see now that I was deranged. Insane. I haven't known what was real and what wasn't since they stood me in the blazing sun for all those days. You think I'm making excuses? Of course you do. You hate me."

"Yes, I hate you."

"You want to kill me. I don't blame you."

"I'm not going to bloody kill you. I'm not going to make this easy for you. Even if you're about to die, you can face what you've done. You can face it and you can give me answers. And then I'm going to consider whether I ring the police." She heard herself and gave a bitter laugh. What would be the point? What could the law do to him that illness wouldn't accomplish within the next day or so?

"Your mother wasn't harming you, was she?" He sounded sad. "Poor little Evie. How could I imagine she'd hurt a fly? Always such a gentle child, good with the animals, too. Yet Martha told me your mother couldn't manage the animals, that they were getting sick and she was finding it hard to look after you alongside everything else. Martha said you were suffering. I had to trust her. She's always been part of my life. She's known me from the day I was born."

That wrinkled face with its staring eyes, always coming upon them while they were playing, talking of the old days, when Robert and Matthew helped their father and Martha was such an important part of their lives. *It's not for me to say but I know that old Mr Winter depended on me for the sheep . . . During the war I was there to keep an eye on things . . . I never liked to leave the farm after your father died, Jess. I know he'd have wanted me to stay . . .*

"The evil old cow." Jessamy struck out with her foot, catching the oxygen cylinder and sending it towards the wall. The mask would be out of his reach now. "You listened to her and let her persuade you to do this." A group of rosellas outside shrieked a kweet-kweet of panic.

"In the camp we'd hear birds make a noise like that when something was going to happen. Sometimes I wonder why I ended up back in the tropics." He sounded far away now. "Sometimes I'm still there, Jessamy. I'm in those forests and I'm trying to run away with Noi but they're catching up with us."

"What's still happening?"

"The little girl, Noi. I didn't look after her properly. But then she had a bad fever and I stayed by her. I think she got well again but I'm not sure. That might have been Evie." He peered at her through his yellow eyes. "Or was that you, Jess?"

"It was me, I had the fever." But Jessamy's thoughts were all with Evie, still thinking her daughter was dead.

**302**

"I could ring her." She glanced at the phone. "I could pick up that receiver and find out her telephone number and ring her. Right now."

"I wanted to protect you, Noi."

"My name is Jessamy," she screamed. "And you stole me from my mother." Her heart was going to burst right out of her chest. "How the hell could you have ever thought you were protecting me by taking me from my mother?"

He shook his head and let it slump to one shoulder. "Tell her . . ."

"I could tell her that I'm in the same room as my abductor and that he was my own uncle. I could tell her that all the pain she's felt over the last twenty-five years was caused by her own brother-in-law." Jessamy thought of her twins, how she felt when they spent holidays without her with their father. But to imagine them gone, dead, vanished, to wait for years without a definite answer . . . She thought she might actually vomit. "How could you do this?" She watched him. "Robert . . .?" He gave no sign of having heard. His breathing was harsh and there were pauses between each breath. She waited for a minute before going over to him and touching his shoulder. No response. She turned away before her hand could pick up a cushion and hold it over his face until his lungs gave out. Or perhaps she could just leave the room and let him die: alone, untended, like a wild animal. Would he realize he'd been abandoned? Serve him right. He was nothing to her, nothing at all. He moaned and muttered something. "Noi? Read . . . letters in drawer. Please . . . read."

"What letters?"

"Drawer . . . by bed . . . please read . . ."

She shook her head, picked up her car keys and walked out of the room, letting herself out of the house. She sat in her car and switched on the engine.

Then she switched off the engine, picked up her cell phone and called for an ambulance.

# CHAPTER
# FORTY

**Rachel**
**2003**

"I was still so angry I didn't want to read them," Jessamy said. "I waited a day or so after his death. He'd addressed them to my mother. It felt . . . weird. As though there was some kind of relationship between them."

"Perhaps there was."

"She was just a kid back in the war." She reached into her rucksack. "Here. Want to read them?" She pulled out a small bundle, held together with a couple of rubber bands.

The offer was made almost offhandedly. But I sensed my cousin wanted me to look at the letters. I took them from her and undid the bands. The letters were arranged in date order, starting in 1942.

"You can save some time by going straight to November 1943," Jessamy said. "That's when things really started falling apart for Robert. The seeds were already sown but he might have come back to England a sane man if it hadn't been for . . ." She nodded at the pile. "Well, you'll see for yourself."

# Kanburi Camp, 14 November 1943

Dear Evie,

Today. It must be today. There's word they'll move us further up into the mountains in another forced march. Matthew will not survive. The malaria has left him so weak and the ulcer on his leg has poisoned the skin so that the bone is now visible. We need medicines and there are none.

I have saved a large amount of baht. "It's not worth it, Bobby," Matthew told me. "Don't take the risk. I expect I'll do just fine without quinine and iodine and all those things."

He didn't mention the leg. He must know that the stench of the ulcer hits us before we've even entered the hut.

"You're mad if you chance it, Winter," said Macgregor from his mat, where he sat counting his snails in their biscuit tin. Macgregor has been farming snails for their nutritional value. He does quite good trade. "Word is the Japs have paid the guards extra to hunt out spies. Spy being anyone they don't like the look of."

"It might be dangerous for the girl, too," said Matthew.

"Don't worry about the Thai," said Macgregor. "Worry more for your own skin. And ours." He gave an apologetic cough. "If they search this hut and find your letters it's the Kempeitai for you."

We see the Japanese security police, the Kempeitai, as Europeans do the Gestapo.

"Mightn't be a bad idea to move the letters, old man," said Matthew.

I know a tree stump by the cesspit, a place nobody sane would insert their fingers for fear of kraits.

## 15 November 1943

Something is happening here. The guards are restless. They search us each time we leave the camp, looking for something. Radios? Three more British officers were dragged out of their huts today.

## Two days later

Still no quinine because there's no sign of Noi. The traders keep themselves to themselves at the moment. Apparently the Nips are convinced that a spy ring is operating here. They think POWs use the traders to pass information God knows where. But I look at my brother and I know he will never again see the farm if we can't get the quinine and something for the ulcer. He is the eldest Winter, the heir. Dad wanted him to have Winter's Copse. I've always known that and accepted it, too.

Just thinking of the cool, clean, green of the Downs is cruel as I sit writing this on my fetid mat, my skin a mass of sores and insect bites, constantly dripping with sweat. Mum would hang out the sheets on a breezy day and tell us the wind shooting up from the west, from the Bristol Channel and the Atlantic itself would act as a natural disinfectant. "Clean air keeps people healthy," she said. This tropical air is like a germ-ridden damp cloth round the body.

I saw Noi this morning with some other children by a stall in the town. The guards were using their bayonets to flick up the cloths covering the stalls. I had to take a chance. Noi gave me a half-smile and looked away. I called her. She gave a slight shake of the head and vanished behind the stall. I cursed, I'd scared her. She was just a kid, for God's sake, same age as Evie when Evie first came to the farm. Unfair to rely on her like this. But then I thought of my brother, shivering on his mat, too sick to come out on the working party. Any day the Japs might take him out and shoot him, "in mercy" as they put it. The thought steeled me. I looked around for another Thai trader. Noi had been trustworthy, wouldn't someone else be?

A middle-aged man arranging mangoes in a basket made eye contact as I walked past. "You want something, mistah?"

I shook my head.

"You need eggs? Soap?" I walked on.

"Medicine?" He almost threw the line away as though he'd given up the attempt to sell to me.

"Quinine," I said. The word just fell out of my mouth.

"You pay how much?"

I took most of the baht out of my pocket, keeping some back. He nodded, looking satisfied.

"On way back to camp tomorrow." His eyes dropped down to the mangoes.

## 18 November

I think the God I prayed to in the cool church back in Craven with the pools of light dripping from the stained glass has left me.

And I deserve to be abandoned. I deserve the broken wrist of my left hand, which I've tried to bind with my shirt so that it doesn't hang loose, and which was the parting present of the guards before they locked me in this cell. I'll write what happened.

The day after I spoke to the trader we were working on the line as usual. The sleepers are nearly all laid now and we were sent on ahead about a quarter of a mile to cut down trees. This work tears the hands. Each cut, each splinter, becomes septic in the tropical heat. Suddenly, from behind one of the carts we use for transporting spoil came Noi, running to me, her face pale. "No buy quinine." She glanced over her shoulder and I saw she was scared. "Japanese look."

"I need quinine, Noi. My brother . . ."

I don't know if she understood the word, she stared at me blankly.

I touched my heart. "Brother ill." I placed my hand on my brow and pretended to wipe it. "Quinine good."

"No!" She shook her head again. "No go for quinine." Then she ran off again.

We finished our shift and walked back to the town along the railway. The stallholders had gone. I looked for the man who'd offered me the quinine. No sign of him. As we reached the teak trees someone stood out from the shadows and pulled my sleeve. "Mistah." The mango seller. The guards had gone on ahead, hidden by a curve in the path. "Quinine in here, is safer." I followed him into the shade. He was right, we were almost completely hidden from the path, I could buy the quinine unobserved.

He led me on through the undergrowth. "Very good iodine. And I have also disinfectant as well as iodine."

I could stock up, be prepared for the next infectious illness.

"Not far."

"Where are we going?" I was growing nervous, too much time was passing, if the guards turned round and counted the prisoners on the track they'd soon spot I'd gone.

"I have other things, too. You like aspirin?"

My temptation must have flickered over my face because he increased his pace so that I was almost running to keep up with him. The macaques in the branches overhead gave warning chatters and swung away from us.

Then she was running towards me. Noi. Hand held out to stop me, she was shaking her head, "Man bad!"

That chattering in the jungle ahead of me wasn't gibbons any more. It was the guards. Even the birds seemed to have grown silent.

Noi pulled me by the hand, dragging me along. "Back to track." Behind us boots pounded. Above us a shot cracked. I pushed Noi towards the trees. Another gun fired. We crouched in the undergrowth. I could make out the caps of the guards above the bushes. A centipede wriggled on a branch just above Noi's head and I longed to swipe it away.

The hand on my shoulder sent me flying face-first into the bush. Thorns pierced my skin. When I stood I saw they had Noi and were dragging her off, a tiny figure, face grey and rigid. "Let her go," I shouted. "She's done nothing."

"You spy too," the guard shouted.

"Child, just ten." I held up my fingers to show them. "Not spy." His answer was to swing the butt of his rifle into my solar plexus. When I could rise to my feet again I was winded.

Noi seemed to have turned to marble in their grasp. Now I understand what being petrified means. More men came towards us. The mango seller and more guards. He nodded towards me and muttered something. "Tell them," I pointed at Noi, "tell them she's not involved."

He mumbled at the guards. One of them laughed. In a movement so casual it might almost have been accidental he aimed the gun at the trader and pulled the trigger while the man was still finishing his sentence. For a second the trader stayed on his feet, looking no more than mildly surprised, before he crumpled to the ground. Noi screamed. The guard holding her gave her a push towards the body on the ground, just as it gave a final twitch.

I saw something small and bright fall from her pocket. The wooden doll I had made for her. Above our heads the frightened gibbons were still screeching a protest and I could hear the urgent flaps of hornbill wings. My lips were still moving in pleas. ~~Noi was looking towards me in appeal, lips opening as she begged me to help her. I was seeing her as I'd first seen her on that barge and also seeing you, Evie, as I'd first set eyes on you, standing in that village hall, a small frightened evacuee, gas mask round her neck. Still Noi called to me and now her voice was yours. But the guards held me tight. I don't think I even heard the shot: my mind was so full of images and memories. Her body was so light there'd have been no sound as she dropped to the ground.~~

I pulled myself from my captors and ran to her where she lay on the forest floor. ~~The red mark on her chest was like a single ruby. It didn't seem enough to have done its terrible work.~~ Her eyes were still open and for a second they shone with the last of her life. "Noi." I held her in my arms. But already the eyes had lost their brightness. I wanted to tell her I was sorry, that I'd never meant this, that I should have looked away from her that day I first clapped eyes on her on that painted barge.

The gibbons stopped their screaming and I could hear the insects again, very loud now, as though someone had turned up the volume. Even as they were dragging me off I wanted to put my hands over my ears to block out the sound.

312

The last thing I saw was the doll, lying among the ferns and mosses. Still with its perfect little smile.

## Later

They haven't searched me yet and I am writing this quickly before they do. I am waiting now, waiting for them to come for me. First will come the forty-eight hours standing out in the sun, perhaps extended to three days if they feel like it. Then perhaps I'll be removed to the town for the Kempeitai to work on me. But more will follow: it is never just the one punishment. And it could end with a bullet to my neck, I know that.

I didn't take care of that little girl. I let her down. I can never make up for that.

Evie, I shouldn't tell you all this, you're just a kid, just thirteen. You'll almost certainly never get this scribble, anyway. If I ever do make it home I'm going to take such good care of you and your brother. And Matthew. I can tell you what I'm frightened of. Evie, I'm afraid I'm losing my sense of what's real. Sometimes you seem to stand in front of me, in this cell. You're holding Noi's doll but I know that's all wrong. I want to hit my head against the floor so that I force myself back into reality. This cell stinks. I do, too. I can't write any more, I'm tired.

God bless you all. Watch over the farm for us. And Fly. He's such a good dog.

I will push this letter through the slats of the . . .

**313**

# CHAPTER
# FORTY-ONE

I finished reading. I didn't know what to say. The picture I'd been building up of Robert Winter as some kind of monster was starting to dissolve. And I saw what? A sad, almost pathetic man who'd tried hard to cling on to his humanity and optimism. "Poor Robert." I spoke so softly Jessamy could hardly have heard me but she nodded.

"He must have known the letters were important. He kept them all. I don't know if he ever reread them, though. I wish he had, it might have helped. Might have stopped it spilling into the rest of his life."

Spilling into *her* life.

She picked up one of the rubber bands and started twisting it in her fingers. "Even if he'd shown the letters to Mum in 1945 it might have made a difference."

"Didn't Matthew read them before he gave them back to Robert?"

She shook her head. "They were addressed to Mum."

Reliable, honourable Matthew: not one to read another person's letters. But perhaps it would have been better if he had done. At least the family would have had some insight into the disturbed man who'd come back home. Would it have made any difference to the way events unfolded? I couldn't be sure.

"Did reading the letters change the way you thought about Robert?" I asked as gently as I could. I sensed my cousin had almost reached the limits of her ability to discuss her past.

"Yes." She blinked. "And I feel disloyal to Mum just saying that. But it did. That little girl in the jungle, I think what happened to her haunted him. They broke his mind in jail and he could never come back, not properly." She'd twisted the band as far as she could and now she let one end go and it spun in her fingers.

"She was about nine or ten, same age as you were when you disappeared." I felt a headache coming on and pressed my fingers against my temples, trying to push it away.

"Robert regained consciousness just before he died. He was actually quite lucid for about an hour. He told me about Noi. After he'd written that letter they took him outside again and made him stand outside the officers' mess in the heat for two days and nights. He wasn't allowed to sit or lie. He was given no water. And all the time he was grieving for the little girl, for Noi. And worrying about his brother. He thought the letters would be safe in the hollow but perhaps it had been risky to tell Matthew where they were."

She shifted her position on the hard kitchen chair. "Lucky for both of them that the Japanese didn't find that last letter he wrote, either. When the two days and nights were up they took him off to the town, to the headquarters of the Japanese security police. They put him in a hutch, that's literally what it was, a hutch, for another day. Still no water or food. Then they started torturing him: half drowning him in a bath. Beating the soles of his feet. They were convinced he was part of a spy ring but obviously he could tell them nothing about it. Finally they gave up and they sent him all the way back to Singapore Island, to a jail so awful that Changi was a holiday camp by comparison. There was more forced labour: breaking boulders, and more torture, and some attempt at a show trial in front of a Japanese judge. But he was so sick they had to let him go to Changi for hospital treatment and he managed to string out his stay there until the atomic bombs fell on Japan and the war ended."

"And he came back here to the farm." And found that life was impossible.

"He couldn't shake off the memories. At night he had bad dreams. Things would set it off . . ." Her voice trailed away. "There was this awful time in Brisbane when he came to take me out of school for the weekend. We were walking along the street. I had an ice cream, a Blue Ribbon Heart, my favourite. There were lots of Japanese businessmen in that part of the world and two of them came out of a hotel. They'd probably been drinking in the bar but they didn't mean to bump into me. The ice cream fell onto my shirt. It was chocolate and the shirt was white. I was upset. They started to giggle. They were just drunk and embarrassed, that was all. Harmless. But Robert . . ." She put her knuckles to her mouth.

"What?"

"He knocked them both down and wouldn't stop kicking them. They were screaming at him to stop and I was trying to pull them off. 'Don't you touch Noi!' he was screaming. 'Don't you touch her!' Someone called the police and they wanted to take him down to the station and charge him. But the Japanese men were really decent about it and said they wanted to let it go. I was crying by them and trying to explain that it wasn't them, it was something that had happened in the war, in Thailand. One of the men told me his brother had been killed in some battle near the Burmese border. He'd travelled along that damn railway that Robert had helped build. 'I hate railway,' he said. Then he was patting Robert on the back and telling him again and again how sorry he was. And Robert was just standing there, completely baffled, as if he didn't know where he was. 'You dropped your doll,' he told me. 'I don't have a doll,' I said."

She retreated into herself, not speaking for a while.

"It must have been so hard for you," I said, as gently as I could. "Not knowing what would act as a trigger. Your life must have been so . . . difficult."

She forced a smile. "I grew up," she said, her voice shaking slightly. "I had a decent education and I was able to go off to college in America and meet my future husband. That marriage was good for quite a long while and it gave me my kids. My business has gone well, too, and that's kept me sane."

I studied her face, still watchful and closed, and wondered. But perhaps it had only been the events of the last month which had forged that expression. Her

317

eyes still sparked in a way that reminded me of her younger self. But that was perhaps the only sign of Evie in her. In maturity Jessamy had grown to look less like her mother and more like her father: the Winter genes had asserted themselves.

"But in all that time before you knew the truth you were never tempted to do what all Australians do and come to England to see the old country and hunt out family? Or visit your mother's grave at least?"

"I thought of the farm, of the village, but I knew that if I came here I'd distress Robert. I wondered about contacting Martha, but something . . ." She wound her fingers together. "Something stopped me. Robert hardly mentioned her. I wondered whether she'd died, too. Then I married and had the kids and it all started to fall apart. We had to work hard to keep our house going and the nursery business solvent. There was never time to plan a trip apart from to far north Queensland to visit Robert once or twice a year."

"You must have been fond of him." I was starting to understand more of the complexities binding the two of them together.

She sighed. "I can't explain the relationship between us. We'd spent so much time together that we were very close, probably closer than most fathers and daughters." She must have caught the look of something on my face. "Not close like that, there was never any . . . It wasn't sexual, Rache."

I bowed my head. I hadn't had Robert Winter down as a paedophile but in our erotically obsessed times it was hard not to see sex in every relationship.

"He was always just like an uncle to me. But we meant everything to one another, God damn him." She came to a halt again and put her hands over her face. I wanted to wrap her up in my arms but didn't dare do it, not yet. She was like a frightened deer and I was scared too much show of emotion would scare her off.

"There was another letter, Rachel." She took her hands away and reached into her rucksack again, pulling out a white envelope. "Written to Mum and dated just weeks before I went up to see him for the last time. Never posted."

## Cardew Plantation, 1 February 2003

Dear Evie,

I see you and I don't see you and sometimes it's you who's here with me and sometimes it's Noi. And sometimes it's Jessamy, too. I think I know which one of you it is, but I don't. And then the drug starts to wear off a little and I remember that you've all grown up and left me and I'm in this bungalow with just the carer. But Jessamy will visit me soon, staying until the end, probably. She's been so good to me.

When I came back from the war you didn't look like the little girl I'd written to. You'd become a young woman. I didn't expect that. Stupid, really. I think I melded your image onto Noi's and made one child I wanted to save. I scared you so badly, didn't I, that night up on the Ridgeway when you hid among the old Sarsens? I scared myself, too. That's why I left so abruptly. I sound sane to myself when I write these things down. Perhaps I should have carried on writing after I left Thailand. Perhaps it would have helped to clear my head.

In 1977 Martha told me that the farm was having problems. She said you were under strain and you were taking it out on the child, Matthew's only child, and that I should come and get her. "She's the last of the Winters," Martha said. The last of the Winters. All those centuries of grinding hard work to build up the farm, all culminating in little Jess. And Matthew wasn't there to protect the girl and look after Winter's Copse, his beloved farm.

How could I believe that you would harm your own daughter, you will ask? How, knowing you as I did, could I possibly think that was true? Hadn't I seen you looking after the animals on the farm, never once losing your temper?

I don't know. Psychotic episodes. That's what I have self-diagnosed by reading. I always was a highly strung lad, I think I told you that in one of my letters. Imprisonment by cruel guards was always going to be particularly hard for me. Not that I'm making excuses. I believe my problems really started in the jungle in Thailand when I saw them shoot Noi. It was as though all the threads in my mind undid themselves and I couldn't retie them again. A stronger man would have been able to pull them back into place.

I sound so logical as I read what I have written here but that is because the pain is pulling me back into reality. I won't take the next dose until I've finished this.

**320**

I watched you from the down in those weeks before the Jubilee. I watched you with the child and I couldn't see any problems. But always there was Martha telling me I was wrong, telling me to look at the bruises on Jess's legs, telling me the child herself had said that you'd done that to her. And who was I to trust myself? I had been so, so wrong about Noi.

Martha seemed like the only person who'd stayed the same. When I came back she was just as I remembered her. I didn't treat her well, Evie. But she was always loyal to me, no matter how I spurned her. She helped hide me when the barn burned down. We forgot about my motorbike, though. I'd left it in the lane. If the police had taken more of an interest in the fire they might have asked Martha some searching questions at the inquest. Be that as it may, Martha helped me get away to Holyhead, where I caught the boat to Ireland.

Perhaps I felt guilty about having turned away from her before, back in the war. That's why I kept in touch with her, writing occasional letters to her from Australia. And I came back to Craven at the time of the Coronation in 1953. You didn't see me, though. I watched you and Matthew. You were happy together. Martha wasn't very happy.

My guilt about her might have been the reason why I paid attention when Martha told me to take the child. "Just for a while," she said. "Do it for Matthew. Let poor Evie pull herself together and take care of things at Winter's Copse. It's hard being a widow and managing it all. Give it six months or a year and then we can see about sending Jess back to the farm."

Just a year, I thought. But then when Jessamy was with me I couldn't let her go. She was all I had: the only thing that wasn't spoiled. When she was with me the voices in my head seemed to die down.

The worst thing I did was tell Jess you were dead.

Thing is, Evie, I am no longer sure whether you're alive or not. Perhaps you did die. I can't always tell which of you is here. I pulled that jasmine plant out of this garden because the smell reminded me of Thailand. But sometimes I still think I'm there.

I know I'm dying. I don't know how to finish this.

I never stopped loving you. You won't believe it, but it's true.

I don't know what else to say to you.

Robert


"Psychotic episodes," I said when Jessamy had finished telling me the contents of the last letter. "He means he was off his rocker." The sympathy I felt for Robert Winter seemed to ebb and flow. I didn't think I'd ever be able to forgive him for what he'd done to my aunt. And to Jessamy.

"But the delusions took the same pattern: he was always trying to look after a little girl."

She put a hand to her mouth and yawned. I sensed that my own weariness had settled like cement into my bones. I could hardly bear the thought of hoisting myself upstairs to bed.

"Where would you like to sleep?" I asked Jessamy. "You can have your old room if you don't mind my sheets. Or . . ." I hesitated, thinking of Evie's bed, which I'd stripped but could be quickly made up. "There's your mother's, if . . ."

Her eyes filled again. "Yes," she whispered. "I'd like that. It would make me feel close to her again. When I was little and had nightmares I used to go into her at night."

I forced myself to stand. "That's where you'll sleep then."

We found sheets and quilt covers in the airing cupboard and with two of us it took only minutes to prepare the bed.

"There's something silly that's been on my mind." She straightened a pillowcase. "I let you think that it was you who dropped that baton in the relay. It was actually me."

I had to think hard to work out what she was talking about. Then I remembered. The races at the Silver Jubilee party, just before Jessamy left.

"I wasn't a very good loser."

"I forgot about that relay almost immediately."

"You were always generous, Rachel."

I laid a folded towel on the end of the bed. "Do you need anything else?"

"Everything I need is here." Jessamy laid a hand on one of the pillows and stared at it as though she could see her mother's face. The lump in my throat threatened to prevent me from breathing.

"Night then." I kissed her cold cheek and wondered how she'd sleep in that bed. "I'm just next door if you need anything. Just call."

"Rachel." She caught my sleeve. "You've been so kind. Thank you."

I shook my head, unable to say more. But as I undressed I knew I'd simply managed to keep some of the doubts and mixed emotions I'd felt under cover.

I fell into immediate sleep, deep and dreamless. I woke with cautious daylight slipping under the blind. Seven-thirty, my watch said. I wondered whether Jess wanted an early morning cup of tea. Last time I'd been in this house with her, twenty-five years ago, she'd woken before me and I'd met her in the farmyard coming back from a walk somewhere. Where had she been? I sat up in bed, trying to remember if she'd told me.

Of course. She'd been up on the hill talking to Martha. Because that's where Martha always was: up on the hill, looking down at us. My heart filled with a cold dread. I dressed quickly and ran downstairs. Jessamy was in the kitchen, pulling on a pair of rubber boots.

"There's one person I do blame even more than him, one person who generated all this misery." She stood.

"Where are you going?" But of course I knew. "To find Martha."

"I have to have it out with her."

The wind was still battering the house, seeming to want to force its way inside. The rain belted against the window-panes. "At least put on a decent coat, that light jacket won't keep out the wet." I sounded like Evie. But Jessamy put on the waterproof when I handed it to her.

"What are you doing?" she asked as I pulled on my own coat.

"Coming with you."

I thought she'd object but for a moment the hard expression on her face slipped. "C'mon then."

# CHAPTER
# FORTY-TWO

As we opened the kitchen door the wind seemed to grab it from us, flinging it open so that wet air gushed through the kitchen, rattling the cupboard doors and sending the papers pinned to Evie's fridge with magnets rustling to the floor.

With difficulty I shoved the door shut and followed my cousin into the lane, wind hitting us from the right, roaring in from the Atlantic and funnelling down the gap between the Downs, the Chilterns and the Cotswolds. I gasped as it hit me. It felt as though I was pushing myself back through the years, through history, almost, to a time when people had lived up on the Downs for months at a stretch, minding the sheep, cut off from the village by the weather and the nature of the work. I remembered Jess telling me unemotionally about Martha's mad Welsh drover forebear and wished I hadn't let that thought slip into my head. I recalled Martha's own stories about the White Horse leaping out of its chalk imprint and galloping over the down to have its hooves shod, and the ghostly drovers driving cattle along the Ridgeway. It was daylight but still these images chilled me. I glanced at my cousin and wondered whether she remembered any of these things.

326

As we climbed I almost expected to see myself and Jessamy as little girls running down the lane towards us, carrying the pots of honey or cakes which Martha'd given us. Rain ran into my eyes and down the back of my coat. We could wait until the weather calmed before making this visit: Martha would always be up here. We could go back and have breakfast by the range. The sky had taken on a dirty yellow tint. Evie had taught me what that meant at this time of year: snow. But Jess's set jaw told me she had no intention of postponing the encounter.

Something brushed my legs and I jumped. Pilot. Once my heart had stopped racing I was glad to see the dog. "Come here, boy." He walked beside me and I rested my right hand on his wet back.

Martha's cottage ought to have been pretty; it was built of the same Sarsen and chalk stone as Winter's Copse and the chocolate-box cottages in the village, with the same muted orange brickwork picking out the outlines of its windows. But green damp patches flecked the walls and the roof lacked several tiles. The gate hung off a single hinge and creaked in the breeze. I forced myself to follow my cousin up the path. She rapped on the door. No answer. Martha had probably risen early to carry out her usual patrol of the hillside. Pilot barked, obviously believing us to be insane to stand here in the wet.

"Let's go back," I said, shivering as the rain ran into my eyes and plastered my hair to my cheeks. But Jessamy's answer was to turn the door handle. It wasn't locked.

The cottage felt damp and probably would have done so even if the sun had blazed outside. "Hello!" Jess called. "Anyone home?" She stood, hands on hips, lips pursed, ready to demand answers. But I noticed how her lip trembled.

Nothing.

She walked inside and I followed. "Stay here," I told the dog, pointing to the front door mat.

Martha's walls sported no pictures. There were no vases or photographs on the few pieces of old, dark furniture in the rooms. "Where is she?" Jessamy scowled. "You'd think she'd come inside from this rain." But Martha and her ancestors had spent their lives up on the hill in all weathers; she'd be impervious to rain. I followed Jessamy through the house and into the kitchen, scrubbed but spartan, with a green lino floor and old Formica kitchen cabinets. An old television set sat on the dresser. I couldn't remember ever coming in here. One of the shrubs in the overgrown garden swayed backwards and forwards in the wind, tapping the windowpane. The kitchen overlooked the down, where the Winters' sheep had grazed for centuries. A perfect vantage spot for one who'd seen herself as the family's sentry, always on duty. The thought made me shiver. I tugged at Jessamy's sleeve. "Let's go. We shouldn't —" I couldn't finish the sentence.

Someone moved behind me. An old woman, all in black, clutching a shepherd's crook, stood in the doorway, her eyes like two searchlights.

"I didn't mean to scare you." One of the old woman's black-clad arms reached out and her hand touched Jessamy's sleeve. It reminded me of a crow's talon. "I've just been out checking the lambs."

Lambs which didn't belong to the Winters any longer; animals for which Martha had no responsibility. Something in her genes refused to let her adapt to the changed circumstances of life in the early twenty-first century.

"Jessamy, my love," she said, staring at her. Jessamy was silent.

"Hello, Martha," I said, to break the spell. "I haven't seen you for a long time. Though I suppose you'll come to the funeral next week." I was speaking slowly, quietly, because Martha scared me. I think she'd probably always scared me, in a way I hadn't noticed because she was always so good to us. Tonight she seemed to be one of Macbeth's Weird Sisters. She could only be four or five years older than Evie, but a hard outdoor life had weathered her skin. Her eyes were still the same strange, almost greeny-blue colour but filmed and milky now. Her gaze seemed unfocused, as though she was looking beyond the kitchen to something we couldn't see.

"I saw you," she told Jessamy. "You were at the house that day. You went to the hospital when Evie was dying. You spoke to her before she passed?"

Jessamy nodded.

"She knew where you'd been?"

"I didn't have time to tell her." I could see a vein stand up in Jessamy's arm as Martha gripped it. "Her heart gave out before I could finish."

The look she gave Martha was penetrating. "I didn't have time to tell her the woman she employed on her farm had conspired to have me kidnapped." She shook herself free.

"Robert wanted the child with him. It seemed for the best." Martha spoke matter-of-factly. "He was family. I knew Jess'd be safe out there."

"You wanted to separate me from my mother?" Jessamy's voice rose. "Why?"

"You'd be better off away from her, my dear. That's what Martha thought." She nodded. "And seems I was right. Look at the woman you've become." She smiled at Jessamy. "Robert did a grand job with you."

"Why? What the hell possessed you?" I asked. "You must have known you were doing something completely evil."

"Evie was no fit mother for you, Jess," she said, ignoring me. "And she wasn't coping well with the farm."

Jessamy and I looked at one another in confusion.

"The cows had TB. Robert and Matthew's precious herd. Built up by their father before them."

"A single case of TB!" Jessamy spat. "Three reactors. So unusual that I remember it after all this time."

"There were other things." Martha folded her arms.

"Don't tell me. She lost an occasional ewe. The fox got into the chicken shed. Things that happen on every farm in this parish."

"Farming is a hard business. Evie found it hard to look after a child and mind the farm." Martha still spoke in the same calm tone.

Jessamy's lips were pursed together. She seemed to be finding it hard to speak.

"Evie was struggling," Martha went on. "That's what I told the police when they came up here to ask me those questions after the Silver Jubilee party."

"What?" I took a step towards her. She eyed me without showing any anxiety. "What did you say to the police?"

"I said there was always trouble at Winter's Copse and had been from the moment Evie arrived in 1940. I said young Jess had probably run away because her mother wasn't able to give her enough care."

Jessamy shook her arm free. "Why did you tell those lies?"

"I was meant for Robert Winter, not her." The old woman spoke with utter conviction.

"You?" I couldn't help the incredulity in my voice. I was comparing my aunt with this dishevelled woman with her staring eyes.

"He and I were in love before he went off to fight. There was an understanding between us."

I wondered whether Robert had allowed himself a last fling with Martha in preparation for the years ahead of him in the army. He wouldn't have been the first young man to take advantage of a willing girl. I felt a kernel of pity for her. Had she waited and waited for him to come back to her, building what had happened between them into a declaration of intent?

"When we were children Matthew, Robert and I played in the farmyard together, jumping off the bales in the barn. I showed them where the adders lie out on the chalk on hot afternoons. I taught them how to save a lamb that was dead to the touch." Jess started to say something but Martha held up a hand. "We went to school together. When they were older they took me out rabbiting in the copse at night. We went to all the country fairs together and Matthew and Robert bought me rides on the merry-go-round. The Winters and the Stourtons belonged together. If I couldn't have Robert I should have had Matthew." Her voice rose on the last words.

"Robert loved my mother," Jessamy said evenly. "So did Matthew. Both of them loved Evie."

"They were taken in by her with her pretty way of doing things and her trim little figure. When I told Robert how things were he saw clearly again."

I glared at Martha, the kernel of pity inside me fragmenting. I could have twisted every bone in her old body.

"I told him that this farm was going to pieces," she went on. "And his niece needed taking care of, Matthew's girl, his own flesh and blood."

"Why?" asked Jessamy, dangerously quiet now. "What was Mum supposed to have done to me?"

"She'd been beating you."

I looked at Jessamy. "Beating you?" I couldn't even remember Evie as much as slapping the backs of Jess's legs or tapping her on the hand.

She looked puzzled too. "Mum never hit me. Not once. Not even a slap." She moved closer to Martha. "What do you mean?"

"I found you with bruises on your legs and black eyes and you said it was your mother."

"Jess would have been joking," I shouted. "You know, a joke, when you say something you don't mean? Children do it all the time."

"You knew I didn't mean it, Martha." Jessamy's face was white. "You knew Robert was sick in his mind and he'd believe your stories."

She shuffled. "Maybe he wasn't himself."

"Maybe? He was probably psychotic." She looked at me blankly. "He should have been having psychiatric treatment," I went on, "not running off with a ten-year-old child."

"I would have done anything to make him happy." This I could well believe. "He was so lonely, living in foreign parts by himself. I thought that having a youngster with him for a visit would pull him out of his troubles." Even now she sounded so sure of herself. "I knew Robert would look after you and it would only be for six months or a year. By then Evie would have gone."

"Gone?"

She looked at me. "I didn't think she'd carry on after Jess left. I thought she'd give up the farm and go back to the city."

My mouth opened to ask her what she thought would have happened when Evie's daughter had returned. Surely she knew that the police would have been called. She and Robert would have gone to prison.

But on Planet Martha Evie would have returned to a city she hadn't lived in for decades, leaving Martha and Robert in the farmhouse together. Perhaps with Jessamy living with them. My mouth opened.

"It was jealousy, plain and simple. You did this to spite Evie."

"I thought he'd bring the child back. I didn't think he'd keep her all those years. It was just to show —"

"Just to show my mother that she couldn't have it all: the farm, the status, the child." Jessamy folded her arms in front of her chest. Her eyes were like shards of glass.

"Did you summon Robert over here in 1977 specifically to take Jess?" I asked.

Martha's lantern-eyes gazed at me as though I were speaking in a foreign language. "Robert wanted to come back for the Silver Jubilee anyway. He always liked the traditions and he'd been home for the Coronation, though he didn't show himself to anyone. Just me and old Mrs Winter." Her expression was smug. "He stayed here with me. But then he went away again. But I wrote to him from time to time. And when he heard what I had to say about Evie he thought the child should go with him. He wanted her to be safe. I told him I'd help him get a passport for her so he could take her away with him."

She'd stolen Jessamy's birth certificate from the house, I guessed. And used it to apply for the passport.

"You preyed on his disturbed state," Jessamy said. "You exploited his broken mind with your lies. You were an accessory. More than that. An accomplice."

"An accessory to the abduction of a child," I said. "That's a very serious crime. Even though you're old now you'll go to court." She was old but I hated her, hated her so much I could have spat at her. "You did a terrible thing. You're responsible for Evie's death. Her heart stopped working when she saw her daughter again after all those years, it couldn't take the strain. You deserve to die in prison."

She nodded, seeming to shrink into herself, suddenly meek. "I see that now. I'm sorry."

Just that one word, sorry. I thought of my aunt, of her years of waiting to hear what had befallen her daughter, wishing herself in a coma until Jessamy reappeared. I saw her watching the TV news each time a child's body was discovered, shaking, wide-eyed. I replayed the telephone conversations I'd had with her each time the police had called her to tell her the body didn't belong to her Jessamy. I recalled the mixture of relief and horror and guilt I'd heard in her voice each time that had happened. "Some other mother's child," she'd whisper. "And I was on my knees, Rachel, thanking God. But now I feel sick with myself because some other mother has lost all hope now. But then a little part of me even wishes it was Jessamy they'd found so at least I'd know."

I thought of Jessamy, fed lies about her mother, uncertain what or who to believe, robbed of home, friends, her pony and dog, the morning walk down the lane to the village school. And I thought of Robert, poor Robert, who'd been damaged beyond repair. I shuddered at the malign conjunction which had placed such a damaged man within Martha's orbit.

I knew Martha was old, probably senile, but I could have struck her with my fists until she bled in front of me and wept for mercy. What mercy had she shown Evie? The police inquiries, Evie's newspaper appeals, all ignored, dismissed because of that corrosive jealousy.

Sorry. Just that, for all she'd done, for the quarter-century of pain.

"I can't stand here looking at you any longer." I got up and walked out of the cottage. Pilot was waiting on the doorstep and followed me into the lane, his ears pricked into courteous enquiry. I walked so quickly I was almost jogging, mindless of puddles and potholes, the dog's paws splashing behind me. My fury drove out any lingering fears I might have possessed about phantom drovers and their flocks. I saw the white walls of Winter's Copse in front of me and broke into a run until I reached the gate. For a moment I stood there, the sleety rain falling gently on me, letting it wash me. I felt calmer just standing in front of the old house. I opened the gate and walked to the kitchen door, heart rate slowing. When I went inside I stood for a second letting the warmth of the place ooze into my cells, as though it was flushing out the madness I'd witnessed in the cottage.

I stood at the window, staring out towards the front garden where the film of the child Jessamy had once been taken. Bushes swayed in the still-lively breeze. I clenched my fists hard then forced myself to let out all my breath.

*It's over.* I almost looked round to see if Evie was really standing there in the kitchen with us; her voice seemed as clear as the church bell.

*Are you at peace now?* I asked her, wordlessly.

I heard nothing, but there was something in the quality of the silence and the deep tock of the clock on the wall which made me believe she was. *All is well*, my aunt seemed to tell me. *Be at peace too, Rachel.*

And I answered her wordlessly. *It will continue, what you and Matthew wanted: your child will live in this house again with her children, maybe even get the farm going again.* Jessamy hadn't said this to me but how could I doubt it? Jessamy's ease in Winter's Copse had proved that although she'd been away for twenty-five years she belonged here completely in a way I never could. Why couldn't she run a plant nursery here?

This recognition might once have made me feel resentful or sad but not now. My life was elsewhere. Something was pulling me towards the future: unknown and slightly scary, but exciting, too. I put a hand on my abdomen, just below my navel and remembered the package from the chemist's. It was still in my handbag.

I plucked the bag from the kitchen chair and went upstairs to the bathroom. When I'd taken the test and it had shown me the result I went to sit at the top of the stairs for a few minutes, just as I'd once done with Jessamy when we were children. I sat motionless while the disordered atoms of my world rearranged themselves into something new.

It felt as though I'd been up there for hours and hours but it was probably only about fifteen minutes later that I came downstairs again. Through the white noise of my own pre-occupations I heard the garden gate click open. Jessamy was back. She came inside. I tried to read the look of concentration on her face, to work out what had happened.

"Have you rung the police?" I asked carefully.

She shook her head. "Not yet." She looked so pale I rushed to her and steered her to a chair.

"I shouldn't have left you alone up there with her."

"She's no danger to me, not any more. Not to anyone." She sounded strange.

"What do you mean, Jess?"

"Martha's gone back up the hill. Without a coat. With that old shepherd's crook of hers, that old crook she used when we went blackberrying."

I remembered the blackberrying.

"The rain's turning to sleet now and the temperature's dropping." She spoke as though she were reading from an autocue. "Martha's tough but she's old now. You could ring for an ambulance, Rachel. It would probably take at least half an hour to get here and we don't know exactly where Martha is. She could be anywhere up on the down."

"Why's she done this?"

"She said she wanted to do one last check on everything, to make sure that all was well. She said goodbye to me and apologized for all the sorrow she'd caused."

She held out her mobile phone. "Go on, ring for help, if you want. Or tell me we should go up on that hillside and find her. Tell me that, Rachel. I'll do it if you say we have to." Her expression was reflective, neither angry nor anxious.

My hand was reaching for the phone but I pulled away. Let Martha take her chances. I thought of the old woman up there, lashed by the wind and sleet from the west, her eyes gazing down the hill towards the farmhouse, watching over Jessamy, watching over the last of the Winters, finally back where she belonged. I thought of Martha turning her face towards the icy downpour, untroubled by the chill, standing there on watch, always on watch.

The picture moved me but not as much as I might have expected. I was starting to feel distanced from it all. Other things mattered almost as much. I hardly dared tell myself what was happening to me.

I took the mobile. "I do need to make a call, actually," I said. "I left my phone at a neighbour's the day before yesterday and the landline's disconnected. Do you mind if I ring my husband Luke?"

"Be my guest." She stood. "I'm going to have a shower, if that's all right. Then I'll ring my kids and you and I can sit down and talk and you can tell me all about your husband."

"Luke . . ." Thank God it wasn't his voicemail I reached.

"Rachel. I've been worried sick, you haven't been answering my calls to your mobile." He sounded frantic. "I thought . . . well, I didn't know what to think, actually. Are you all right? The weather sounds dreadful there. The forecast says you're in for snow."

"It is dreadful but some very exciting things have been happening." I hesitated, not knowing how to start. "Are you sitting down? You won't believe this."

He didn't. Not for about ten minutes. "Jessamy's come back?" he kept saying. "She was alive all this time? Where did she go? Why did it take her so long to come back? I don't understand. Tell me who Robert Winter was, again." Finally I managed to persuade him to stop asking questions long enough for me to paste the facts together into some kind of recognizable narrative. "Pyschiatrists would have a field day with this," he said when I finished. "That sad and crazy man. And that jealous woman. What an appalling thing to do: take revenge on your love rival by helping to abduct their kid."

But something else was on my mind now.

"Martha's gone up on the hillside," I said. "It's snowing here now. She's over eighty. What should we do?"

There was silence. "She's a shepherd?"

I could almost hear his logical mind working on it.

"Her family have lived in Craven for centuries, she knows what conditions are like up there." I heard his out-breath. "Let her go, Rachel."

"I think she's a bit senile. She may not be mentally switched-on enough to know what she's doing."

"Do you know her well?" he asked sharply.

"Not really."

"Well then, it's not for you to decide on her frame of mind. Let her stay up there," he said. "For all you know she might already be back home by now."

But I knew she wouldn't be, she'd still be up there with all the ghosts, talking to people who'd died years ago, inhabiting the weird world she'd created from her broken mind. Dragging her off that hill, taking her to hospital and subjecting her to police questioning, a trial, perhaps, would be a just consequence of what she'd done to Jessamy. Just, but harsher.

"The person I'd be more concerned about is Jessamy," he went on.

"I just hope she can stop punishing herself for giving her mother such a shock." I relayed what had happened when Evie had seen her daughter again.

"Probably inevitable that Evie would react violently, no matter how Jessamy'd broken the news. Perhaps she really did have something wrong with her that wasn't picked up."

"Perhaps."

"Jess'll have to see lawyers, of course. Probably the police too. They'll want her to make statements."

Somewhere in a filing system there'd be an open file on Jessamy's disappearance that would need to be taken out, dusted off. And closed.

"You must feel wrecked, darling," Luke went on.

"I am tired. But apparently that's not unusual."

A silence.

"What are you talking about? It sounds highly unusual to have your long-lost cousin come back —"

"Luke, I just did a test. It's a very thin line but . . ." It was there, as pale a blue as a spring sky. "I'm . . . pregnant." Finally I let myself say the word. I was expecting a child. If all went well, I'd hold Evie's great-niece or nephew in my arms in about nine months. *When? How?* I let the questions buzz between Luke and me, unspoken, unanswered, because neither of us knew. Perhaps that last despairing night with the takeaway curry and the bottle of Rioja when we'd behaved like a pair of teenagers. For the first time in months and months I felt myself produce a sound that could only be described as a giggle.

Again there was a silence.

"You know, I think I must have guessed." His voice quivered. "I must have worked it out subconsciously. Perhaps that's why I needed to speak to you so urgently. I just can't believe it."

"Nor can I." I let my heart give a little skip. The excitement felt delicious. I hardly dared to enjoy it after all the years of disappointment. "But I don't under-stand how it happened. The dates . . ." I shrugged.

"Bugger the dates," said Luke. "For the last year all we've done is worry about dates, the right date for this injection or that blood test or this new fertility drug. And now — this. You star, Rachel."

The lump in my throat threatened to render me dumb, something that had never before happened in the seven years of our marriage. We exchanged a few more words, half choked by emotion, and finished the call.

342

Jessamy came downstairs, her hair still damp from the shower. She'd borrowed my towelling dressing gown. When we were children we'd swapped clothes all the time: my smartly labelled French skirts and cardigan for her Marks and Spencer trousers and hand-knitted jumpers.

"Sorry," she said. "I wanted to ask if I could put this on while my clothes dry but you were on the phone. Do you mind, Rachel?"

My answer was to pull her into my arms and hug her. "I have missed you so much," I whispered. "You can have no idea."

"Yes I can." She shook her head, relaxing in my grip. "Every single day I thought of you."

It was what I had needed her to tell me.

"Every time I came down here to stay I'd lie up in that room of yours and think it must be a game, that you were hiding in the cupboard or under the bed." I shuddered, remembering. "It felt..." I couldn't tell her what it had felt like but the image that came into my mind was of a three-legged stool, missing one of its legs and never balancing properly again.

"You're going to crush me," Jessamy protested, between laughs. But we stayed, arms round one another, for minutes. Then we let one another go. She watched me preparing the food and picked up the kettle. "Let's use the famous Winter Jubilee mugs and brew up more tea." She pointed to her rucksack. "I've got mine in my bag."

Almost as a reflex I was going to remind her that the mugs were only ever brought out on high days and holidays, Coronations and Jubilees, for example. But what could be more of a celebration than today?

# Acknowledgements

Not for the first time I would like to thank Becky Motew, Jill Morrow, Barbara Derbyshire, Kristina Riggle and all the members of the Newplace writing group. My thanks also to Jane Cooper and Johnnie Graham.

My gratitude goes as well to the Vale and Downland Museum in Wantage, especially to Howard Fuller for showing me the photo archive, and to the inhabitants of Kingston Lisle and Uffington for being so generous with information about rural life now and in the past.

Two books were particularly useful to me in researching the story of the POWs working on the Burma — Siam railway: *The Railway Man* by Eric Lomax, and *Secret Letters from the Railway: The Remarkable Record of Charles Steel, a Japanese POW*, edited by Brian Best.